THE DARK ISLAND

BOOKS BY

V. SACKVILLE-WEST

The Dark Island

Family History

Thirty Clocks Strike the Hour

All Passion Spent

The Edwardians

King's Daughter

Twelve Days

The Land

Seducers in Ecuador

Passenger to Teheran

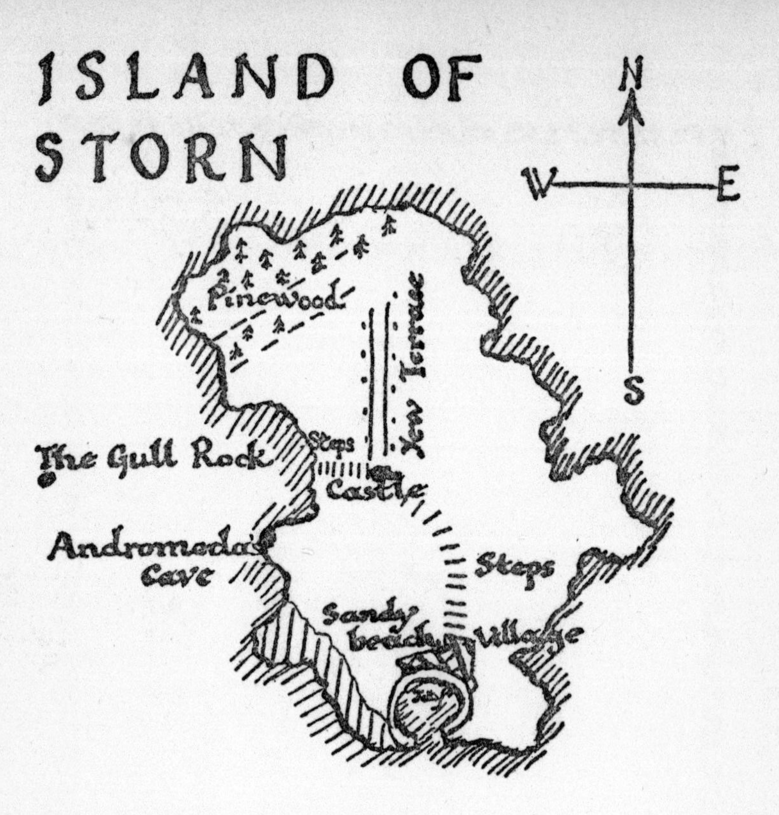

Scale of Miles

0 ½ 1 2

THE DARK ISLAND

V. Sackville-West

1936

Doubleday, Doran & Company, Inc.
Garden City, New York

PRINTED AT THE *Country Life Press*, GARDEN CITY, N. Y., U. S. A.

FOR

GWEN ST. AUBYN

CONTENTS

NOTE:

The name Shirin should be pronounced Sheereen.

PART I

SIXTEEN

I

MR. AND MRS. WILSON took their children away every year to the same place for their summer holiday. That habit began the trouble which ended in two persons losing their lives and in one criminal receiving an expression of sympathy from the coroner instead of a sentence of death from the judge. The inability of Mr. and Mrs. Wilson to vary their settled routine of life might thus be held originally responsible for the complicated disasters entailed upon their nearest kin, disasters of whose implications Mr. and Mrs. Wilson fortunately never became aware.

In fairness to them it must be said that every year they made the same pathetic attempt to vary their routine and thus to avoid the tricks which destiny had in store.

"Now really we mustn't be so silly," Mrs. Wilson said regularly once a year in June. "Of course we all like Port Breton, but isn't it rather unenterprising of us never to go anywhere else? What about Dieppe for a change?"

Mr. Wilson replied that he didn't like foreigners; they couldn't speak English and they didn't understand about breakfast. These appeared to be his principal reasons for his objection to foreigners. Mr. Wilson was blind, so special consideration had to be accorded to him. It was accorded with some exasperation by his family.

"Well, Philip, if you feel like that about it. . . . All right, then we won't think of crossing the Channel. But there are other places in England, after all. Or Scotland. The West coast of Scotland? The Kyles of Bute? Mrs. Morison tells me that it isn't true to say it always rains."

Mr. Wilson replied, fretfully, that the return journey to Scotland, for five people, was too expensive. The exiguity of his pension constituted as permanent a grievance as his blindness, and made as great a demand upon the patience of his family.

They surveyed England methodically, geographically. The East coast? Too bracing. Bournemouth? Too relaxing. Mrs. Wilson suggested them all in turn, conscientiously, knowing full well that they would decide in the end on Port Breton again. The discussion was simply a ritual that had to be gone through. They all knew that it would be Port Breton in the end. They were used to Port Breton; they knew what time the train left London, and from which station; they knew exactly the cab which would meet them; the way the old cabby would raise his hat; the look of the lodging-house when they got there; and the warmth of the greeting they would get from Mrs. Jolly. In common with the majority of their fellow-bourgeois, they found such cognisance reassuring. It saved effort, and, again in common with their fellows, the idea of effort was repellent to Mr. and Mrs. Wilson. They preferred the known to the unknown; familiarity to novelty.

It was perhaps strange that Port Breton should ever have established itself as their habitual haunt. That wild coast, you would have thought, was scarcely attuned to the Wilson temperament. Mr. Wilson, of course, could not see it, and Mrs. Wilson, who could, might reasonably have been expected to recoil in almost physical dismay from the savage austerity of the place. It is hard, indeed, to discern what pleasure either of them derived from their expedition. The probability is, that their principal satisfaction lay in proving to their neighbours that they could afford to remove themselves and their children to the sea for a month every summer; that they were doing their duty by the children in question; and then in the final comforting reflection that they were going to what Mrs. Wilson called "a home away from home." She was pleased with that phrase, and pronounced it always with a special voice, indicative of great affection. It had helped her, in her own mind, to tame Port Breton into a respectable, cosy, seaside resort, honoured during the month of August by the presence of a solvent English family on its annual holiday. Thus adopted, docketed, labelled, and pigeon-holed, Port Breton served its purpose in Mrs. Wilson's scheme of life, though Bournemouth with its chines and pines (but for the chance which had first led the family to Port Breton and the stranger chance which had sent them there again and again) was really her spiritual home away from home.

The decisive moment, committing them more firmly than ever to Port Breton, came when their eldest son secured a job from Messrs. Block and Arrowhead, Solicitors, and discovered that that respectable firm had for three generations been concerned with the affairs of the le Bretons, lords of the island of Storn. Mrs. Wilson loved coincidences. They gave her something to exclaim about, and she enjoyed pointing out how things that you wouldn't believe true if you read them in a book did really sometimes happen in real life. Here was a coincidence after her own heart. She never tired of asking her neighbours, wasn't it funny that she should have taken her children every year to Port Breton for five years before Paul got into the firm that had so much to do with those parts? Her neighbours always, and gratifyingly, agreed. Like Mrs. Wilson, they loved coincidences, which belonged, for them, to the region they vaguely called "uncanny."

Mrs. Wilson usually waited until her entire family was assembled, before introducing the subject of the holiday. It was not a particularly united family, and indeed was held together, as in the case in many families, less by the ties of affection than by those of convenience and convention, but for the purposes of discussion Mrs. Wilson liked all its members to be present. She liked the maximum number of voices raised in disagreement, for there were few things that her cheaply cantankerous nature enjoyed more than a good wrangle. This her sons and husband could always be relied on to provide, although her daughter might cut the fun short in an untimely way by suddenly waking up to the argument in progress round her, growing impatient, and settling the matter by one of her quick decisions. Not one of the family was proof against Shirin's decisions, neither her mother, nor her father, nor her brothers. The fact that she always laughed in no way diminished her influence.

The recurrent subject of the holiday, however, cropped up this year between Mr. and Mrs. Wilson as they sat alone. The children were all out, keeping unspecified appointments. Nothing but the usual faint querulousness disturbed the peace of the dining-room, where Mr. and Mrs. Wilson sat although it was not yet time for supper, because that was the only room in the house where they allowed themselves a fire on a chilly evening. The sense of security induced by the knowledge that their house was one in a row of identical houses, for they lived at Dulwich,—was pleasant to Mrs. Wilson; it would have disturbed her to reflect that her house differed from its neighbours any more than one postage-stamp differs from another. Even to the stained glass in the front door, it was comfortably and conformably the same. Its geography could have been predicted from the moment you entered the hall.

"We were really very lucky to have got this house," Mrs. Wilson remarked as she had remarked a hundred times before; "it really suits us very well."

As "To be let or sold" boards figured permanently on half the houses in the street, it was a little difficult to see why the Wilsons should consider themselves favoured by so amazing a stroke of fortune.

Mr. Wilson made the invariable reply. He said, "Getting a bit small, now that the children are growing up."

"There you go, Philip, always grumbling. You know very well that we can't afford a bigger one. Besides, it isn't."

"Well, I think Shirin ought to have a sitting-room."

"At her age? Ridiculous! How you do spoil that child. She's only sixteen, and what can anybody want with a sitting-room at sixteen? Hasn't she got the drawing-room to sit in, with me? Things are coming to a pretty pass, nowadays, if a chit of sixteen wants to get away from her own mother. Really, Philip!"

"If those people had treated me decently," said Mr. Wilson, referring to the Company which had employed him as a clerk for twenty-five years in Persia, "we could have afforded a bigger house. Easily."

"I dare say, but they didn't. They treated you abominably. Considering that you lost your sight from the dust in that horrible country. It was your own fault, though. If you hadn't let yourself be put upon. . . ."

"I didn't let myself be put upon," said Mr. Wilson, his masculine sense of loyalty to his employers rising against this feminine attack; "it was very decent of them to give me a pension at all."

"Nonsense, Philip. You know quite well that you always did all the work for everybody else. Don't you remember how I was always telling you not to work overtime, or if you did, to see that you got properly paid for it? And did you? No, never."

"Yes, I remember," said Mr. Wilson wearily.

The topic lapsed. Mr. Wilson's blind fingers skilfully refilled his pipe.

"Philip, must you really fill the dining-room with pipe-smoke just before supper?"

"I'm sorry, dear," said Mr. Wilson, knocking it out and putting the tobacco away again very carefully into his pouch. On the whole, he was the meeker of the two; or perhaps, being a man, the more accommodating over small matters.

A pause ensued, while Mrs. Wilson looked round for another grievance.

"Those children are late again."

"Oh no, dear, surely not? The clock hasn't struck seven."

"Five past," said Mrs. Wilson severely, looking at her wrist-watch. "And it does upset things so, if one is always unpunctual."

"My dear, Shirin is never unpunctual."

"No," said Mrs. Wilson reflectively; "but it's odd that

she shouldn't be. It doesn't seem to go with the rest of her."

"I don't know about that," Mr. Wilson began.

"Oh yes, she's perfect, isn't she? Just you wait. We shall have trouble with that child before long, mark my words." Mr. Wilson hated it when his wife said *mark my words*. It was one of her ready-made phrases, which she contrived to sharpen into a little barb of sinister and disagreeable import. In order to avoid further discussion of their daughter, whom his wife secretly and jealously adored, but whom she must constantly and naggingly criticise, Mr. Wilson plunged reckless into the only topic which he knew would certainly divert her attention:

"I suppose," he said, "that we must take them all away somewhere as usual this year?"

"You *suppose* we must, Philip? But of course we must! You aren't seriously suggesting that we should keep those children for the whole summer in Dulwich? Really, I sometimes think that you have no idea of your duty towards your children. I won't even mention myself, though I must say I should have thought you might realise by now what it means to a woman to struggle with a house and a family, year in, year out, never able to afford even a theatre in London, and three children to think about,—what with their boots and their mess and Roger's ridiculous affected ideas and Shirin's wanting to be a nurse and go in for goodness knows what horrible indecent training and the expense of it all and never a bit of fun for me and now you want to give Shirin a sitting-room of her own which just means extra work for Gladys even if we had the room which we haven't, and what would it lead to anyhow? just to Shirin entertaining a lot of young men who'll all be round her like flies round sugar in a year or two if they aren't already, you mark my words."

Mr. Wilson knew these tirades. He waited.

"And now that the boys have taken to bringing home their friends it'll be worse than ever. This is only the beginning of the end. Of course you can't notice as I do, but I can tell you that any boy who comes home with Paul or Roger gets caught up by Shirin within the first five minutes; she's only got to look at them once. I promise you, Philip, it isn't a responsibility that any mother worthy of the name would take lightly. You don't seem to realise it at all, but then of course I suppose one couldn't expect you to. You'll realise it fast enough in another two years."

"The question is," said Mr. Wilson, ignoring all this, "where are we to take them?"

"Well, I've been thinking about that. Really it seems rather unenterprising to go back to Port Breton again. I was thinking, we might make a change. I was thinking . . ."

The slamming of the front door interrupted her.

"That'll be Shirin," said Mr. Wilson. His face lighted up.

They both listened. The sounds of arrival in the house were familiar to them, from long habit. On how many evenings had they sat, as they were sitting now, and listened to their children coming home! But the habit and the familiarity had bred staleness rather than affection. Or perhaps it would be truer to say that habit and familiarity were substitutes, almost synonyms, for affection.

"It isn't Shirin," said Mr. Wilson, hearing steps go upstairs, "it's Roger."

"When will Roger learn to shut the bathroom door?"

Mrs. Wilson said peevishly. Her life was made up of similar small grievances.

Roger's appearance belied his virile name. Fair and slender, wearing a blue shirt with an open collar, he came gracefully into the room. Mrs. Wilson often wondered how she and Philip could have begotten such a son, but dismissed the problem by the reflection that no one could account for what young people were coming to, nowadays. Moreover, Roger had a taste for drawing and went to art-classes in the evenings, where he met a great many young men of his own type and a great many young women on whom his mother, not approving of such companions at all, put half the blame for Roger's eccentricities.

"So there you are," said Mrs. Wilson with implied reproach. "We won't wait for Paul or Shirin. If they like to have their supper cold, that's their affair. Tell Gladys, Roger, to bring supper."

The boy said, "I'm going out afterwards."

"What, going out again?"

"You can't expect me to sit at home every evening."

He looked sulky, but sulkiness was not unbecoming to his blue eyes and sullen, sensual mouth. He pushed back a drooping lock of corn-coloured hair.

"I wish I could get out of this place," he said as he went out of the room.

That was the disagreeable, upsetting kind of thing that Roger always said.

In the hall he met his brother, just coming in with another young man.

"Hullo, Roger. This is Tracey. He's come to supper. Tell Mother, will you, while I take him to wash? And you might tell Gladys to lay another place."

Roger knew very well that his brother was merely delegating an unpleasant necessity; he nodded politely to Tracey, giving Paul a meaning look meanwhile, of the kind that members of the same family do give one another when private motives are, to them, so ludicrously transparent. Paul tried to reply with a gaze of blank innocence. Tracey, catching both looks, wondered how to interpret them; they puzzled him, for to him in his easy home it was a natural thing to ask a friend back to supper. *How amusing it always is,* he thought, *to come suddenly into the middle of somebody else's family! Roger,* he thought, *looks more interesting than Paul, who is strong and dark and rather ordinary.* Roger, with his pallor, his slight figure, and his bright clothes, was certainly an odd product for this very orthodox home in a suburban street.

"Paul has brought someone back to supper," Roger said, reappearing in the dining-room. The pleasure of vicariously annoying his mother on Paul's behalf compensated him for the petulant outburst which would, and did, ensue.

"Who is it, anyway?" she asked in conclusion, crossly.

"Man called Tracey. I can't tell you more about him than that. And I've warned Gladys."

Mrs. Wilson had fully intended to be rude to Tracey when Paul brought him in; but instead of being rude she suddenly became quite polite; she even produced the only bottle of sherry and offered him a glass. For Tracey was not a person to whom one could be rude; he reminded Mrs. Wilson of a nice black retriever with trustful eyes. If a trifle clumsy, upsetting the cigarette box on the floor, he redeemed his blunder so charmingly that he was instantly forgiven. By the time they were seated round the table, the atmosphere in the room was more genial than it had been for many a day.

He was interesting, too. It appeared that he worked in the same solicitor's office as Paul, and was willing to talk legal shop in a manner which held Mr. Wilson's attention; frank, modest, and intelligent, it transpired that he had evolved theories for himself, beyond the dull routine of an ordinary clerk. Mr. Wilson loved such conversation; it took him away from his family; it took him back to the days when he, too, had known something of public enterprises; it took him back to Persia, which he had rather pathetically loved, so that he still minded when his wife referred to it as that horrid dusty country; it took him back to the days when he had played a tiny part in the concerns of a big company. Mrs. Wilson became aware of an unwonted stirring of affection as she noted the animation of Philip's sightless face, usually so grey and pinched and bored.

It was surprising, how friendly they all became. Even Roger, usually so sullen at home, displayed something of the mischievous gaiety which made him welcome, though feared, at the studio; he could feel that Tracey liked him, and, responsive, improved upon the flattering impression by a slyly-placed word or glance. The simple goodness of Tracey influenced them all. Before very long, they found themselves submitting the problem of their holiday to his arbitration; "Now let's ask Mr. Tracey and abide by what he thinks," Mrs. Wilson exclaimed quite archly. She had even forgotten to worry about her daughter's continued absence, although, as Philip had observed, Shirin was never unpunctual. Only once had she said, "Where *is* that child?" and had immediately followed up the remark by telling Gladys to keep the supper hot, a concession appreciated with amusement by both her sons.

Tracey, thus appealed to, waited expectantly for the problem to be put before him. He looked from one to the other as though he were really interested, smiling enquiringly at them with a kindliness surprising in one so young. He could not be more, Roger thought, than twenty-two or three; about the same age as Paul. Unhappy eyes, thought Roger; and he hasn't once spoken about himself. —But before Tracey could be consulted, they heard Shirin's laughter in the hall.

"Shirin," said Mr. Wilson, raising his head with an expression of pleasure.

"So her ladyship's been pleased to come home at last, has she?" said Mrs. Wilson, but she said it without any real ill-humour. "This is my daughter," she explained to Tracey. "She goes to her Junior Red Cross classes in the evenings, and I expect she's been kept." She did not want Tracey to think that any daughter of hers would be allowed to wander about the streets, even such respectable streets, alone after dark without a very good reason. "She comes home by bus, door to door," she added.

They heard her say something to Gladys, and then a fresh peal of laughter,—Tracey had never heard anyone laugh so merrily or so frankly; it did not seem to accord with a person who went to Red Cross classes,—and then the door burst open, and Shirin looked in.

"Sorry!" she called. "But I *must* wash,—down in a minute,—don't wait," and she came in quickly, gave her father a kiss on the top of his head, noticed Tracey, looked a little taken aback, gave him a swift half-smile, and was gone, calling out to Gladys as she went.

In that brief moment of her entry, Tracey observed with surprise a smear of fresh blood on the ruffle of her white shirt. It was more than a smear; it was a long stain. *No one else*, he thought, *has noticed it. She herself appears to be unaware of its existence. She must discover it*, he thought, *as soon as she looks into her mirror upstairs. Then she and I will be like conspirators, since she and I will be the only persons conscious of the once-existence of that red stain.* He desired with inexplicable ardour that she should discover it before she returned to expose herself once more to the scrutiny of her family.

The Wilsons brightened visibly with the return of their daughter, though they had been amiable enough before.

Shirin, taking her place beside her father, gave no explanation for her lateness, and Mrs. Wilson, as a concession to Tracey's presence, for once exacted none. He saw with relief that she had changed her white shirt for a blue one. He wondered, however, whether she was always so pale, and whether her eyes were always so dark and wild. She was extremely gay and animated, taking control as though she gathered up all the strands into her own childishly fragile hands, plaiting them into some kind of unity; he observed, too, how she immediately took her blind father under her own management, putting the things he needed within his reach, looking after him efficiently but unobtrusively, whereas the other members of his family had looked after him in a grudging and inadequate way, as people who perform a tiresome but accustomed duty, so that he had several times been obliged to ask for one thing or the other, which Tracey divined to be a humiliation for him, especially in the presence of a stranger. Shirin tended him differently, forestalling his needs, now giving him a fork when he lacked one, now pushing his cup of coffee gently against his hand when he seemed unsure where Roger had set it down, yet all the time without glancing at him or interrupting her chatter or the laughter that came so readily to her lips. Tracey was puzzled: she seemed so intensely aware of everything that was going on, *and yet in some curious way*, he thought, *she is not really in this room at all. To myself she accords no special attention, beyond an occasional glance that includes me in the circle; but that is her good manners*, he thought; *she doesn't want me to feel out of it.* Why he should have been so sure of her good manners, he could not have said; he simply knew that about certain things in Shirin one could be instantly positive, whereas by other things one would remain forever perplexed. Thus he accepted her inclusive glance as the ordinary courtesy she would accord to any possibly shy stranger, and was grateful to her for the kindness that prompted it. Suddenly, however, she looked him full in the face across the table, and he was startled as never in his life before by the wide gaze of her eyes, so extraordinarily brilliant in that particular illumination of the lamp. "Starry," he said to himself, inventing the cliché for himself, as inevitably as though it had never been used before; "starry, that's what they are," and he gazed back at her, so that he imagined himself and her both caught together into the same intense moment of time.

By such false intuitions are we misled.

Disconcerted, stirred, upset, Tracey receded from the circle into a haze of his own. He thought about the different eyes of all the people sitting round that table: Mrs. Wilson's mean little boot-buttons, set too close together, so that they appeared to be trying to gimlet each other through her nose; Mr. Wilson's sunken sockets, from which the light was for ever extinguished; Roger's sullen rebellious blue; Paul's ordinary, empty brown; Shirin's sudden starry gaze, that promised so much and (probably) meant so little. In this catalogue, naturally, he forgot to include his own which Roger had thought unhappy and which had reminded Mrs. Wilson of a faithful dog. Indeed, he had never thought much about eyes before, until this moment of an intenser consciousness produced by his brief union with a child of sixteen.

With an effort he brought himself back, and heard them again, still talking about their holiday, that problem which he, apparently, was to resolve for them by giving the casting vote. It was funny to think of Paul Wilson going on a holiday,—Wilson, whom he scarcely knew save as a fellow-clerk, and whose head he had seen bent always over a ledger, and who had so unexpectedly asked him to come home to supper. He wondered what Wilson would wear, down there by the sea, for he gathered that the family's customary resort was somewhere by the sea; a fisherman's jersey, perhaps, and grey slacks; no cap, so that the wind might blow through his hair. Shirin? she would wear no cap either, covering her rough curls; and he wondered whether he might not join them, but sighed then, remembering that he could not possibly take his holiday at the same time as Paul Wilson. He could imagine the head-clerk's face, if he asked for it.

He had not been listening properly.

"Port Breton?" he heard himself saying; "yes, of course I've heard of it. You see, I have a job in the same office as your son." He said *your son* because he did not know how otherwise to refer to Paul, whom he had never called by his Christian name. "And we look after the le Bretons' estate for them,—but of course," he added hurriedly, "he's told you that."

This was an opening for Mrs. Wilson, and Tracey got the benefit of all her reflections on coincidences, which her family had heard frequently before, but endured again patiently.

"The lodgings are very comfortable," Mrs. Wilson wound up, "and Mrs. Jolly,—that's our landlady,—is very nice to us always, and Shirin manages her wonderfully, I must say," said Mrs. Wilson; "I'm not saying the contrary; still, it does seem a bit unenterprising. . . ."

In the end it was of course settled that they should go again to Port Breton. Tracey noticed how skilfully and with what rapidity Shirin piloted her parents towards this decision, considering Mrs. Wilson's manifest desire for prolonged argument.

"Then I'll write to Mrs. Jolly tomorrow," said Mrs. Wilson with final relief, though she tried to make a belated grievance by adding, "You see, Mr. Tracey, their father and I, we always put the children first, and if they want to go to Port Breton, to Port Breton I suppose they must go."

Paul scowled. He did not like being included among "the children" in Tracey's hearing. Still, Tracey was a kind-hearted chap; he wouldn't snigger about it at the office next day.

Tracey got up finally and said he supposed he must go. He did so with extreme reluctance, for although he easily liked people and found them amiable and friendly in their relations with him,—an amiability and friendliness which his diffidence would not allow him to attribute to his own merits,—yet he was unaccustomed to the surprising stimulus which some influence in the room was giving him. Then they all, except Shirin, expressed their hope that he would come again. Mr. Wilson especially was unaffectedly cordial; and Tracey, looking at Shirin, believed that she also would not be displeased were he to do so.—*Incredible,* he thought, *that she should be only sixteen!* But, as people frequently realise only in retrospect the moment at which they have fallen in love, he walked home without realising in the least what had happened to him.

With his departure the customary flatness descended on the family, a flatness usually dispelled, at least in appearance, by Shirin's undisciplined laughter. Tonight she was so quiet and abstracted that her mother nagged at her out of the flatness to know if she were tired, though she might have learnt from experience that that was the last admission ever to be expected from Shirin. No, not tired, said Shirin, rousing herself as she always roused when an appeal was made to her and as she always repulsed her mother's prying solicitude; for a few moments she reassumed the mask of her habitual self. And what did she think of Paul's new friend, her mother asked? and Shirin, sparkling once more, said that he was like a hearthrug, the black shaggy kind. Oh, said Mrs. Wilson, pained, I thought him more like a nice dog. But dogs can be black and shaggy too, said Shirin; a nice dog, then, lying warm and comfortable in front of the fire; or the remains of a favourite dog, that someone has made into a hearthrug after death. Shirin, what dreadful heartless things you say! Fancy anybody turning their favourite dog into a hearthrug! Well, said Shirin, running on, some people like to preserve the memory of their dog, and there isn't much to choose between a dog's cemetery in the back-garden and a dog's pelt spread for ever, or until it wears out or gets the moth in it, in front of the fire. Paul, who was getting sleepy, yawned, and said he couldn't bear Shirin when she said things like that for effect. Privately, he was annoyed by the way Tracey had looked at her; he had seen that look too often in the eyes of young men when Shirin was in the room. He had seen it, with a difference, in the eyes of older men also. Being just old enough to know what it meant, he was also just young enough to wish to snub his sister for her own good. I hate you, Shirin, he said, when you show off and try to be clever; and getting up he went crossly out of the room. Roger said, yes, really, you do get above yourself at times, Shirin; but he looked at her as he said it, in such a way that they both smiled, and she wondered with a new interest what Roger's private life was really like. In that moment a new sympathy between them was born, which had never existed before. I like Paul's friend, said Roger. He's too soft and woolly, said Shirin, answering Roger. Mrs. Wilson said firmly that she had liked him very much, and that nothing would give her greater happiness than to think that Shirin might marry such a good man. She said this, because she was always afraid that Shirin with her ideas of nursing and what-not, and her funny reserved ways, and her scoffing ideas about people, might get it into her head that she would refuse ever to marry at all, the worst disaster, according to Mrs. Wilson, that could befall a woman. Mr. Wilson also expressed his approval of Paul's friend: nice boy, no nonsense about him; you could hear from his voice, said Mr. Wilson, that he was a nice boy. He seemed disposed to say more, but Mrs. Wilson was getting the house ready for bed, raking out the fire and setting aside such bits of coal as were preservable; shaking up the cushions and giving them a thump as much as to say, they had better look out for themselves next time they were used; twitching the tablecloth straight and emptying the ashtray into the grate. Now come along, she said to her family, it's time for bed; there's Paul gone upstairs already, and as for you, Roger, you seem to have forgotten thank goodness that you were going out and it's too late now, and as for you, Shirin, you're as white as a sheet and I don't wonder with these ridiculous classes keeping you till all hours of the night . . . and so saying, with a great deal more, Mrs. Wilson shepherded her family, as she had done many times before, to bed.

After the necessary banging of doors, silence enveloped the house.

Mr. and Mrs. Wilson lay awake for a short time in the darkness, which was the same as the light to Mr. Wilson, congratulating themselves on their wise decision to go once more to Port Breton. Or, rather, Mrs. Wilson congratulated herself, while Mr. Wilson, only half awake, dutifully listened. Then they had a word or two about Tracey, and about the desirability of Shirin finding a nice husband for herself like that, else there's no telling what she might be up to, said Mrs. Wilson; the sooner she gets a good man to look after her the better pleased I shall be, but at the same time she sighed, thinking how empty the house would be without Shirin, and Mr. Wilson sighed too, with more reason, not sharing his wife's feminine interest in the marriage of her daughter, but thinking only of how much he would miss the touch of Shirin's hand on his forehead and her watching over his needs and her ringing laughter in the house.

Roger went to the room he shared with Paul, who was already asleep, and, getting quietly to bed without waking his brother, thought without regret of the party he had missed, since Tracey in his sincere and simple way seemed so far more worth while than all the rather precious gang he would have encountered at that party. Roger hoped that Tracey might become a friend. Tracey wasn't very exciting, perhaps, but so likeable! Roger was surprised at himself for liking Tracey so much. Tracey was not of the type that Roger usually liked at all. Still trying to puzzle out why he liked Tracey so much, Roger fell asleep.

On the top floor, Gladys snored contentedly, her alarm-clock beside her bed set for half-past six.

Shirin alone moved about her room while the others slept. She was not thinking of Tracey. From a leather note-case hidden among her handkerchiefs she extracted a photograph of the sea, taken from the coast near Port Breton. The foreground was all sea, with a path of sunlight leading up it and ending in the dark island of Storn. As the island lay some two miles out from the coast, no details were discernible in the photograph, only the silhouette of the island and two rounded tower-tops of the Norman castle. She had never regretted that her photograph should reveal so little of the island; had never attempted to obtain one that should give a nearer view. It was enough for her that it should lie, dark and suggestive, at the end of that path of sunlight, symbol of all romance and of all escape from the humdrum weariness of life, from its meannesses, its falsity, and its pain. It was the secret, undetected refuge from her family, from Dulwich, from herself. It was the sanctuary she never desired to enter, save in spirit; so precious a treasure that the austerity of her self-discipline allowed her to look at the photograph only on limited occasions, not as a self-indulgence, but as an invigoration when the need for invigoration became imperative. This evening she felt to be such an occasion, and, taking out the photograph, she looked at it long and seriously. Then having put it away, she took up her shirt stained with blood, and carefully washed the ruffle in her basin. In the midst of doing this, and observing the water turn pink, she sickened suddenly and was obliged to sit down on the edge of her bed to let the weakness pass. She pressed her fingers against her eyes to exclude the vision of the child running out under the lorry in the ill-lit street,—the unknown child she had picked up and held with all the poor skill of her slight training until the ambulance-men came and took it away to the hospital. That was a thing she would never tell to anybody, except, perhaps, to Mrs. Jolly. She would never tell anybody how the injured child had moaned uneasily, moving in her arms, or how the blood had trickled, horrifying her and yet fascinating her. Even Mrs. Jolly should never know those details. Mercifully her mother had not asked her why she came late, so that she had not been obliged to lie. Mercifully, too, she had kept her head and had refused to give her name or address to anyone but the policeman, to whom she had given it only because he said she might be wanted as a witness. Mercifully, above all, no one at home had noticed the stain on her shirt; she had not noticed it herself until she ran upstairs to wash her hands before supper. She was safe now, she thought, from any enquiry. Even the policeman contemplating her youth with evident sympathy, looking down from the height and solemnity of his helmet on to her head, had promised not to call upon her unless such a demand should become necessary. It was a dark, private, terrible experience which she could not have borne to have exposed to the light.

She knew that. What she could not quite analyse was her own attitude towards the happening, and this inability to understand her own feelings was perhaps partly responsible for her ardent determination to keep the accident and her own share in it entirely to herself. There had been other occasions in her life when a similar instinct had prompted her to absolute secrecy, nor had the instinct ever given her cause for regret. Already at sixteen, she had evolved the guiding principle that it was better to keep your own counsel. Oh, by all means! Revelation invariably brought regret in its train. It was better to be secret, very secret, even though for secrecy you had to pay the price of loneliness. It was better not to let anyone know how much you loved the shadow of a bough on a wall, or a swirl of dead leaves falling past a street-lamp; better not to let anyone know how vividly you retained the memory of a sunrise in Persia, or the chatter of the Persian servants; better, above all, not to let anyone know how much you loved the sea and Port Breton. That inner knowledge which told you that life was cruel, told you also that life, just for mischief, might take away such things if it suspected that you loved them. Loneliness was not so very great a price to pay for such security; she would call it privacy rather than loneliness. And, respecting herself with a kind of savage pride, she esteemed her privacy beyond all her other possessions; esteemed it the more, perhaps, because other people from outside always seemed to be attacking it, other people who seemed to have no sense of privacy, no decency of reserve, neither her mother with her overflowing volubility and her avidity for endless "good talks" with her daughter, nor the men, old and young, who tried to kiss her and to paw her about. In her immature philosophy, the first tenet was to shut yourself away in a stony fortress and then to consider what system of bluff would best defend you against the importunities of the world.

Curled up in front of her little gas-fire,—her brother Paul always scolded her for her inability to sit straight like an ordinary person, though other men, yes, and women too, teased her affectionately about it as though it amused them,—she tried hard and honestly to understand the puzzling thing that had been happening within herself all that evening, since the child had run out under the lorry. To fall short of honesty towards herself was already in her eyes the worst of offences, a real sinning against the light. In the confused way of sixteen, she was aware that something not very pretty had revealed itself within her that evening, for she could not and would not pretend that the accident had filled her with nothing but horror and compassion. Compassion she had felt, yes, for the little quivering body; but horror at the sudden destructive danger, no. Rather, an answering mood had risen in her to respond to it. Was she cruel, then? was she coarse? Had she really enjoyed seeing the red threads of blood trickle from the temple down the white unconscious cheek? Yes,—she faced the admission,—the brilliant contrast under the lamplight had pleased her, the violence of life and death had stirred her and had taught her something that she needed to know. Harsh, then, was she? harsh, and rather cruel? she realised then, once and for all, articulately, that she preferred harshness to sentimentality.

Life itself was harsh, and sentimentality only a cowardly human invention for escape. If one dared to be harsh towards oneself, one could afford to be harsh towards others also; one could exact from others any price, however heavy, that one would not hesitate to pay oneself.

Looking at her own reflection in the mirror, she felt grateful to a fate which had bestowed on her an appearance so thoroughly at variance with such a nature. Those soft contours, those tumbled curls, provided her with a ready-made bluff. She brushed the back of her fingers lovingly across the softness of her cheek. Quite detachedly, she surveyed her own attractions. Warm as a little animal she was; yielding as a kitten. Surely, with such a physical advantage, it ought to be possible to deceive anybody? and, in a conspiracy with oneself as sole ally, quietly to remain unguessed, unknown, and thus to protect oneself against the pain of life.

II

HERE you are," said Mrs. Jolly, handing them the sandwiches, "and now off you go and enjoy yourselves, and mind you don't let me see any of you again till supper. And as for you, my beauty," she added, addressing herself to Shirin, "mind you behave yourself, and don't get yourself into trouble, and don't get drowned, either." She nodded her head at Shirin, in the minatory, proprietary way she adopted towards the whole family, but for Shirin she made a difference, since Shirin was her pet, her darling, and never had anybody chaffed Mrs. Jolly as Shirin chaffed her, though everybody chaffed Mrs. Jolly, and never had anybody loved Shirin in exactly the way that Mrs. Jolly loved her, though everybody loved Shirin.

Happy on holiday, the family moved off, having received its lunch done up in newspaper. Paul carried the lunch in a string bag; Roger slouched along, carrying nothing because he was selfish, but looking picturesque enough to please anybody, and to make anybody forgive his selfishness, in a fisherman's blue jersey; Mrs. Wilson walked alone, picking her way with difficulty and dignity over the rough path; and Shirin piloted her father, without seeming to do so, up and down the narrowness of the path between the boulders. It was a rough coast, and a lovely day. The sea lay twinkling and enormous in the sun. Anything less like Dulwich could scarcely be imagined. Streets had disappeared, and their houses with windows and chimneys and front-doors all exactly alike, houses inhabited by people all leading the same kind of life. Here was liberation; here was the thing that none of the Wilsons except Shirin and Roger would consciously call beauty. Still, although the others did not consciously call it beauty, they were happy. "Nice, isn't it?" said Mrs. Wilson, forgetting to be the ill-tempered Mrs. Wilson of Dulwich, picking a piece of thrift as she passed.

The gorse was hot in the sun; hot, and scented. It loaded the air with its scent. The wild coast sloped steeply to the sea. Down on the edge of the sea, little green pools slept oily among the rocks. Not a person to be seen; not a boat on the sparkle of the water. The tiny cluster of houses called Port Breton had disappeared round the bend of the hill. Only a few sea-gulls swooped above the pools, and drew the lovely line of their open wings against the flatness of the sea. "It isn't often," said Mrs. Wilson as she had said regularly on a similar occasion every year for ten years past, "that one gets a day like this."

She was slightly out of breath. The path went up and down, accommodating itself to the exigencies of the hill rather than to the convenience of its users or to the inadequacies of Mrs. Wilson's middle-age. It was no municipal path, such as Mrs. Wilson might have found at Bournemouth, but merely a path that had grown into existence under the tread of fishermen and cottagers for generations. Mrs. Wilson, accustomed to the asphalt of Dulwich, found it trying. "Let's stop for a minute, shall we?" she said, sinking down on the bank. A stunted gorse bush pricked her, and she jumped, resettling herself to sit more comfortably, furtively poking the gorse bush aside as though she had not noticed it. Shirin deposited her father carefully beside her mother, and the three children stood looking down upon their parents. "It's only eleven o'clock," said Paul, consulting his wrist-watch and shifting the string bag to the other hand. "Well, we can't have lunch till one, that's certain," said Mrs. Wilson, as though that were a law of nature, measurable by the tides. She was still slightly out of breath, although she tried to disguise it. "Now why don't you children go off and explore for a bit?" she said, "and we'll all meet at one o'clock down there by the cove." She pointed down at the cove in question with a gesture that might have seemed vague to a newcomer, but which was quite explicit enough to the children who had known the cove for the last ten years as a place of appointment. Her children, and rightly, interpreted the gesture as meaning that she wanted no more physical exertion to be demanded of her for the moment. They themselves were relieved to be so easily rid of their parents for a couple of hours. Youth was exuberant on a morning like that, and grew restive under the necessity of measuring its steps to the pace of the elderly and the blind.

"Sure you'll be all right?" said Paul, who was a dutiful son. "Roger and I will go and bathe. We'll leave the lunch down by the cove."

"It'll get stolen, mark my words," Mrs. Wilson said, rousing herself to the suspicions and complexities of Dulwich.

"My dear mother, there isn't a soul within miles!"

They left their parents seated side by side, very contented, Mrs. Wilson fanning herself with a newspaper, Mr. Wilson sitting with his legs stuck straight out in front of him, his boater tilted slightly forward on his head, and his sightless eyes gazing out to sea,—a respectable British couple taking their holiday according to the instinct which leads the most confirmed cockney to the shores of his native island at one moment or another during the summer months. So Mr. and Mrs. Wilson remained there, more or less comfortably seated, but their children, leaving the path, plunged downward over tufts and boulders and short grass, till they reached the boulders dark and slippery with spray where the long waves came in sonorously, washing in and out of the curving creeks.

"I shall bathe," said Paul. "Coming, Roger?"

The brothers went off together, linked by their masculinity, which could go and bathe naked and alone. Shirin went away by herself up the coast. The path had ceased to exist, down by the water's edge, and she had to jump from rock to rock, making for a little cove a mile away, a little cove which many years ago she had claimed from her brothers as her own. That had been on the first occasion of their visits to Port Breton, when Shirin was six and Paul fourteen and Roger twelve. Shirin, discovered by the boys in her retreat, had flown instantly into one of the rages for which they delighted to tease her. "You shan't come here," she had cried; "this is mine, mine, mine." Paul enquired sarcastically who had given it to her; was it the Ranger, he asked, alluding to old Sir Dominic le Breton, who lived out on the far-away island of Storn? There was no one, he added with the superior knowledge of a schoolboy, who had any rights over that coast save the le Bretons, and since they seldom emerged from their island it was improbable that Shirin should have obtained the rights of a vassal over that particular cove. In order to annoy his sister, and also to impress his younger brother, he mentioned all the applicable terms he knew. "Have you a charter?" he asked grandly; "do you hold it by tenure or seisin?" for he had just been reading an historical novel, which had taught him that ownership of land was connected with such things as tenure and seisin, and dancing about from one foot to the other, he chanted "Vassal! liegewoman!" asking whether he and Roger should do homage to Shirin or whether Shirin herself had already done the necessary homage to the Ranger. By such methods do schoolboys traditionally irritate their sisters, but not always are they repaid by their sisters with a pelting of stones about the head. A small, furious figure dominant on a rock, Shirin defended her rights with all the missiles she could collect.

She recalled this incident now, as, exuberant in her solitude, she scrambled her way towards the cove. She smiled to remember how childish they had all been then; how silly. The incident seemed to have happened a long way off, in another life, yet at the same time it had its bearing on this present life when the cove by tacit consent was hers and she no longer had to defend it with showers of stones flung in handfuls against the offending head of Paul. Paul was a reasonable person now; she was really quite fond of him. But she loved the cove with quite another part of herself; not at all the part that made the best of Paul and endured a lukewarm affection. Affection, for Shirin, counted very little. She was prepared to give it, when people, like her father, seemed to rely on it, but it was not to be classed with, say, the feeling that she had about the cove. Ardour was what she prized and recognised as the only worth-while force, and the fact that she loved the cove with ardour made it into one of her most hidden and treasured places.

She could see the island of Storn lying out to sea. Every year she knew she would see it again, yet every year it was a surprise to her to discover the island still lying there. The enchantment which had put it there might just as easily have swept it away. She stood still, shading her eyes with her hand, the breeze blowing her skirt against her bare legs. At this distance, little could be discerned on the island, quite two miles away; only the pink cottages of the village down by the breakwater, and the rosy fortress of the le Bretons' castle rising in a piled mass above the village. That sufficed Shirin, who had never seen the island except from the mainland. She had no wish to visit it and risk destroying its illusion. She held, indeed, an intense and clearly formulated determination not to do so. She knew of course that tourists went out from Port Breton and from the neighbouring villages, chugging round the shores of the island in a stout little paddle-boat incongruously named *Daffodil* while they leant over the taffrail and pointed; but fortunately her mother, who fancied herself a bad sailor, had never suggested joining that ungraceful company. Rumour said that round on the other side of the island were dark pine-groves descending to the sea, but Shirin would not believe that the island had another side, any more than the moon. She scarcely believed that it was tethered to the floor of the ocean at all, but preferred to think that it might drift away in the night, to reappear someday among the Cyclades or the Sporades, or, more likely, never reappearing anywhere.

The boys had been across to Storn, and had wanted Shirin to come with them, but at the last moment she had been unaccountably missing. And when they returned in the evening, chattering about the sights they had seen, Shirin was not there to listen. They supposed that she was hob-nobbing as usual with Mrs. Jolly in the kitchen, not knowing that she had stolen out alone along the coast, to look at Storn once more by moonlight and to apologise to it for her brothers. "I wouldn't go," she cried to it passionately; "no, I wouldn't, not for the world."

So peculiar a feeling had she about Storn, that she would no more have cheapened it by exploring and exploiting its secrets, than she would have betrayed through indiscretion the intimate life of a person she loved. The idea of going to Storn on the *Daffodil* with her brothers and a horde of tourists, offended her as just such a cheapening would have offended her. Storn to her was sacred, secret, set apart; it was like love, love which she had never known.

She was nearing the cove, when she discerned a small boat hauled up on the beach of white sand. Such a thing had never happened before in her experience, and she looked at the boat with the same red rage as had hurled the stones at Paul and Roger ten years previously. Only, this time, because she was older, instead of picking up a stone she went forward with her hands clenched and a real despair at her heart. She saw then a boy, perhaps two years older than herself, red-headed, freckled, tanned, sitting on a rock mending a fishing-line. He was rather an ugly boy, she thought, but not unpleasantly ugly, for he was spare and thin beyond all belief; so thin, that she thought he must be ill; his figure was concave wherever it ought to have been convex, as though emaciation had eaten him away; there seemed to be nothing but bones inside the belt that hitched up his trousers; he was sharp and bony all over, with his pointed face and his pointed ears, and the peculiar grace and ease that governed his limbs, the peculiar insolence that inspired his every movement and attitude. She liked him, yet she hated him. She was surprised to find how instantly she could like and yet hate a person, at first sight.

It was not within her policy ever to betray her feelings. Jumping down on to the sand, she came to a pause as though she had only just caught sight of the intruder; stopped; looked at him; and smiled. He looked back at her gravely, without smiling. Then he bent again over his line and went on mending it, making her feel that she was the intruder, and ought to go away.

The sand was very white and the water very thin where it washed over in lazy ripples. The sea-gulls swooped and cried up in the air. The boy whistled softly to himself, his fingers deftly busy with the line. He took no notice whatsoever of Shirin, and she, half amused, half angry, and wholly determined not to be driven away, sat down on a rock and stared at the distant island of Storn.

The rock she had chosen was flat, and presently she lay back full-length on it, her hands clasped behind her head, the sun warming her thinly-clad body all through. The sensuous indulgence pleased her; and such was her power of abstracting herself that she forgot the boy's presence, losing herself in the warmth of the sun, the lapping of the water, the cries of the gulls, and the faint but honeyed smell of the gorse; all her senses became mixed in that general sense of well-being. The start she gave when the boy spoke to her was unassumed. "I hope," he was saying in a voice thick with suppressed fury, "that I haven't disturbed you. I'm going now and you can have the cove to yourself."

Shirin sat up; one glance at his angry face, and she broke into peals of the laughter she had never learnt to control. "Oh, I'm sorry," she said, realising that this was not very polite, "but you did look so cross."

The boy relaxed a little, seeing that she was scarcely more than a child.

"That's all right," he said, not disagreeably; "only, you see, I'm not accustomed to finding anyone here. Of course you have as much right to be here as I have. And one must expect to meet people in the summer."

"Do you live here always, then?"

"Yes," said the boy, his pale eyes becoming suddenly dreamy; "yes, I live here always."

He must be the son of a fisherman, she thought, *and yet he doesn't speak like one.*

"Do you come from Port Breton?" she asked, for although reluctant to let other people find things out about her, she was always ready to find things out about other people.

"No," said the boy, spinning a flat pebble, ducks-and-drakes, into the sea; "no, I don't come from Port Breton."

He's holding something back, she thought; *he's embarrassed; now why? I like his thin sulky face and his thin brown hands.* But she could not think of anything to say, and suddenly she laughed again.

"Why do you laugh?" said the boy, looking curiously at her.

"Because I couldn't think of anything more to say," she said, her eyes dancing, "and if you don't want to tell me where you live, I don't see why I should force you to tell me. That's simple, isn't it?" and mentally, for somewhere within the inarticulate depths of her being lay the realisation that half of her life must be spent in warring with men, she registered the value of an unexpected gesture of frankness in a sticky situation.

"There's no secret," said the boy; "I live over there." He pointed to the island.

"On Storn?"

"Yes, on Storn.—I see you know its name."

"I ought to know it. I've been to Port Breton every year for the last ten years."

"Ten years? But were you born, ten years ago?"

This was so much more like the bantering tone to which she was already accustomed from young men, that a shadow of the well-known brand of weariness crossed her, yet at the same time she felt better able to respond, better equipped through experience to deal with this kind of familiarity than with the previous aloofness of the boy. Instantly she liked him less. He had been distant and angry; now he was accessible and ordinary. Very well: she would become accessible and ordinary too. She answered him in the same tone, taking her note from him.

"How old, then, do you suppose that I am?"

He considered her. She had forced him to consider her. Up till now, he had tried to keep his eyes averted from her, but for that one examining look when she had laughed.

"Oh,—twelve?—fourteen?" he said, and instantly she liked him better again, knowing that he was deliberately trying to offend her.

They were both very childish.

"You're wrong,—I'm only eleven." Would he take that lie seriously?

"Of course you're more than eleven. Anyhow, you're very pretty."

"Am I? What an obvious remark."

"You've heard that sort of remark before, I see."

"And shall hear it again, no doubt."

"You seem very sure about it."

"So sure, that it doesn't interest me very much."

"You won't hear it again from me at any rate, you may be sure of that."

"Shan't I?—Aren't you," she said, "being rather common?"

"Damn you," said the boy, flushing, and he seized her wrists and twisted them, hurting her.

"Is that the way you usually behave to people you don't know?" she said, while he still hurt her. "Rather schoolboyish, perhaps, aren't you?"

"And now," he said, ashamed, dropping her wrists and standing back from her, "I suppose you'll cry?"

"It would take more than you and more than that to make me cry."

They stared at each other, she mocking, he breathing deeply, because his loss of temper had upset him.

"You *have* got a bad temper, haven't you?" she said, smoothing her bruised wrists.

"Haven't you too?"

"I hate lack of control," she said coldly, evading the question; "I hate people who let themselves go."

For the first time, she was putting a new point of view to him, and a severe one at that. He was accustomed to people who let themselves go whenever they felt inclined, which was often, in his own home.

"How sure you are," he said, but without a sneer. With admiration, rather. *She hates lack of control, does she? Well, she is probably right. Only the people who have no control feel the need of it. The others are safe without.*

"What sad wisdom," he said, sneering now; but then, "Look here," he said, sitting down beside her, "I'm sorry if I hurt you. I'll apologise if you like."

"I really don't mind whether you apologise or not." Then she laughed. "It's quite all right," she said; "I only thought you were being rather silly,—and rather cheap."

Anger blazed again in his eyes for a second; she had managed to humiliate him, who was not accustomed to humiliation. But only for a second. "I couldn't help myself," he said; "I never can. I'm sorry."

"Don't be sorry," she said; "I hate people who are sorry for what they do. Either you don't do a thing, or else you do it and aren't sorry for it afterwards. You can't have it both ways."

"You seem to have made up your mind about a lot of things. Wisdom of the East, one might almost call it," he said, rather pleased with the phrase because he had only recently discovered Rabindranath Tagore. "Look here, I don't mind telling you the truth if you like: I was angry with you because . . ." he stopped.

"Because?"

"It doesn't matter," he said, spinning a flat pebble into the sea again, making ducks-and-drakes.

"I'll tell you why," said Shirin; "it was because you didn't like anyone but yourself coming to this cove."

Her perception startled him.

"How on earth did you know that?"

"Because I was angry with you myself for the same reason. I hated finding you here."

"Do you like this cove, then?"

"I like all this coast," she replied, surprised at herself for answering him so frankly, "and yet I don't live here, —I've got no right to like it,—it doesn't belong to me in the same way as it belongs to you."

"It doesn't really belong to me yet," he said, misunderstanding her, and answering her with apologetic modesty.

She, for her part, was puzzled by his embarrassment. "How do you mean, it doesn't really belong to you yet?"

"Well, my grandfather is still alive, you see," he said, kicking the sand with his toe, and he stooped to pick up another flat stone, and span it again.

"I see. Then you must be Venn le Breton."

"Yes, that is my name. How did you know?"

"Our landlady told me about you; Mrs. Jolly. You are the person whose grandfather she calls the Ranger, and you the young Ranger always, but she did also tell me your real name. All the fishermen talk of your grandfather as the Ranger and of your grandmother as Madame."

"Yes, I know, he's called that because he is Ranger of the moors,—a silly sort of hereditary thing, you know, —Crown lands, and all that." He blushed and changed the subject. "Have you ever been across to Storn?"

"No, never," she said; reservedly, he thought. Then she came to meet him once more with a gesture of frankness. "If you want to know, I wouldn't go. I should hate to spy on people's places, like all those trippers who go off every day in the boat."

"That's nice of you. I hate the trippers myself,—I should like to pick them off one by one with an air-gun." He said this with such savagery that she sympathised.

"So should I, in your place."

"Look here," he said,—it seemed to be a favourite expression of his, and he pronounced it with decision and arrogance,—"would you like to come across, now, with me? I'll take you in my boat, but only if you are a good sailor."

To his surprise she did not leap at the suggestion.

"It is very kind of you, but I think I won't."

"Why not?" Now that she held back he became determined to take her. "I can send a message to your people, if it's them you are thinking of," he said, rather kindly and patronisingly, "for I imagine that you aren't staying at Mrs. Jolly's by yourself? I know that, because you said *our* landlady."

"I wasn't thinking of my people. If I went with you, I shouldn't tell them at all, either before or after."

"How queer you are, do you always do exactly as you like?" Seeing that she made no reply, he went on, "Then why won't you come?" and nearly added "Damn you" again.

"Do you really want to know?—No, I can't tell you. I'm sorry, I was just going to tell you, but I can't tell you."

Because she saw that he loved the island and because she knew what she would herself feel about the pine-woods if they were hers, she would not add herself to the offensive trippers, even at his invitation. But she could not tell him this.

He considered her once more. He was older than she was, and although he had little enough experience of the world it did just cross his mind that she might be refusing for purely conventional reasons. He discarded the idea as soon as it was born. There was a depth and a warmth and a secrecy about her which eliminated such considerations; they were not, and never would be, her guides in life. The only guides she would follow were her own principles and her own decisions. He became confused then for an instant, wondering just exactly how grown-up she was, or how childish, for at one moment she seemed in full possession of her intentions and at the next moment seemed baffled herself by some nearly-expressed impulse which an inner instinct warned her to suppress. Meanwhile she was, as he had said, very pretty, sitting on her rock with her curls blown about by the breeze; but there, again, her prettiness was confusing, for it held a greater danger in it than mere prettiness could ever hold. *She is a difficult person to get hold of*, he thought; *indeed, I doubt if one could ever get hold of her at all, and that's the maddening part of her,—she is there, and then one turns round and she isn't there; she has slithered away. Is she beautiful*, he thought? *no, she's not beautiful,—beauty is a more dignified thing and is apt to have an aquiline nose;—is she pretty? yes, but many girls are pretty, especially at that soft age; is she lovely? yes, she is really lovely, for she changes the whole time, and every new light on her face gives it a new meaning; there are moments when she looks almost plain, and then she turns her head and the shadows come differently, and she is lovely again, with a loveliness one wishes to seize, and cannot.* "What is your substance, whereof are you made, that millions of strange shadows on you tend?"; he would, and rightly, have applied the quotation to her, had he but been acquainted with it, but he was not a person who read poetry. *And then*, he went on, *at moments she is friendly, and at other moments she goes away into herself.* "Look here," he said, "I want you to come to Storn."

"Seriously, do you?"

"Seriously I do. Don't you want to come?"

She wanted to, more than anything she could think of, but she said only, and rather coldly, without enthusiasm, "Yes, I'll come, if you mean it."

"Come along then."

They went.

They were both quite irresponsible. *My family*, she thought, *shan't know;* for she had without hesitation decided that her family should hear nothing of her day's occupation. *I couldn't endure Mother's questionings*, she thought; and having thus arranged the situation in her own mind, she as usual cast all qualms aside with a grand recklessness. Sitting in the bow of the little boat on the dancing waters while Venn pulled steadily and strongly at his oars, she felt so sharply happy that she longed to catch the moment, hold it, keep it for ever, like a note of music, vibrant, eternal; a secret which no one should ever prise out of her; not even Venn, though in a sense he shared it with her. *But he doesn't really share it, for he doesn't know, he can't know, what I am feeling.* No one could ever know, exactly, the precise shade of what one was feeling. He accompanied her in body but not in mind. *Nobody*, she thought, *can get into one's mind, if one is sufficiently determined to prevent them. Admission is by privilege, not by compulsion. Only to the person I love, if ever there is one*, she thought, *will that privilege of admission ever be granted. I don't want to grant it*, she thought; *I dread being obliged to grant it; I don't understand that thing called love, still less that thing called intimacy; I don't even want to understand it, since apparently it robs one of all independence, and independence is the only thing worth preserving, and the one thing most difficult to preserve. Thank God,* she thought, *I have always kept myself separate hitherto.* She looked at Venn, liking him now, not hating him, liking him all the more because she held a secret against him, several secrets: her own desire to walk at last on Storn; her own satisfaction at having kept herself away from it for all those years; her firmness in the refusal to go there, even at his invitation, until she was quite sure he would not resent her presence. She liked him, too, for another reason, of which he was also unconscious: for the satisfaction that he gave her by the rhythmical movement of his body, bending to the strong stroke of the oars, backwards and forwards, his muscles swelling and then subsiding under his jersey. Rhythm in any form gave her a sensuous satisfaction always. And the boy was beautiful in a way, beautiful in body though not in face; beautiful in body because he was young and hard and spare and just as he ought to be; but her satisfaction in him was quite impersonal; she watched him much as she might have watched the action of a young horse; not with any thought of him as a young male; for although she possessed a certain experience of men, even beyond her years, and had acquired a certain superficially competent manner in her dealings with them, who invariably treated her as sheer woman already, not as an independent person irrespective of sex, so that she had to act up and behave in the way expected of her, she yet remained untouched and unaware whenever her defences were not being called into play. They were not being called into play at this moment. This moment, for her, was compounded of a dancing sea, a small boat, herself alive in it, a rhythmical creature bending to a pair of oars, and Storn in the distance, Storn which for ten years she had,—and how wisely!—refused. The moment was as pure as a draught of water, a note of music. All tiresome, impinging complications introduced into her life by young men, or old men too for that matter, were for the moment mercifully absent. Venn was simply the healthy creature, rowing, and taking her to Storn. He was part of the boat and the water, and part also of the tin of bait and the dead silvery fish lying at the bottom of the boat, and he was also the person who was taking her to Storn; but he was not a real person to her, and her thoughts were utterly withdrawn from him. Her thoughts were not thoughts at all, but simply a haze of feeling.

His voice interrupted her unexpectedly, so that she jumped.

"I don't suppose you like that bait, do you?" he was saying. He was saying it in a sneering way, not in the courteous way of a young gentleman being considerate about the feelings of a girl he has taken out in his boat. He spared a hand from the oar to point at the disgusting mess of bait tangled slimily in the tin at the bottom of the boat, and rescued the oar just as it was about to slip into the sea.

"I don't mind it in the least, if that's what you mean," she replied, looking at the bait; "why should I?"

"Well," he said, rather disconcerted, "I thought women didn't like worms."

"Yes," she said, suddenly amused and breaking into the ringing laughter that her family knew so well; "yes, you thought that women didn't like worms, and you had a preconceived idea that I was squeamish, hadn't you?"

"Well," he said, considering her while he rested on his oars for a moment, "you look like a squeamish person."

Oh, she thought, *if he only knew the sights I see in the children's ward! If he knew the things I force myself to look at! If he knew how I shrink, and refuse to allow myself to shrink! But he has never seen such sights; he has never seen children in pain; he is soft; he is sheltered. He thinks me squeamish, does he?* And bending forward she took up a handful of the bait and allowed it to drip back through her fingers.

"I say!" he exclaimed, shocked, "you shouldn't have done that."

"Why not, if I wanted to?"

"Your hands," he muttered; "they're too small, too . . ." Delicate was the word he wanted, but either he did not find it, or was reluctant to use it.

"Oh, they will wash," she said lightly, and trailed them in the water.

She could see the island better now, with its little harbour and fleet of fishing-boats, brightly painted, idle in the sun; and the pink-washed cottages whose green shutters gave them a curiously un-English appearance; and the ruddy mass of the Norman castle high up above its terraces; and the pine-trees going down to the sea. She could see fishermen standing about on the jetty, watching Venn's boat, and a dog or two, snuffing at a heap of garbage. All rather pleasantly lazy, with an air of noonday about them; rather foreign, even the dogs, mongrels who belonged to nobody in particular; but she, who had never been abroad since they had returned from Persia when she was five, did not know about things being foreign; she just thought it was somehow different from anything else she knew; different from England, although they had left the coast by only a couple of miles. But Venn was not making for the harbour, he was rounding the island, so that the village disappeared from sight and nothing was left but the tops of the rounded towers and the dark woods going down to the sea. This, then, was the other side of the island, the side in whose existence she had never quite believed. It was rocky down by the water's edge, with many little inlets and creeks, overhung by sombre, twisted bushes of box and myrtle growing out of the mossy rocks, and the gleam of the water in between, all very deep and rich and shadowy on this bright day when the rest of the world lay out in the sunshine of the ocean, sparkling in diamonds on a pavement of blue. Cool and green and gloomy, and extremely secret, in contrast with the diamond sparkle of the open sea; and then rising up out of the little secret inlets and creeks to the height of the pine-trees that mounted the hill to its summit and were blown crooked by the gales until it seemed that their tops had all been shaven to a slant by the single swish of an enormous scythe. Her frank happiness had left her now, and had been replaced by a deep unfathomable excitement. She felt as though she were about to set foot on enchanted ground,—really enchanted, where anything, physically, might come along, and where anything, spiritually, might happen within oneself; where one might feel and act the most incalculable things, though whether good or evil, who could foresee? but in any case unescapable. A coward spirit would draw back, a brave and reckless spirit go forward.

"We'll land here," said Venn, and pulled in, where a little pool of dark still water lay triangularly between a cleft in the rocks. He knew the way exactly; he knew each stroke of the oar necessary to bring them in. She liked his skill. Shipping his oars, he leaped ashore and helped her out of the boat, and as she stepped for the first time on the soil of Storn,—very soft too, on the peaty thickness of the pine-needles,—she knew that he did after all resent her presence there. The very touch of his hand was sullen. She said nothing; she didn't say, as she felt impelled to say, "You don't want me here,—let us go back,—let us go away again,—let us go back even to the cove where we hated each other so much at first": she said none of these things; she merely landed, without fuss or protest but with the help of his hand, on the island he had brought her to. She stood under the pines, silent, motionless, aware of the angry boy at her side and of the peculiar resilience of the soil beneath her feet.

"Well, what do you want to do now?" he asked. He would have spoken really roughly, but that his innate good-breeding prevented him. As it was, he added with such show of hospitality as he could command, "Shall we go up to the house, or what?"

By "the house" she knew he meant "the castle." And, sympathising with him because she herself would have resented the presence of a stranger on her own island, she unexpectedly became gentle towards him. "We'll do whatever you like," she said; "I don't particularly want to walk about; let us stay down here if you like; and then you can take me back."

Touched, he suddenly saw her as very young, very vulnerable. He knew that she had been happy, five minutes earlier, and now was not happy any more. In some way or other he had spoilt her happiness for her. And his own happiness was spoilt too; he had enjoyed rowing her across the sea, he had enjoyed bringing her to his own private landing-place, evading the boatmen watching him from the jetty, he had looked forward to taking her up through the pines by paths he knew; but now everything had gone flat; he no longer wanted to do anything at all. Looking up at the sky, he expected to find the sun gone behind a cloud. It had done nothing of the sort, but was blazing as cloudlessly and serenely as ever above the sparkling sea. Only the creek where he had brought her and moored his boat was dark and shadowy and overhung by the sombre trees, blotting out the sun so as to make him believe that it had gone behind a cloud.

"Just as you prefer," he said, sulky; angry with her because on her account he felt he had somehow behaved badly; angry with her because he wanted to restore her happiness and his own also, but lacked the skill to do so. "Ne sachant pas comment s'y prendre," he said to himself, because he was working up for a French exam. and had got certain idioms into his head, which muddled him because at times they seemed to have no bearing on real life and at other times a great deal. "Ne sachant pas comment s'y prendre," he thought again, fixing the phrase in his head at the useful moment when it could take on a new significance and could mean something definite, instead of meaning nothing outside the green phrase-book which he had in his pocket and which bored him.

"No, we won't stay down here," he said, jumping up. "Come on. I'll take you to Andromeda's Cave."

"Andromeda's Cave?"

"That's only my name for it," said Venn; "don't call it that to anybody else, or they won't understand what you mean. I call it Andromeda's Cave because it has iron rings fastened into the rock so that one can tie up a boat there, and when I was a kid I always imagined it as the sort of place Andromeda might have waited for the dragon in. Of course that was before I realised that Andromeda's rock was really out in the open, not in a cave at all." He said this as though anxious that she should not underestimate his present erudition. "One has to wade into it, by the way. Shall you mind?"

"Of course I shan't mind."

They set off, and their happiness came back. They were both happy again, with the simple childish happiness they had both known in the boat. Venn especially was happy, because he felt that by letting her see his beloved cave he was making reparation for his unkind and unreasonable resentment. And he must admit that she scrambled along as nimbly as a boy. True, every now and then she stretched out her hand for him to help her over a difficult place, but he did not mind that: he liked the cool touch of her hand, and he liked the implication of her dependence on his superior strength. So he cheerfully dragged her up and down the rocks. The coast of the island grew steeper and steeper here, so that only a narrow strip of sand ran between the foot of the cliffs and the lipping of the sea. Myrtle and box had been left behind, and nothing but red valerian, pink thrift, and grey-green sedum coloured the face of the rocks. They did so in profusion. Shirin, throwing a glance upward, looked up into a curtain of tumbling rosy loveliness.

"You'll have to take your shoes and stockings off now, I'm afraid," said Venn, sitting down on a boulder himself to give the example.

Barefoot, they splashed onwards through the encroaching sea. The thin little waves came licking the base of the cliff. They were lazy little summery waves, with scarcely enough energy to break themselves against the resisting land. They just arrived, turned over once, and fell, listless, languid, spent. But Shirin thought how magnificently they must roar against the cliff, in storms when they ceased to be little summery waves and became Atlantic breakers.

"This is the way," said Venn, leading her, stopping to roll his trousers higher. "You must pick up your skirts," he said, showing some solicitude for her, "it gets a bit deeper here."

They splashed into a little creek where the water rose to their knees. The mouth of the cave appeared, black and high and narrow in the cliff's face. "Don't be frightened," said Venn, reassuring her; "the water doesn't get any deeper after this."

They were in the cave now. Shirin liked it. It was dark and cool in there; paved with black water; rising to a high and jagged roof. As her eyes accustomed themselves to the half-light, she discerned the roof and the iron rings of which Venn had spoken. They were secured into the opposite wall of rock, with a black pool of water making the floor of the cave beneath them. *Poor Andromeda,* thought Shirin with sudden sympathy for another woman; *it would be worse to wait for a dragon in here, than outside in the sun and the open air; one could better bear to die in the sun than in the darkness.* All her fear of the dark made her sympathise with Andromeda, yet at the same time she felt exhilarated as she always felt exhilarated when life became mysteriously and inexplicably dangerous.

"Well, there you are," said Venn, resentful again now

that he had brought her to his secret place; "that's Andromeda's Cave."

Shirin said nothing; she was under a spell.

"Look," said Venn, angry because she said nothing, "there are the rings I told you about. They were put there hundreds of years ago."

"Yes," she said, "I see."

"I should like to chain you up to them," he said; "yes," he continued, suddenly and savagely possessed by something he did not understand, "I should like to chain you up to them naked and beat you and beat you till you screamed.—I told you the rings were there so that one could tie up boats, didn't I? Well, that was true in a way: we do use them now for boats. But it wasn't entirely true, —at least, I don't think it was. Tradition says that some old le Breton put them there originally to chain up his woman because she'd been unfaithful to him. They say, he left her there for a whole week in the winter,—it's pretty rough here in the winter, I can tell you,—and at the end of the week she was found hanging dead by some fisherman who had taken his boat into the cave for refuge. God knows what he'd done to her in the meantime. History doesn't relate that."

"Had he beaten and beaten her till she screamed?" asked Shirin, on whom the words appeared to have exercised some unexpected fascination. She was staring at the rings as though she saw the body of the old le Breton's woman hanging there.

Venn laughed.

"I say, you are queer, aren't you? Just because I tell you that old story. . . . Come along, let's go back. We shall have to go back the way we came, I'm afraid: there's no path up the cliff. Come along; don't stare at those rings any longer. I'm sorry I told you that story. I'm sorry I said I should like to chain you up there. Of course I was only joking. You didn't take it seriously, did you? People don't do that sort of thing, nowadays." She had such an odd look in her eyes, that he felt he must reassure her. Still, it was true that he had wanted to chain her up; and that odd look in her eyes did nothing to diminish his desire. He still wanted to tie her, helpless, to those hard rings. He had experienced a curious pleasure in frightening her. It reminded him somehow of the curious pleasure he had experienced when, as a prefect, he had first thrashed a lower boy at school. He had been ashamed, then, of his own relish; he was ashamed again, now, of his relish in frightening the unknown anonymous girl. He couldn't think what had impelled him to do it. But, having done it, he felt he must make amends; he felt he must make her happy again; must comfort her; reassure her.

He enjoyed the power of reassuring her just as much as he had enjoyed the power of momentarily alarming her. Besides, he liked being happily at ease with her: she was clearly a person with whom one could be happily at ease, though at the same time a person whose danger was never absent. "Come on," he said; "let's go."

They made their way back along the coast, on the best of terms once more. They went up the hill under the pines. They went scrambling up the brown slope between the trees, and he paused to tell her that owls nested in the holes high up in the trunks and that recently he had found a young owl fallen out of its nest which, although uninjured, fell over on its back and died of rage and indignation at his approach. There were squirrels too, red ones, not grey ones such as Shirin was accustomed to seeing round London. But here, of course, isolated, nothing could ever have contaminated their true breed. She noted inwardly that their red fur matched the colour of the pine-trunks, and thought what a blaze of reddish-brown the trunks must turn to, when the light of sunset struck them from the west. Loving pines as she did beyond all other trees, this was the first time she had ever seen them in actuality as she imagined they ought to be, very tall and grave and like a temple, on a sloping hill with the sea glittering between their trunks, and their boughs spread out like hands in a dark benediction over the gay waters. But as she never made comments about anything which affected her, she kept these reflections entirely to herself. "Thank God," thought Venn, "she doesn't chatter."

Strangers were not admitted to this part of the island. Strangers, indeed, were very savagely regulated by the morose old bullying Ranger. He could not prevent them from chugging round his shores in that old tub of a paddle-boat the *Daffodil*, which provided a convenient object for his scorn when at a loss for anything else to disdain; nor could he prevent them from landing at the jetty and invading the few shops that supplemented their living in the summer by picture-postcards, bulls'-eyes, and teas, but he could and did prevent them from setting foot on any other part of his property. A posse of keepers in his pay, vigorously abetted by his grandson Venn, pounced on any impudent straggler and chased him in humiliation out to sea again. The Ranger, although he did his duty in various ways by the county, was devoid of any truly democratic instinct. He hated democracy even more vehemently than he loved privilege, and consequently had a double hatred of trespassers on his own private island. His grandson Venn had inherited these prejudices to their fullest value. Both the old Ranger and the young Ranger were as unaccommodating as they well could be, and understood one another over that, though they might quarrel over other things.

"Oh Lord," said Venn, "there's my grandmother."

A very beautiful old woman was approaching them down a path. She walked cautiously, leaning on a stick. Shirin saw at once that she was very beautiful, or had been. She had all the grace and assurance which old age achieves when it has enjoyed an exaggeration of beauty and charm from youth onwards throughout the processional years of life. Although she leant now on a stick, she still walked with all the confidence of young beauty coming into the lights of a ballroom. That was a grace, an assurance, and a confidence which would live after death in the memory of those who had known her.

"Look here," said Venn hurriedly to Shirin, "I don't know your name."

He introduced her then to his grandmother. Lady le Breton, rather taken aback by the presence of a stranger in those sacred woods, though authorised by her fierce and fastidious grandson, gave two gracious fingers to Shirin and liked her instantly; she liked her for the soft warm touch of her hand and for the half-veiled, half-candid lifting of the starry eyes. She liked her for the mixture of sophistication and wild innocence. Two women, they took each other's measure across the chasm of the years. Shirin wondered what the old woman had known, and Lady le Breton wondered, more wistfully, what the child would have to learn. Neither of them put it into those words, but the flame of an inner knowing flew between them.

"But, my dear children," said Lady le Breton, concerned, "have you had any luncheon? It's nearly three o'clock."

Venn saw that his grandmother was in her best mood. She had other moods, as he knew well; more exciting, perhaps, but also more alarming; less charming, less amiable. Even in her charm at its maximum lurked danger, which intensified it.

"Now run up to the house," Madame continued, "and get Graves to give you something to eat. I'll follow you, but my steps are not so quick as yours."

"Grandpapa?" said Venn.

"Asleep," said Lady le Breton, smiling and nodding.

"Come on then," said Venn as he had said before, and Shirin followed him because outwardly she always did as she was told unless she had any very good reason for not so doing, but inwardly she minded leaving Madame, who held her and fascinated her.

The castle, seen from this side, was less forbidding than from the sea, and its sun-flashed walls more amiably rosy. This was partly because one approached it on the level, instead of seeing it towering above one. One approached it along the famous level terrace-walk of turf, stretching between yews several hundred years old, cut into fantastic shapes of wild animals barely recognisable today in their original design: an elephant under its howdah, a leopard leaping onto the back of a crouched gazelle. In their grotesqueness and extravagance and gnarled antiquity, they made the word topiary seem vulgar and silly; pettily elaborate, and reminiscent of plants in tubs at a flower-show.

"We call this the Zoo," said Venn, vaguely waving his hand. He seemed to be apologising for it, but she guessed the pride under the deprecation. He did not add that he himself had invented the expression at the age of six; an expression received with amusement by his grandfather in place of the reverential attitude usually adopted towards the famous terrace by his family and kinsmen. Venn's irreverent nickname had become a standing joke from the moment the Ranger first heard it. That childish joke dated the moment when the Ranger first began to like his heir.

How lucky, she thought, *that the Ranger's ancestors had not trimmed their yews into pheasants and tea-pots!* The fantasy of the wild beasts distorted by age into apocryphal semblance, completed the fantasy of the red castle hung above the sea. Shirin was silent, taking it in. There was no garden, properly speaking, she noticed; no garden, in the sense that she had been accustomed to consider gardens, although she had always hated them; no pretty, garish beds or borders; no real attempt to tame Nature; nothing but the severity of the mown turf and the high terraces and the dark enormous yews. And then the castle with its rounded towers, sunburnt and barbaric, of an undefinable colour, varying and capricious, as pink as old brick where the sun caught it, but far more temperamental; as sinister as dried blood in the shadow. Its walls could blush or darken; it shared the quality of both a warrior and a girl. Its colour reminded her of something else she had recently seen; and, groping round in her mind, she found it: the colour of the pine-trunks in the sun, which might be merely brown until the sun touched them, and but which then turned red as they started up into life. Rose-red and dark-green; that was the symphony of Storn, dashed with the blue of the sea beyond.

Lady le Breton came in while they were still eating in the big dining-room. They were eating hungrily, with the appetite of the very young who have let their usual hour go by. Shirin, by nature frankly greedy, liked her meals; she could forget about them until they became due or overdue, losing herself readily in other and far less mundane things, but once recalled to the actuality of breakfast, luncheon, or supper, she started to think about them with the urgency of a hungry puppy. So now she looked up at Madame, bothered by the remembrance that Madame half an hour ago had held her and fascinated her as a new and unexplored experience. Regarding her now from another standpoint as an interruption to her luncheon, she wished rather impatiently that life might allow one to keep one's pleasures separate, and that this excellent cold pie secreting hard-boiled eggs so beautifully yellow, and jelly so beautifully brown, should not coincide so inconveniently with the reappearance of this important and preponderant old woman. For there was no escaping Lady le Breton. She eclipsed; she ruled. Whether in her good and charming mood, or in her bad, she left no place for anybody else in the room.

So Lady le Breton came in, leaning on her stick, and Venn the defiant and the independent made a grandfilial gesture to help her to a chair, and Graves the butler hastened forward too, and she accepted their deference as her due, imposing the obligation upon them and allowing them to deposit her dominantly at the head of the table. She propped her stick against the arm of her chair, and sat there, beautiful and alarming, talking to the children while they ate. She talked to them casually and charmingly, passing from one thing to the other, describing now the way an enamoured bull-fighter had once tossed a bull's ear into her lap; and then the way that William Morris in his exuberant fashion had told her exactly what he would do with Storn if it were his. She sat there, entertaining the two children by these anecdotes, new even to Venn who had never heard those particular stories before; he wondered, in fact, why his grandmother should lay herself out to be so charming and amusing, telling stories he had never heard her tell before, not realising that Shirin by her silent presence and eager eyes made her tell them, working on Madame with the same unintentional attraction as she used on young and old. Venn knew only that his grandmother was in her best mood, not scolding Graves even when he clattered the plates as she usually scolded him, but displaying all the graces of a woman of the world who is determined to charm.

Oh, thought Shirin, making another discovery to add to the sum of the short experience which she was always carefully and deliberately increasing, *what a depth and richness there is in women! This old woman could tell me everything I want to know. It mightn't be accurate and it probably wouldn't be true, but it certainly would bear more relation to truth than anything Father Weakes at Dulwich told me when I went to him for guidance and he made me kneel with him in prayer at a horse-hair sofa and I picked out the long wiry hairs while he prayed. This old woman, beautiful and wicked and good, with a power of charm beyond reason, holds more danger and wickedness, beauty and goodness and wisdom in her than anyone I have ever met.* Nevertheless, fearless, inquisitive, and recipient though she was, she underwent a moment of alarm when Lady le Breton bore her off, after luncheon, saying, "Now I am going to steal her from you, Venn, for half an hour," and found herself in a sitting-room overlooking the sea with a window-seat in the recess of the window. But in spite of the sea and the recess and the sense of being very high up and of looking out over nothing but the immensity of waters, it was not really at all the kind of room which she expected to find in that stern and lovely fortress. She had expected bare stone walls and sparse, rough furniture; even bare floors, perhaps, whereas this room was deeply carpeted and so crowded with furniture and objects that one entered it in fear of knocking something over. She realised then that this was Madame's private room, remorselessly overburdened with its owner's personality. She was amused. On principle she hated rooms stuffed full of comfort and objects; she hated rooms which revealed anything of their inhabitant. Her own room, she had always determined, and her own house, if ever she had one, should be as coldly and discreetly non-committal as possible. Never should it express or betray anything of herself. Yet her amusement at this room affectionately overcame all her prejudices. It supplemented and completed so exactly and rightly all the impressions she had received of Lady le Breton! It was like a life stuffed full of memories; a life not only full of memories of the past but also full of the activities of the present. There were photographs of bygone friends, both men and women, on every shelf and table; and those were dead; but there were also evidences of an untiring, continuous zest for living, witness the picture-frames made of sea-shells, the unopened parcels with which tables and chairs were heaped and littered, the door-stops made out of anchors, the lobster-pots transformed into waste-paper baskets. An active ingenuity was at work, which ordered things from shops and then forgot to unpack them, or turned things to uses for which they had never been intended; an energetic mind, running sometimes to waste; yet a mind which created its own world, keeping no contact with the world of real life. Nor desiring it. Madame, on her island, led an existence divorced from the world of real life by something more than a mere expanse of sea. On a lesser and more feminine scale, a creativeness was at work as novel and original in its own way as the creativeness which had once imagined the wild beasts tortured out of yew on the terrace-walk.

Shirin looked at Lady le Breton and loved her. She saw the extraordinary contrast between Lady le Breton and Storn, and her own home at Dulwich. She saw Dulwich spelt with two *ll*'s. She saw fantasy for the first time incarnate, and recognised it as something she had always desired. At that moment she looked up and met Lady le Breton's eyes. Both she and Lady le Breton smiled, out of the deeps of their understanding. "Well?" said Madame.

Shirin had nothing to say. She could find conventional things to say as a rule, but here they were stopped dead, in the queer encumbered room with the deep old woman and all her unopened parcels and her photograph-frames made of shells. So, wisely, she said nothing; she simply kept her eyes on the old woman's face.

"You have very beautiful eyes, my child,—have you been told that before? Yes, I see you have. Of course you have. They are expressive and yet secret; deep, and yet mocking. You laugh a lot, and yet you think. You are gay, and yet you can be unhappy. You are friendly and merry, and yet you give nothing of yourself. You are a most misleading person, and a very attractive one.—You must not resent my saying these things," she added, with the charm that had turned many hearts; "I could be your grandmother, you see, as I am Venn's, though I never can see why that should give one an excuse for impertinence."

"I don't resent it," said Shirin truthfully, realising at the same time with amusement how indignantly she would have resented it from anybody else.

"Yes," said Lady le Breton meditatively pursuing her thought, "an easy life is not for you. Life is never easy for those who are obliged to make themselves hard in self-defence.—Now come," she said, patting the window-seat beside her; "sit down and tell me something about yourself. Oh, not about your real self! Even though I could be your grandmother, I wouldn't ask you that. But about where you live and where you met Venn and why he brought you to Storn and where you are staying? for you are a foreigner, I think?"

"A foreigner?" said Shirin, surprised. She thought Lady le Breton was alluding to her Persian name.

Lady le Breton laughed.

"Perhaps you didn't know that in this part of the world we have a way of referring to everybody as foreigners who come from another part of England? Our local patriotism expresses itself most contemptuously, and I have caught the trick myself in all the years I have lived here, more than three times the number of years you have spent on earth. Besides, I am not a foreigner myself; I was a cousin of Venn's grandfather before I married him. This is a very peculiar part of the world, you know, and very peculiar things happen here. What else could you expect from a coast accustomed to wrecks? The standard of life alters, when danger becomes ordinary and every-day. Most people forget that life is dangerous, but down here we are never allowed to forget it.—Anyhow," said Madame pulling herself back, "I was asking you to tell me something about yourself, wasn't I? I wasn't meaning to talk to you about the dangers of life."

"Please go on, though," said Shirin. She really wanted Lady le Breton to go on. She had never met anyone before whose ideas she wanted to hear, except the ideas of people like her friend the hospital matron, who was practical by intention and poignant by chance; or the ideas of people like Mrs. Jolly who was rich and thick and human and humorous and cynical and warm-hearted and vulgar turn and turn about. Lady le Breton was a new experience; Shirin did not trust her,—her charm was too good to be true, too true to be good,—the ice was thin, always,—yet in spite of the mistrust she was fascinated, won over; there was some quality in Madame which made her want to explore it and squeeze it to the drops of its wisdom and, possibly, of its mischief.

She was startled, later on, to hear Madame saying, "Venn will be as black as thunder by now; do you know that we have kept him waiting for two hours?" *Two hours*, she thought? *is it possible that I have talked and listened for two hours? In one sense, it seemed ten minutes; in another sense, five years.* Even then, she was not decided whether to regard her companion as divinely good or magnificently wicked, —for, being sixteen, she still believed that people, and especially all very definite people, could be sorted into those two categories. Wicked or not, Madame had certainly had a strange effect upon her: she had made her talk. And this was the strangest thing of all: that although she mistrusted Madame, and knew her to be capable of the darkest mischief, she had responded with a frankness she had never accorded to human being before. She had answered questions with the utmost truthfulness and candour; questions which affected the most secret parts of her life. She had explained exactly why she wanted, when she was old enough, to train at the hospital. She had explained exactly why she loved Storn and hated Dulwich. She had talked about Persia and the little that she remembered of it; the precious, treasured, romantic little. She had even told Lady le Breton about the child that had been run over; and about other things too. The only reservation she had made had been one of loyalty towards her family; there, she had just answered that they were all "very nice," and Lady le Breton, recognising the instant curtness of her voice, had let the subject go. She had revealed herself in this way, because she knew that Madame (in spite of her mischief?) would never get her values wrong. And values mattered to Shirin more than anything in life.

"Venn is an impatient person," Lady le Breton was saying, "and may well have taken himself off by now. Never mind, I will ring for a boat to take you back." (*Ring for a boat*, thought Shirin? *she says that as somebody else might say Telephone for a cab*. And was there, *was* there? —a note of malicious amusement in her voice as she indicated that Venn might be annoyed?) "I do hope," Lady le Breton continued, "that your parents have not been anxious about you?" Her manner had suddenly become conventional, though kindly; making Shirin shrink back into her little-girl self. The magic shrivelled; she was just a girl to whom Lady le Breton had been kind for an hour,—two hours.

III

VENN was annoyed indeed; he was more than annoyed; he was furious. Furious on several counts. (But then he was so easily made furious; and hid it in himself, darkly.) First he turned sullen because he was kept waiting. Then he started to rage against his grandmother, because she had done it on purpose. He knew his grandmother,—oh yes! he knew her well, the artful old woman! Then he raged against Shirin, which was most unfair; but he raged against her only superficially, not deeply, because she meant nothing to him at all; she was just a girl he had picked up in his young-lordly way. Finally he shrugged his shoulders and went down to the harbour to talk to the fisher-boys. When his grandmother wanted to get rid of the girl she could ring for a boat. He, Venn, refused to wait about any longer. For the girl he had no personal feeling one way or the other; but there was more personal feeling than was comfortable between himself and his grandmother, whom he hated and adored and despised and respected and fought. They clashed and wrangled all the time. This stealing of Shirin, and keeping him waiting, was just another clash and wrangle. So what was there for him to do but to go down to the harbour and talk to the fisher-boys?

Shirin saw him there, when she went down the path to find the boat that Lady le Breton had ordered for her after calling without much hope for Venn. She would willingly have avoided him, not because she was afraid of him or his temper, but because she was already so full of impressions that she felt she would overflow. She wanted now to be alone with her thoughts of Storn and Lady le Breton. But he saw her too, and sauntered up, looking insolent.

"So she's finished with you at last, has she? And how did you get on?"

"I like her," said Shirin. She was not going to be intimidated by Venn. Wherever her loyalty was given, it was passionate.

"Do you? Well, good luck to you in your liking. Of course you like her; everybody does, when she means them to. She took a fancy to you, I could see. Anyhow, she never leaves Storn, so you're not likely to see her again."

Is he being deliberately rude? I shan't tell him that she has asked me to come back.

"Probably not.—I must go now, and thank you very much for having brought me over."

She made a movement towards the boat that she saw waiting for her. It rocked slightly as the watchful boatman with the painter in his hand pulled it in closer to the jetty steps. He waited for the young lady. But as she made ready to step in, Venn caught her by the wrist.

"Don't go just yet."

He added under his breath, so that the boatman should not overhear, "You shan't go just yet."

The boatman waited, patient, holding his boat by the painter close to the steps. He looked amused, as though he were used to the ways of the young Ranger; the other boatmen, lounging round, looked amused too.

"All right, Matthew," he said aloud to the boatman; "you can wait a bit."

He took her away, towards the pines. He still led her, as it were unconsciously, by the wrist. They went out of sight of the harbour, round the corner of the island.

"Look here, you have a damned cheek, haven't you? Going off with my grandmother, and keeping me hanging about like that?"

"It wasn't my fault," said Shirin. She was frightened of him now, but she still kept her loyalty towards his grandmother, whom she had for two hours loved. "It wasn't my fault," she said, "if your grandmother took me up to her room."

"No, it wasn't your fault, I suppose," he said, dropping away from her. They were standing now beneath the pines, detached, and very separate from one another. "No, it wasn't your fault," he said, not angry any more, but suddenly sad. His temper had receded from him, and his rage; he looked merely tired now, and worn out.

"Look here," she said, unconsciously adopting his phrase, "I'm sorry I kept you waiting."

"That's all right," he said, school-boyish again.

They were both unhappy. Uneasy they both were. They stood under the pines, not knowing how to get things right again between them. Now that he had let go of her wrist he felt that he had no more contact with her. She stood there, soft and desirable and available, but now that he had let go of her wrist he had no more contact with her; she was separate; cut off. They were both separate; cut off.

Their lives were separate, and could never join. So he was sad; not angry; just sad.

"You'd better go back," he said, in despair.

"The boat is waiting," she said, making another movement as though in obedience to his words, a movement away from the pine-wood, back towards the harbour.

"You shan't go just yet," he said again, catching her. Liveliness had revived in him.

"Why shouldn't I?" she said, resisting him.

"You shan't," he said. He had caught her by the arm this time, but in order to get a better grip without bruising her he caught her now by the hand. Her hand went to nothing in his; it fell together as though he had caught a bird. It went so soft and narrow, as though it could slip through his, leaving him with nothing to hold her by.

Then with a sudden twist she was free of him. She was free, running through the trees. She ran faster than he would have believed possible, so that it cost him quite a little effort to come up with her. And when he caught her he was excited, strung up, with a new quivering which she did not understand, but which she knew was not exactly anger.

He pushed her down onto her knees, playing the childish trick of slipping his fingers between hers and forcing her downwards, till she knelt, reduced, unwilling, at his feet.

"Now say you're sorry," he said, unbelievably childish.

"I won't. I've nothing to be sorry for, and if I had I wouldn't say so."

"You shall. Say 'I, even I, dirty worm of the earth . . .' go on, repeat it after me."

But he was laughing now; it had turned to a joke. Still,

it remained a dangerous joke; danger was not far off; it was ready to leap out again at any moment.

"Is that what you make people say at school?—Are you at school, by the way?" she asked, still kneeling on the ground where he held her, and looking up at him with a new interest.

"I was. I left at the end of last term. I'm going to Germany now, in October, for two years,—damn it."

It was a queer little conversational interlude, conducted while he still held her kneeling on the ground.

"Don't you want to go?"

"I do and I don't. I do want to live for a bit in Germany, but I like being here most, you see; here at Storn."

"Yes, I see. Of course you do.—How old are you?"

"Eighteen. How old are you?"

"Sixteen." But she resented giving away anything about herself, even so simple a thing as her age.

He went on, "Where do you live, generally? When you aren't staying at Port Breton, I mean?"

"Oh,—near London." Her instinctive secrecy prevented her from saying precisely where.

"How horrid."

"Why, horrid?"

"Well,—I don't know." But he knew quite well what he meant, and she knew it too. "I shouldn't like to live in London or near it," he added lamely and inexplicitly.

"No. Well, I don't like it much, either. I think you are quite right to prefer Storn."

"You like Storn, do you?" he asked, pressing her fingers a little more severely, because he minded so much about Storn.

"Yes, I like Storn."

They paused, contemplating each other, still in the same attitude which was becoming ludicrous as it became prolonged but from which there appeared to be no escape unless one of them made a movement either of release or of evasion.

"I like you for liking Storn."

They paused again.

"Are you ever going to let me get up?"

"Lord, I hadn't noticed that you were still on the ground."

He released her hands, and she began to get up.

"No, don't get up," he said, pushing her down again; "you look nice there, on the ground; you look as though you belonged to it," and suddenly he threw her right down on the earth, and lay beside her, panting.

She was frightened; so was he.

"I like the pines,—do you like them?" he said, holding her close.

"Yes, I like them,—you know I do," she replied, feeling as though he tore something very private out of her.

He held her close to him, so that she felt his heart beating extravagantly.

"Venn,—what's the matter?"

She called him by his name without realising that she did so; she held his head against her breast, in order to comfort him. She pressed it close, and felt herself much stronger than he.

"Venn," she said, stroking his head; "don't worry, you'll come back to Storn."

"Of course I shall," he said, raising his head, ashamed of his weakness, and as he raised it he saw her looking down on him, propped on her elbow above him; she was looking at him with a half-smile and a quizzical expression, half tender, half critical, in her eyes. She was flushed, and her short curls tumbled wildly. Brown and rosy she was, with something touchingly young and immature about the soft curves of her face, contradicting the sophistication in her eyes.

"Lord, you are pretty!" he said involuntarily, and putting up his hand he touched her cheek. She smiled frankly then, amused by the naïveté of his admiration. Just for that second, he was a boy and she a woman.

"How queer you looked, just now," he said. "What were you thinking to yourself? How did you know I suddenly couldn't bear the thought of leaving Storn?"

She gave a little shrug. His question seemed so elementary as to be scarcely worth answering. It was on a par with his crudely expressed admiration of herself.

"How does one know things?" she replied.

"That's what I'm asking you: how do you know things? I never do. I never know things about other people. You seem to. You've said several things today. . . . How is it done? I wish you'd tell me. I feel at such a disadvantage, sometimes, not being able to follow what goes on in people's heads."

"I expect you are always too much taken up with being violently yourself," she said, still amused, but expressing herself carefully.

"Lord!" he said, startled; "Lord!" he said again, having thought it over; "yes, I believe you're right. But how do you know? you *are* a queer person. Wisdom of the East, again. Go on; tell me some more."

She laughed, realising that he now wanted urgently to talk about himself, a desire she had already recognised as apt to arise in men. She had recognised it so often that it no longer interested her, although—as part of the game, —she was usually ready to subscribe to it. One subscribed to it; bored perhaps, but polite; one appeared to listen, and meanwhile one could think of other things; it was very little more than the small change of intercourse.

"I won't tell you any more today. Another time, perhaps."

"Another time,—is there going to be another time?" He sat up, ruffling his fingers through his hair. "Am I going to see you again?"

"Do you want to?"

"Do I want to!" he exclaimed. "Yes, I want to," he continued more calmly; "I want to see you every day you are here; we can meet at the cove if you like.—Look here," he said, with the earnestness of one who has hit on an idea really worth putting forward, "I'll teach you to fish. I'll take you out in my boat every day and teach you to fish. You didn't mind the bait, as most women would, so you can come."

She was enormously amused by this,—by the condescension, by the implication that he knew all about women, and by his quick arrangement of the circumstances to suit his own wishes while pretending to confer a benefit upon her.

"Thank you so much," she said gravely. Then she laughed at him. "You know quite well that you would hate to see me every day, or anybody else for that matter; you know you like having your boat and your cove and your Storn, all to yourself. Come now, don't you?" She looked at him, teasing.

"I did," he said, staring back at her, very earnest; "yes,

I did; you're right in a way. But now I don't any more; I do really want you to come out with me in the boat and fish. You will come, won't you?" he added, appealing. "You'll be here for another three or four weeks, and you'll come out with me every day?"

But she would not promise; she would say only that she would think about it, for she was not at all sure, herself, whether she wanted to meet him again or not. Above all, she was not sure that she wanted to return to Storn.

"I must go," she said, stirring.

"Wait a minute longer." He put his hand on her shoulder to keep her down.

They were still lying on the ground, on the soft pine-needles smelling deep and warm. The sun splintered the branches overhead, and lay about in flecks and splashes as dappled as a fawn. Everything was so still that a rabbit put its head out of a bury, but, seeing them, withdrew it quickly. They looked at each other and smiled. Perhaps the rabbit would come out again; they lay quite still, hardly breathing; watching the bury.

The rabbit remained hidden, and Venn, growing restless, began to speak. She laid the tip of a finger against his lips, to keep him silent. In that gesture, he noted how the tips of her fingers turned back. *She is double-jointed,* he thought; and, amused, he took her hand away and looked at it; he looked at it closely and curiously, examining it; he took each finger in turn, bending each in all its articulations; then he held the hand up to the light, and saw the pink transparency against the sun, as thin, he thought, as the petal of a flower; but where, he wondered, was the difference between this hand and other hands? and then he saw the quality of the skin, so smooth, without roughnesses or visible pores, and then he looked at her throat which had the same quality too, as smooth as cream and as silky, so that he curved his own hand round her throat, and fitted the fingers of his other hand into hers, constricting them rather too unkindly because he liked to feel their flexible fragility cracking under his strength. He pressed harder, hoping to make her give a sign of pain, but she gave none; she only looked without flinching into his pale eyes with hers that were so dark and thickly fringed. He noticed then that in one place her eyelashes went crooked, making a darker blotch, and he touched that place too, learning to know her intimately in small ways, intensive as though he examined her under a magnifying-glass; yet he remained detached, even in this intimate discovery of her. He was detached, even in this very close and intensive examination of her. He saw her very closely, looking at her hand and into her eyes and feeling her throat rounded within his hold; he saw the smoothness of her forehead, and the fringing of the young hair that curled downy and almost golden on the edge of the brown curls. *She has a lot of red in her hair*, he thought, *where the sun catches it; it's as glossy as a horse-chestnut, and as strong and thick as bracken. How alive it looks, and how unruly. What would it be like*, he thought, *to bury one's face in her hair, and holding her close, to feel her come closer of her own accord until she lay as though she had been blown against one's body?*

Turning himself a little, he slipped his arm under her shoulders and held her, as the slow sleepy sensuality of the summer earth and the warm sun crept through them both in the silence. They came nearer to one another, as yielding and as innocent as young animals. In fact they were very like young animals, furry and boneless and flexible, lying together as though tired out after play. Less innocent than she, the thought crossed his mind, *She has lain like this before;* and he began to breathe more deeply, desire mounting in him as he began to doubt her essential innocence. He was scarcely to be blamed, feeling her instinctive movement towards him; her body so softly recipient of his caress. "Shirin!" he whispered, making his limbs touch hers in all their length, so that their thighs and their knees touched, and her face was pressed against his shoulder. A weakness which she had never known overcame her; she lay against him, bewildered by the beating of her own heart and his, so near together, thumping against one another; bewildered too by the weakness which affected all her limbs, a weakness amounting almost to pain, as though she had fever and were going to be ill. Her ankles ached, her wrists and knees and the curve of her spine; her breathing became difficult to control. *Am I swooning?* she thought, the absurd word coming oddly into her mind; *am I dying perhaps? am I drifting away from the earth altogether? Is this heaven?*—for she was religious in a confused, undecided kind of way, believing obediently in the cleft of difference between heaven and earth. *Is this heaven?* she thought, *or does it remind me only of what I feel when I hear music? What is it? Oh God, what is it?* she thought, losing herself and not associating this extraordinary experience at all with the compliments that men paid her or with the kisses that they tried to give her and sometimes against her will succeeded in giving.

And then she suddenly became aware of his hard young masculinity pressed against her, and possessed by the horror of a half-understanding she sprang away from him, gone before he could catch her back to him. She was standing up, above him, smoothing her hair, putting her palms against her warm cheeks. "I must go," she was saying, frantic to get away; "I must go"; but, polite, and anxious not to betray her own confusion, she added pitiably, "and thank you so much for being so nice to me."

He got up too, brushing the pine-needles off his clothes. The spell was smashed; he luckily knew better than to try to revive it. "I'll take you to the boat," he said uncomfortably. He wished now for one thing only: that she should go, and go quickly. He felt it would be days before he could come to the pine-wood again. He hated her for having spoilt his private pines, for having seen Andromeda's Cave, and for having chipped his independence.

Mrs. Jolly put Shirin to bed. Her mother had been cross to her all the evening, and Mrs. Jolly with her few but firmly-established ideas assumed as a matter of course that young people minded their mothers being cross to them. Her shrewd, elementary intuition had discovered Mrs. Wilson's crossness as the cause behind the especial gloom dimming the room at supper, which even Shirin's laughter, more irresponsible than usual, had been inadequate wholly to dispel. Mrs. Jolly, naturally enough, was incapable of estimating Shirin's indifference to anything her mother might express or imply; Shirin, if only Mrs. Jolly had known it, was preoccupied with quite other matters. So Mrs. Jolly, good soul, seeing that something was wrong, threw all her talents into the mission of comforting her darling. Engaged in clearing away the supper, she cast her eyes over Shirin and announced that she looked tired; "You're not accustomed to being in the open air all day, you folk from London," she said as she swept the crumbs off the cloth into her apron, "and that child, if you'll take my word for it, ought to go to bed early." So she took Shirin upstairs, rather more motherly than usual, and fussed over her, turning down her bed and stuffing a hot water-bottle into it. "Now you get undressed, my beauty," she said as she bustled about, twitching the curtains across, and setting things straight on the dressing-table. "Why, now! aren't you an odd fish!" she said, looking round to see Shirin taking off her clothes under the shelter of her dressing-gown; "why so chary, all of a sudden? You usen't to be so precious with your old Jolly. What's come over you?" and she came lumbering across the room to Shirin and looked closely at her; "now just you take off that dressing-gown," she said, "for if you're going to become precious with your old Jolly you'll go right away into yourself and never find the way out again, not even if some man tries to take you out.

"Why, what's wrong?" she said, as Shirin hesitated in silence; "just you take off that silly thing and put on your nightgown as God and your mother meant you to. What does it matter if you're standing in your chemise or your skin or what?"

"Oh, Jolly!" said Shirin, turning away. She was filled with a terror she could tell to nobody, not even to Jolly.

"There, there, what's the matter, what's the matter?" said Mrs. Jolly, patting her. "Something's upset you, I can see that, and natural enough it is too, at your age. Your mummy was cross to you, wasn't she? and something else upset you too, I dare say. Things do have a way of upsetting one, and not only at your age, believe me. They go on upsetting you for years and years, only luckily it gets less bad as the years add up. That's one of the few compensations, I always think, for getting older: you get further and further away from the age when things seemed to matter so terribly much. Never mind about that now; just you go to bed and let Jolly massage you to put you to sleep."

"*Massage* me, Jolly?"

Mrs. Jolly gave her rich chuckle.

"Why yes, didn't I ever tell you I was a massoose once? properly trained too, and they said I had the hands for it, and the muscles so that I never got tired. No, didn't I tell you? Oh well, I dare say there are lots of things I haven't told you, but they'll all come out in time."

"I like you for that, you old wretch; I hate people who tell you everything about themselves at once."

"There, happier now, are you? Well, jump into bed and let yourself go all soft and don't worry. Don't even tell me what it was upset you, if you don't want to. You're one of those, too, who don't tell everything about themselves all at once. Only, with you, I doubt if it'd come out even in time."

"Jolly, you are good to me; I think I'd tell you anything."

"Not you!" said Mrs. Jolly, her hands beginning to take skilful possession of the girlish body. She left the bedclothes drawn up, so that her craft might be exercised with the utmost discretion. She knew that Shirin was in no mood as yet to lie stripped and acquiescent. It would take at least five years of London before Shirin would allow any expert to exploit and develop her beauty. She could feel a certain tautness still, a certain shyness, a withholding, an absence of relaxation in the soft limbs. For Jolly knew those things; her hands, though coarsened by house-work, were still intuitive.

"Jolly, that's lovely, that's perfect,—how do you know exactly what to do?—you make me stretch like a cat in the sun,—and do you know, I couldn't bear anyone else to touch me,—I can't bear being touched,—I hate it when people try to touch me."

"You like that, honey, do you? I thought you would. It makes you feel like a cat in the sun? So I've heard other people say, only they didn't put it so well. Makes you feel sleepy, does it? What a silky skin you have, haven't you? and I haven't even powdered it, though I had a lot of talcum powder put aside somewhere, old muddle-head and lose-things that I am and always was. Cool, too; I can see, you're one of those who would never be either so hot as to get sweaty or so cold as to get lumpy with goose-flesh; you'd always be just perfect and smooth for your lover, be he husband or what-not. I always said and maintained, some women have a proper gift of skin and temperature, and those are the women, I always said, who were meant for love. Born mistresses, as you might say, dressed or undressed, lovely in summer or winter, at any hour of the day or night.—No, you needn't shrink away from me; remember how I used to give you your bath when you was six? A plump little thing you was too, and you're still plump, although you're small. Small bones," said Jolly, delicately feeling the delicate hips; "you're smally made, and yet you'd breed fine babies, broad as you are, for the pelvis is the important thing, as the doctor told me when he took my baby away from me (but you mustn't repeat that, or I might get into trouble even yet);

yes, you'll breed fine babies to some young man, for you're healthy enough; your skin shows that, to anybody who knows about skins as I had to, being once a massoose; and I know about bones too, and about the pelvis, being as you might say, a mother although an abortive one. But as for you," said Jolly, "you're not one of those skinny modern misses, thank goodness. A French figure, I should say. Dimples everywhere. I remember I had a French patient once,—well, patient isn't quite the word, she wasn't ill, and she certainly wasn't patient, she just wanted a massoose in order to get thin. You see, she'd come to England on a profession you don't know anything about and she thought it wasn't the fashion here in England to be soft and round. You're just a fool, I said to her; far better stay yourself and not try to be like everybody else, which you can't, not even if you went in for diet which I don't believe in. It's a great mistake, I said to her, to want to be like everybody else and spend a lot of money doing it; far better stay what you are than waste your substance making yourself into a bad copy. So I lost that job, but I didn't care because I knew I'd done right in telling her,—helpful, as you might say, and economical too,—and anyway I had lots of other jobs on people that really wanted me; but I've often wondered since if she went on with her silly ideas or if she took to heart the words I'd said to her. Not but what she hadn't got a lot of money to squander on massooses if she wanted them, and that was very nice for the massooses, only it was going to be for those who was less outspoken than I was, and how she got the money I didn't enquire, but I knew very well, or at any rate with my experience I could make a pretty good guess. She was one of those as men can't leave alone,

French figure and all, even in England where she thought it wasn't fashionable. And you're going to be one of the same, honey, in fact you're the same already, for it starts young: you're one of those as men can't leave alone."

"Oh, Jolly, what a bore."

"Yes, dearie, you're right there, though how you know it already at your age beats me: it *is* a bore, but take my word, having once been cursed with that bore by God in Heaven you wouldn't be without it. You may hate it, but on the whole it's the one bore a woman doesn't want to get away from. You wouldn't believe it perhaps," said Mrs. Jolly, still stooping professionally over the bed with her hands beneath the bedclothes, kneading vigorously, "you wouldn't believe it perhaps, but I was like that myself once. They all said the same thing,—and Lord, I did get tired of hearing it! It sounded lovely the first time, I dare say, but oh they did seem to say the same thing over and over again. It's extraordinary, the little imagination men have. *Say* the same thing, and *do* the same thing, without ever seeming to get bored with it or want a change. The only change they ever seem to want is a change of woman, and yet what's a woman but the same thing again, only a different body? and even bodies are the same when once you've got the hang of them. I used to get to know the look in their eyes, and then I knew it was coming. Yes, I used to think to myself: I know just what you're going to say and what you think you're going to do, and you're probably right, and I could tell it you all in advance, but I suppose I've got to let you think you've invented it for yourselves and for the first time of asking, and just listen and pretend I've never heard it before."

"Jolly, you've never told me so much about yourself till tonight."

"Haven't I, honey? no, I dare say not. Well, I haven't told you much now. You wait till you're a married woman and I come and nurse your first baby, and I'll tell you a lot more then."

She felt Shirin shrink under her hands, and shudder; a tremor shook her whole body, and turning her head aside she hid her face in the pillow. Mrs. Jolly misunderstood her gesture, attributing it to modesty.

"Don't you mind what I say, dearie," she said comfortably; "don't you take any notice. I dare say I've outrun you a bit, seeing I forgot you're so young. I told you I'd always been a bit too outspoken. Put it down to the company I've kept, if you like; though I must say, my company whatever it was always took the tone from me and not me from them and I always pulled them up when they went too far. 'No,' I used to say; 'there's decency and there's indecency, and each one has got to judge for herself where the one stops and the other begins.' I'll admit that my level of stopping was pretty high, according to some people's ideas, for I couldn't see why the things that everybody knows shouldn't be said outright and no whispering of them down a rat-hole; but I'll say this for myself, that nothing was ever said in my house that couldn't have been said straight out in company at the bar of a public house, though I wouldn't say that it would have went down well in the House of Lords. Though, if you ask me, I don't believe a lord is any more particular than any other man, and that's not saying much; it's only when a lot of lords get together and set themselves up to govern the country that they put on their grand airs. There's always a deal of solemnity and show-off when a lot of men get together, whether they're lords or not, and they seem to think it's up to them to pretend that we aren't all made the same way, God bless us and where's the shame to us? since God invented the making of us and is answerable for the consequences and not poor us at all?"

"It isn't that, Jolly. I never mind what *you* say, though I do mind horribly when other people say things. It isn't that."

"What is it then, my soul? You haven't been getting yourself into trouble, have you? Come, turn round and tell me, and don't go burying your face in that pillow for I can't hear a word you say,—though I must say you look pretty enough to tempt an archangel out of Heaven, with your curls all wriggly on your neck and the promise of all the rest of you under the bedclothes."

"I couldn't tell you, Jolly; not even you."

"Now don't you be silly," said Mrs. Jolly, ceasing to massage and becoming brisk and sensible; "there's something on your mind, and I've got to know what it is. I never did believe in people smothering things back into their insides and not letting them come out: that makes ideas breed like mushrooms in a shed, nasty things sprouting on manure in the dark. I never liked mushrooms much except the ones that grow in fields in the open air, and even those not much, considering they flourish on the droppings of cows. A nasty idea, I think, though I must say I like gathering mushrooms in the early morning; but there is a difference, I always say, between fresh droppings and those that get turned into manure in a shed. They still seem to have the dew on them, somehow, which those in a dung-heap haven't. They seem more personal, somehow, when they're fresh and separate, which they lose when they all get mixed up. And you needn't fear I'd ever repeat anything you told me,—I don't believe in repeating, not even when it's onions, which I always avoid in my cooking, though I like them well enough for myself, but I've always had to avoid them even for myself because . . . well, never mind about that. It's enough to say, some people couldn't appreciate them. Just you tell me, straight out, what's on your mind."

"I couldn't, Jolly,—not unless you stoop down and let me whisper."

"Aren't you a caution! Well, you are a one! well, all right, whisper if you must," and Mrs. Jolly bent down, approaching her ear.

"Don't laugh at me, Jolly, or I won't ask you."

"I'm not laughing at you, my honey, my beauty, my lovely one," said Mrs. Jolly, taking her in her arms and nursing her, because she saw that something had gone seriously wrong. "If you knew the things that I'd been told in my life, and kept to myself what's more, you'd know I was as safe as Joanna Southcote's box in the vaults of the Bank of England. Take a deep breath and come out with it. There's a great value in taking a deep breath and holding it; I never know why. Or you can hold your nose if you like, like for medicine, while you say what you've got to say. Whisper away, as long as you must, but don't tickle my ear. I never minded what else they did with me, but I never could stand being tickled. It makes me laugh, and I don't hold with laughing at what I don't think funny."

Shirin put both her arms round Jolly's neck and whispered; it was a long whisper, omitting all names, and Jolly disengaged herself at the end of it, looking grave.

"You must tell me more, honey; I can't answer you just on that," she began.

"No, Jolly! you mustn't ask me questions; I couldn't bear that," and Shirin put her hands over her ears.

"Don't be silly, honey, now you've gone so far; it's serious, or may be," and she put some questions, then plumped down on a chair with her hands on her knees and rocked and roared with laughter.

"Oh my poor innocent lamb! don't you worry, you'd have to do a lot more than that,—but do you mean to tell me your mother never told you anything? and you just the sort that would be taken advantage of in a twinkling? Well, your mother can be as mad with me as she likes, but I'll take the consequences rather than that *you* should. Just you listen to me. . . ."

"No, I don't want to, Jolly, not if you're sure it's all right this time; I won't listen; I hate that sort of thing."

Mrs. Jolly took Shirin's hands and held them down.

"Hate it or not," she said firmly, "you've got to listen, or you'll be coming to me one of these days and asking me to take you away to Switzerland for three months. The man won't do that, my dear; they never do. Have your fun and then be off before you have to foot the bill, is their motto."

Mrs. Jolly's explanations were not couched in the most delicate language, but at least they were graphic and left no margin for error. There was something moreover in her solid and common-sensible acceptance of facts, as she sat there on her wooden chair very stout in her print dress and kitchen apron, talking honest monosyllabic English, that made it possible for Shirin to listen to her without shrinking away altogether, though she felt her childhood dropping behind her and a whole new world of horrible and incredible experience opening up before her, an experience which (it appeared) would have to be endured.

"And some day," Mrs. Jolly wound up, "he'll knock a fine baby out of you, though who he'll be I can't tell and nor can you; but what you may be certain of, is that he hasn't done it today, although you're one of those as you need only to shake a pair of trousers at, as the saying goes."

At that moment Mrs. Wilson, distraught and indignant, burst into the room.

"Isn't that just what happens!" she cried. "There's your grandmother dying, Shirin, and we'll all have to go back to London by the first train tomorrow morning, and all our holiday spoilt after one day, because we can't possibly afford the fares all over again, and I do call it too bad and just the luck we always have."

She rattled on, explosive, outraged, recalling herself now and then enough to pretend to a decent show of feeling and to dab at a tear which was not there.

Thank God, thought Shirin, stopping her ears against her mother, *I shan't have to see Venn again.*

PART II

TWENTY-SIX

I

SHE did not, in fact, see him again for ten years, when she caught sight of him at a dance and recognised him instantly. That he did not recognise her she could tell from the first glance he gave her,—a glance of interest indeed, but the same kind of interest as she was only too well accustomed to arousing in most men. There was no recognition in his glance; only an awakening desire for introduction. She knew well enough that sooner or later he would cross the room under escort in order to make her acquaintance,—such an old, familiar proceeding that from anybody else she would have welcomed it only with a weary sigh. But it amused her to see Venn again. That childish episode retained significance for her only in so far as it was associated with Storn; Storn which she still loved in her most secret heart; the sight of Venn himself disturbed her not at all, nor the recollection (which made her blush and smile) of their childish and dangerous behaviour; she knew how to manage such things now. Watching him across the room while she continued to lend just sufficient attention to satisfy the man at her side, she saw him approach his hostess.

Venn, also, superficially, knew how to manage such things now. He had grown up in those ten years. Besides, he knew his hostess, who was also his cousin, very well. He knew her well enough to ask a question he wanted to ask.

"Minna, tell me, who is that woman sitting over there with Gerald Hanbury?"

Lady Lester, very stiff in mauve brocade and diamonds, put up her lorgnon and narrowed her short-sighted eyes to look.

"Oh, that," she said. "That's Shirin Vane-Merrick. I wonder you don't know her, at any rate by sight. But then, of course, you never go to parties. Pretty, isn't she?"

"Very pretty. Shirin. What an odd name. I seem to have heard it before, but I can't remember where. Any relation to Vane-Merrick the M.P.?"

"Yes, if you call it a relation. His ex-wife. He married her seven or eight years ago, when she was barely grown-up. His family was very angry about it because they thought he was marrying beneath him,—you know how old-fashioned they are, and what frightful snobs."

Venn could see that Lady Lester was embarked on one of her favourite topics.

"How do you mean," he said, "marrying beneath him?"

"Well, he found her in the suburbs somewhere, or at a charity dance, I forget which. The Three Arts Club, or something. The Albert Hall perhaps; she has a brother who is a painter. He fell in love with her at first sight, and simply carried her off. No one ever knew the ins and outs of it. There seemed to be more in than out," said Lady Lester, who liked hearty jokes, and sometimes made them, when they occurred to her. "Anyway," she continued, "they got married, and before long Shirin had the whole of Miles' family under her thumb, even the old father,—

especially the old father, perhaps I ought to say. They couldn't resist her, and very soon gave up trying to. Then the trouble began, because nobody else could resist her either. People fell in love with her right and left; the most surprising people, men who notoriously loathed women or couldn't be bothered with them, men who had always thought themselves too busy to waste their time over any woman, men that women had tried to catch and failed,—well, Shirin, who never tried to catch any of them, caught them one by one; we heard the oddest stories, of how somebody or other would go to dinner with Miles and Shirin, and would come away declaring that she was the only woman they ever could have loved,—not that Shirin herself ever said so, because, to do her justice, she never boasts of her scalps, but the men themselves let it out, as though they were half proud of having been sharp enough to hit on such a prize. Instead of being ashamed of their failure to get her, it became a sort of brag to have aspired for one evening to Shirin Vane-Merrick. It became the fashion almost, like wearing the right sort of hat. Nobody ever knew what Shirin herself thought of it all. For the dozens she turned down, she may have favoured three or four. I don't know the rights of the whole story, nobody ever did; Shirin is one of the darkest horses I've ever known; she's one of those women who have God knows how many lovers but no friends, merely because she doesn't want them,—anyway her marriage with Miles ended as everybody had foreseen it would end, in divorce. They had lots of children, first. The funny thing was, that he divorced her, and not she him. Most unusual, and I never think quite so well of Miles now for having allowed it. After all, in spite of modern ideas, it does still harm a woman, and it doesn't yet harm a man. But I dare say they agreed upon it, and it's their business after all, not mine. And I believe that she and Miles meet quite often; have luncheon or dinner together, you know; he told a friend of mine the other day that every time he sees Shirin he realises she was the only woman he had ever cared for or would ever really care for. He said that once one had got Shirin into one's blood one couldn't get her out of it, and yet Miles is a selfish freak, if ever there was one."

"Except for the last bit, it sounds rather a commonplace story."

"Oh, Shirin is quite commonplace really; she just happens to have that curious power of attraction, nothing to do with looks, but the sort of power that makes unknown foreigners send a note across the restaurant by the waiter. Apart from that, I should say she was quite shallow. Flirtation and admiration, that's all she wants," said Lady Lester, who wanted neither and got neither, being entirely taken up with horses, to such an extent that her face itself had become as equine as her teeth.

"You don't like her?"

"Oh yes, I like her, she's so gay one can't help it, and then she's so useful in a party, she does make things *go*," said Lady Lester; "I only meant that there perhaps wasn't very much *in* her, if you know what I mean; she doesn't care for games, and she doesn't ride, in fact she doesn't seem to care for anything except clothes, and dancing, and playing about with men,—though that's a whole-time job for some women, I admit," said Lady Lester with a shade of acerbity in her tone.

"It's a job she seems to have mastered pretty thoroughly. Will you introduce me to your siren?"

"Actually, Venn, for once you're behaving like a human being! What a pity you don't come to London more, instead of remaining always stuck down in that barbarous island of yours. Yes, of course I'll introduce you. Come along."

Shirin looked up as Venn and Lady Lester arrived together. The man at her side looked up too, annoyed, for he had flattered himself on conquering her attention: she had been laughing at his jokes for the past ten minutes. *That is the worst*, he thought, *of Shirin Vane-Merrick: no sooner has one got her to oneself, than somebody else comes up to snatch her away. And, damn her, she always lets herself be snatched. It is as though one face were as good to her as any other face. Yet so long as she is talking to you, or listening to you, which is more in her line than talking, she makes you feel you are the only person she wants to be with.*

Gerald Hanbury was irrationally annoyed.

"Hallo, Shirin," said Lady Lester, in her breezy way. "Enjoying yourself? Having a good time? That's right. Hallo, Gerald. Shirin, I want you to meet my cousin Venn,—Sir Venn le Breton, Mrs. Vane-Merrick."

So the old Ranger is dead, and Venn is the Ranger now, she thought; *Venn has got Storn to himself; how happy Venn must be.*

Still he has failed to recognise me, she thought; *his bow was one of purely conventional acknowledgment. He has changed remarkably little. He seems more polished, of course; the roughness and uncouthness have gone out of his manner; his hair is brushed smooth, and he wears evening clothes instead of an open shirt. But for the rest he is the same, still reddish, still freckled, and still so incredibly thin as to give his clothes an effect almost of emptiness, of containing no body. He has become exaggeratedly elegant, dandified really, his clothes exquisitely cut; his figure, still concave where it ought to be convex, must be the joy of his tailor's life. His elegance is in strange contrast with the background of Storn.*

His eyes, contradicting his elegance, searched her out as she looked up.

Would she give him a dance, he was asking her? The third from now? He thanked her gravely. She knew he would not forget. Men never forgot, when she granted them an assignation. Venn, this polished, civil Venn, would not forget any more than the ordinary young man of a London ballroom. She rather hoped he would, to raise himself in her eyes; she was so tired of eager meetings.

"But surely, surely," he was saying, "I have seen you somewhere before?"

There! she thought, *he is making the usual gambit; he is a cheap person after all.* They had been dancing, and she danced in such a way that he wished never to let her go out of his arms; at the same time he felt that he meant nothing to her, no more than an automaton which also danced well so as to satisfy her sense of rhythm, just the necessary complement to her own dancing, the complement that impersonally held her for a space. "Surely," he said, longing for the touch of her cool flesh again and the suppleness of her body blown against him, "surely I have seen you somewhere before?"

"At some party probably."

"I never go to parties."

"Don't you? You are at one tonight."

He frowned. She liked him the better for his frown.

"Minna made me come," he said. "She caught me on my way through London and made me promise to come. I'm fond of Minna, so I did it to please her. Besides, I had nothing else to do."

"And you hate it," she said, "now you are here."

"I rather hate it,—yes."

She was grateful to him for not saying "I hated it until I met you," as most young men, met at a dance, would have said.

"What do you do as a rule, then," she asked, "when you don't go to parties?"

"Me? What do I do? Oh, I don't know. I'm not very often in London. I'm going home tomorrow." He stopped. She, who knew so exactly what he meant by home, respected his reticence. She knew exactly what his return to Storn would mean to him; she knew exactly where the launch would meet him at Port Breton, and how he would go across the sea, steering himself, coming into the little harbour when the sun was sinking low. She knew that the castle and the pines would be turning red from the western sun. But then, because life had hurt her and because she had pushed Storn and the dream of Storn right away into the background of her heart, and because she had tried during all those years to turn herself into a different sort of person, shallow, chic, superficial, in self-defence, she refused to let herself dwell on what his return to Storn would mean to him, and only laughed outright at his last remark. She, to whom Frenchmen, Spaniards, and Italians had unsuccessfully laid siege, laughed outright. "Why does that make you laugh?" he asked. "Look here," he added, puzzled, "I know I've met you somewhere before. When you laughed just now, I was sure of it. Won't you stop making fun of me, and tell me? But first tell me why you laughed."

"Why I laughed? Well, you weren't very descriptive, were you? I asked you what you did as a rule, and you said, 'What do I do? Oh, I don't know.' I was only thinking how little eloquence we had, as a race, and how differently anyone but an Englishman would have answered."

She would not tell him that she had been thinking about Storn.

"A criticism, I suppose?"

"No; a compliment."

"Never mind about that. Do help me," he said, leaning forward, "by telling me where we might have met. It's worrying me; I can't get it straight."

"Like a tune you can't quite remember?"

"Exactly like that; the shape of it is all somewhere at the back of my head, but it refuses to come forward."

"I can't help you, I'm afraid; and anyhow, why not let it be?"

They were sitting out; he stared at her very intently. *She is young,* he thought; *not more than twenty-five or twenty-six; but beyond her obvious youthfulness of years there is a curious mixture of ages: caught at certain angles she looks almost childish, not more than sixteen or seventeen, so soft and immature are the contours of her cheek and throat, especially of her neck where the short curls break free of their careful setting and lie darkly against her skin; but caught at other angles she looks fashionable and sophisticated, able to cope with life that may have treated her well or harshly.*

Scantily dressed in brown satin, from which her arms and shoulders emerged rounded and gleaming, without a single jewel beyond their own transparent lightness, she enjoyed some quality which made her appear even more naked than she actually was. She had, he noticed, a trick of sitting with her hands clasping either shoulder, as though by her crossed arms she defended her breast from assault, and leant her cheek against her own shoulder, as though no flesh but her own had the right to caress her flesh. Looking at her very narrowly, so that he saw every detail as in a close-up photograph, even to the way her hair was planted on her temples, he told himself a story, a habit to which he was privately addicted, in which she became half a seal and half a woman, a new sort of mermaid, washed up on the rocks of his native Storn, sleek and dark as a wet seal, he thought; sleek and white as a woman ready for the taking. He almost put out his hand to touch her throat.

She looked at him then, a frank, not a covert look, and he suddenly remembered the tune he had forgotten; it came back to him as fresh as a peal of bells in the early morning. It came back to him the moment he looked into her eyes and saw again the patch where her eyelashes went crooked, making a darker blotch,—that odd little peculiarity which brought back to him the scent of the pine-trees and the lapping of the summer sea. Still, for all the relief that the recollection brought him, he was not going to give himself away. Not at once. He liked having a secret against her, as she had a secret against him. *We are both people*, he thought, *who like each other the better for having secrecies and dangers.*

He had not realised the duration of their silence, until

her voice came to him from far off. "Well," she said, "are you remembering your tune?"

Was she mocking? was she serious? And why did this direct challenge not embarrass him more? He was awkward with women as a rule, avoiding them as far as possible.

"I was thinking," he said, turning to her, "how oddly one's senses are mixed up. Haven't you noticed," he said, hurriedly covering up the shyness and awkwardness which abruptly overcame him, "that sometimes when you smell a scent it takes you back to a place you have known? or when you hear a sound unexpectedly it takes you back to some scene or situation you thought you had forgotten?" He was trying to put it as impersonally as possible, and she herself was inwardly laughing at him for the platitude of his observation, but the nearness, the strength, the importance of her personality broke through all such artificial protection. She said nothing, but even her silence shamed him.

"No, I won't pretend," he broke out; "I remember perfectly well; I *have* remembered. Why do you make me talk real, instead of false? You always did, even then. But then, that day, we were meeting in a real place, and we were both young enough not to know better. Now we're meeting in a false place, and God knows what has happened to us both in the meantime, yet you make me feel real again, and say things to you which I would never dream of saying to anybody else."

"All right, get angry with me," she said, smiling.

"No, I'm not angry with you,—yes, I am,—no, I'm not," he said, more like the Venn that she had known. "Anyway," he added, his sudden charm coming out, "I don't know you well enough, do I, to get angry with you even if I want to? I've only just been introduced to you at a dance, and we can't leap back over how long is it? nine, ten years? Tell me, all the same, why did you disappear like that, without even letting me know? We had made an arrangement, do you remember, that I should teach you to fish?"

"A very vague arrangement, wasn't it?"

"Still, I thought you had agreed to it."

"I forgot all about it, I'm afraid."

"Do you always forget all your arrangements, even now? or now more than ever? Or do you remember only those that you want to remember?"

"There aren't very many of those." She laughed, slipping away from him. He thought then of Lady Lester's remarks about her shallowness, and wondered how much truth there might be in them. Was she, in fact, only a shallow flirt? Her whole appearance endorsed such a definition, from the top of her sleek brown head to the top of her sleek brown shoe. She looked the kind of woman who does not emerge from her bedroom till noon, and spends the intervening hours between the dressing-table and the telephone. But was this the whole truth? And if this was the whole truth, why did he feel such a savage desire to take her back to Storn, to isolate her from this world of London, and to make her suffer until he had broken her elusive spirit into irreparable fragments?

"Have you never been back to Port Breton?" he asked.

"I forget; we may have been back once or twice; no, I think we always went abroad; it's so long ago, I forget." She would not tell him that she had ingeniously forced her reluctant family across the Channel every year, to

Dieppe which she loathed, rather than go back to Port Breton and run the risk of being carried off to Storn by him again. It was not so much him that she had wanted to avoid as Storn itself.

"Mrs. Jolly must have missed you."

"Mrs. Jolly? Oh yes, I remember: our landlady at Port Breton. Is she still alive?" She had a letter from Jolly in her hand-bag at the moment.

"Of course she's still alive; whenever I see Mrs. Jolly I think she's immortal, not the sort of person who could ever die." The mention of Jolly brought them a moment of intimacy which made them look in a more kindly way at one another.

"We've got a funny common background in Mrs. Jolly, haven't we?" he said spontaneously. "Why did you pretend you didn't remember her?"

"I can't imagine," she replied, meeting his frankness with frankness. "Habit, I suppose."

"Habit," he repeated; "what a good word, meaning such a dangerous thing. But do you . . ."

"Wait!" she interposed, holding up a finger, and again he noticed how the tip of her finger turned back, precisely as he had noticed it when she had laid her finger against his lips to prevent him from frightening away the rabbit, that day on Storn; he remembered how he had slowly observed the delicacy of her hand, one of his earliest adolescent experiences; "wait," she said; "what did you mean by 'habit' being a good word? Do *you* feel like that about words, too? Are there certain words you like, so that they thrust into you whenever you hear them spoken?"

"There you are," he said; "talking real again." And

he thought what a mixture she was, of candour and pretence; of passion and control.

She longed to ask him questions,—to learn whether his grandmother were still alive or not, and whether he now spent all his time on Storn,—but refrained because she shrank always from talking about the things that mattered to her. Instead, she made him talk, and listened to his ideas coming out in their odd, jerky way, now with a rush of confidence, now with a withdrawal which was almost uncouth, almost rude; and meanwhile she thought how life arranged itself into a pattern, like a scroll drawn by an artist capricious in his penmanship, beginning with a thin fine line and continuing through curves to a final flourish bearing no apparent relation to the thin fine line taken separately, but which taken together grew into an unpredictable unity. The trouble was, that the unity declared itself only when the design was completed, and that the first fine line gave no menace of the eventual development. So many hair-strokes of fate left off short; among the many broken ones, scored by the unknown penman, only a few came to fulfilment. So how could a poor mortal tell one kind from the other? Yet, looking back on that one day with him on Storn, she recognised now that a certain fear had warned her, else why should she have henceforth shepherded her family away rather than risk the addition of another curve to that incipient arabesque?

A bray of music, resuming, interrupted them. "Oh damn!" he exclaimed, with a flash of the anger and impatience she had known on Storn, "must you go?"—for he saw another man making his way towards her, and the polite answering smile in her eyes. "Look here," he said urgently, "give me another dance, can't you? or at any rate give me your address and let me come and see you tomorrow?"

"I thought you were going back to Storn tomorrow?"

"I'll put it off if I can see you again."

She hesitated. The pattern was developing too quickly for her pleasure. Besides, these things had happened to her too often; they no longer amused her, for their own sake.

"I should go back to Storn, if I were you." She spoke gently, almost maternally; protectively.

The other man was hovering, uncertain what to do. She smiled at him again, keeping him quiet, bored by the prospect of sitting out with him, for he danced badly beyond the bourne of her endurance; she knew only too well that if she refused to dance with him he would use up the whole time importuning her to marry him. "Yes," she said to Venn, "you'd much better go back to Storn; Storn in April is much nicer than London in April; you go back to Storn, and give it my love if you like."

In spite of her good advice, he did not go back to Storn next day, but, making a pretext to himself of a long-deferred visit to his solicitors, remained in London. He was in that curious and disturbing state when the mind, refusing to examine the possible truth, uneasily invents excuses for its own uncertainty. Somehow he could not face the prospect of his own company on Storn, nor yet the prospect of his grandmother's company there, she having grown more eccentric and more exacting with the years. But he blamed his restlessness on London, not on the true cause. A mere two days of the damned place, he decided, was enough to unsettle a man from his chosen shape of life. How anybody could coop himself up between houses, leading that rackety, futile existence in the noise and stench and jostle, when not compelled to do so, he couldn't imagine. He himself never came near London unless business took him there, and he saw to it that the business which could take him there should be as reduced in character as possible, concentrating all his necessary contacts with the outside world, estate agents, public works, even doctors and dentists, down in his own domain by the sea. His grandfather had been proud of boasting that, so long as the damned Government would let him, he would live as a gentleman had always lived, doing his duty indeed, but doing it in the decent retirement of his own territory; and, as ferociously territorial as he, Venn held on to the same tradition. London was spiritually as far removed from him as if he had been obliged, in an earlier century, to reach it once a year by road and by coach. He exulted in the isolation and the intensity of living which such a seclusion provoked.

Friends he did not desire, nor women. His only friends were the fishermen and the people on his estates. With them he had a really close understanding. Women bored and embarrassed him, though they gave him enough flattery and interest, whenever they got a chance at him, to satisfy the vainest of men. But Venn was not vain. Over his own realm he was king, and intended to remain a king, but apart from that he was self-sufficient and truly solitary, asking no better than to be left alone. Besides, he had something of the Ishmael in him, knowing himself to be different from other, more easy-going people; he preferred to keep the dark recesses of his nature to himself. That was why he could endure to live with his grandmother, for, quarrel though they might, and did frequently and with great violence, some sympathy of temperament and blood preserved the mutual respect that carried them securely through all their storms.

The very intensity of his habitual living, turned inwards upon himself, prevented him from analysing a motive so far removed from the usual run of his experience. If he must remain in London, as remain he felt he must, not understanding why, then he would explain it to himself by making an obligation of it, in the shape of a dutiful visit to Block and Arrowhead, whose offices he had seldom entered since his grandfather died. He would not for an instant admit that he remained in London because London offered the chance of seeing Mrs. Vane-Merrick again. Block and Arrowhead alone should be loaded with the blame.

He had never even seen young Block, who had only recently stepped in partnership into his deceased father's shoes. He found young Block neat, brisk, energetic, and communicative, the reverse of old Block, who had been dirty, dilatory, sluggish, and reserved. In fact, he was not a chip of the old Block at all. Venn took a fancy to him at once, seeing that he could despatch business, which he abhorred, very quickly with this young man, and moreover be treated as a human being as well. It had been impossible to behave as a human being with old Block; old Block, he felt, had always regarded him as a mere nuisance to be endured because he put money into the coffers of the firm, but otherwise as an interruption to his maunderings into greasy papers with Thomson his greasy clerk. How well Venn remembered those occasions when his grandfather had sent him up to London to interview old Block on his behalf! How well he remembered the waiting-room with its linoleum floor, its vast legal tomes, and the bead curtains over the window, which had lost half their beads and now were little more than grimy dangles of string! How well he remembered the times he had been kept waiting, when he ran the few remaining beads and the string between his fingers, looking out on the drab prospect of the city street and thinking meanwhile vaguely at the back of his boyish mind of Storn and the boats rocking idly in the harbour, and of the long night-journey which lay between himself and London and Port Breton! Then, he had been a mere presumptive deputy; now, he came in his own right, to be welcomed civilly by a younger clerk whose name he did not know,—what had happened to Thomson? had his services now been consecrated to the always invisible Arrowhead, a personage whose existence, it seemed, was limited exclusively to the imprint at the top of the firm's writing-paper?—now, he came in his own right, and after only two minutes' delay in the waiting-room, while his name was taken up to Mr. Block, the young clerk returned and said would he please come straight upstairs? Still, he had had time to notice with appreciation that nothing had been changed, neither the linoleum nor the legal tomes nor the stringy curtains with the few beads still strung on them across the window. It all retained the atmosphere of the respectable family solicitor's office, even to the musty smell and the Dickensian sordidness,—although, Venn reflected, they must pocket enough profit from the Storn estates alone to refurnish their offices yearly from top to bottom.

That was one of the things which predisposed him to

the liking of young Block, the fact that young Block, although so brisk and efficient in contrast to his father, had yet had the sense to leave his office as it was. Even the deep red-leather sofa in Block's room was the same, and the huge writing-table with the rectangular stacks of documents piled neatly upon it like tricks in a game of cards. It all gave the same sense of continuity and security, with the added comfort of a younger and more competent grasp. The black tin boxes, painted in white letters with the names of different clients, also gave the sense of continuity and security. He observed that his grandfather's name had not yet been changed on the box which occupied the place it had always occupied, any more than V.R. had been changed to G.R. on the pillar-box at Port Breton; *Sir Dominic le Breton*, it said on the black tin box, *Storn Estates*. He was well used to seeing the box and its inscription, yet it always gave him the same slight shock to see the word Storn painted in square white letters, there in the London office so remote from the reality of Storn as he knew it. In that box reposed unintelligible title-deeds, settlements, leaseholds, what-not, all with scarlet seals and some with the Great Seal of England; God and the solicitors might understand them; for his part, he knew only that they made Storn his own, and imposed upon him the obligation of going once a year to Buckingham Palace (or Windsor, as the case might be) to pay his tribute in person to the Crown in the shape of a golden nugget supposed to represent a rock off the western coast of Storn, the Gull rock, he supposed, a custom dating back to the reign of Elizabeth, a custom which might have proved difficult as to its fulfilment, since golden nuggets are less readily obtained in London than in Australia, but that the

Goldsmiths' Company had undertaken the difficulty for the le Bretons so far back as the reign of Queen Anne; since when the problem had been simplified for the le Bretons, and their tribute punctually provided. True it was, that by an ancient courtesy the nugget was returned every year to the le Bretons by the Crown, so that the le Breton of the moment could, if he so chose, and as on special occasions he did, decorate his dinner-table with golden nuggets in front of every plate. But, since a niggardly and dissentient le Breton after the execution of Charles the First had played an unforgivable trick upon a republican government by returning the previous year's nugget as the following year's tribute, the custom had also arisen that a corner should always be chipped off before the restitution took place.

Absurd anachronism, thought Venn as he listened with only half his attention to young Block's rapid exposition of the business that needed his consideration; and as he listened, letting his eyes wander, he was startled to observe another name on another tin box: *The Hon. Miles Vane-Merrick, M.P.*

"I had better get my clerk up, now that I have sketched out the preliminaries," Block was saying; "he has all the figures and details at his fingers' ends," and so saying he rang a bell on the table beside him.

A clerk promptly appeared,—far more promptly, Venn noted, than in old Block's day, when discipline had evidently been lax.

"Ah, Wilson! it's Mr. Tracey I want; ask him to come up with Sir Venn le Breton's papers, will you?"

Mr. Tracey came, already known to Venn; he had always liked Tracey, who in a subtly sympathetic way seemed to understand how intensely he, Venn, disliked the necessity for coping with business. Wilson he could not remember ever having seen before; Wilson no doubt was a mere scrub, Tracey the trusted and confidential senior. Dealing with Tracey made matters easy and less distasteful, for Tracey in his gentle and unobtrusive way always suggested what line he ought to take, and Venn invariably found himself in acquiescent agreement. This was a relief; he felt that he could always lean back against Tracey's common sense.

"Well," said young Block, as the door closed behind Tracey, "that's very satisfactory. I think we've cleared off everything." He did not actually rub his hands together, but Venn felt that he would have liked to do so.

"Nice chap, Tracey."

"A very good chap," said Block. "I can't think what I should do without him. In fact, he practically ran the office during the last years of my poor old dad's life. Now, of course, I've taken things in hand myself, but still, I must admit, Tracey is a great stand-by, a very great stand-by; yes, a useful man, Tracey."

He wants me to go now, thought Venn, *he's got other matters to attend to; he's not the sort of man who likes wasting time.*

"I see," he said casually, pointing, "that Vane-Merrick is a client of yours."

"Vane-Merrick? ah yes," said young Block, following the direction of the finger; "we act for his father too. You know Vane-Merrick, do you? yes, no doubt, no doubt, of course you do. A coming man, they say. A pity, isn't it, that his politics shouldn't be more sound?"

Young Block, thought Venn, *although he doesn't like wasting time, is prepared to talk. He is even prepared to be indis-*

creet. He hasn't been at his job long enough to have learnt the game of professional discretion; not altogether, although he may put up a show of it.

"No, I don't happen to know Vane-Merrick personally," he said, "though of course I know him by reputation. And I don't quite agree with you about it's being a pity that his politics shouldn't be, as you say, more sound. I think on the contrary that there ought to be more men of his type in the Labour party."

"I see what you mean: men like Vane-Merrick give ballast, don't they? Ballast; balance. Yes, balance. That's it. Because Vane-Merrick, although a Socialist, some people say even with leanings towards Communism,—very Right indeed, I have heard,—Vane-Merrick, in spite of everything, still belongs to the old school, Eton and Oxford, you know; all that. Yes, possibly you're right: the Labour party needs men like Vane-Merrick. A damn good farmer he is too; runs his farm down in Kent on really scientific lines. A bit too sentimental, perhaps; he shirks getting rid of bad tenants; instead of getting rid of them he tries to turn them into good ones, a hopeless proposition as you know yourself, Sir Venn, if you'll allow me to say so,—look at that man Manktelow down at Port Breton. . . ."

"Tracey backed me up over that," said Venn, smiling.

"Tracey would. That's my only quarrel with Tracey: he's soft. After all, one must consider one's own interests first, and it's part of Tracey's job to consider the interests of our clients."

"Vane-Merrick married, didn't he?"

Young Block shot a look at Venn out of his shrewd little eyes. Did le Breton know Mrs. Vane-Merrick? He,

Block, knew her, and, with the humanity not yet dried out of him, knew that no man could come within her range without danger.

"Yes, he married.—Oddly enough," he continued, carried away on the impulse of indiscretion he had not yet quite learnt to control, "he met his wife in this very office. Funny, wasn't it? And then we had to arrange his divorce for him. Ha, ha! That always makes me laugh.—But I suppose I ought not to be telling you these things. Still, they won't go beyond these four walls, will they?"

"But how on earth did he meet his wife in this office?" asked Venn, who had been told by Lady Lester that Vane-Merrick had found his wife in the suburbs or at a charity ball.

"Quite simply.—I wouldn't like you to think that I gossip about my clients' business, but Mrs. Vane-Merrick isn't my client, only Vane-Merrick himself, and anyway there's nothing discreditable about it to either party concerned, so I don't see why I shouldn't tell you. She came here to see her brother, who happens to be one of my clerks. In fact the one who answered my bell just now and whom I sent to fetch Tracey. Wilson, his name is. Well, Vane-Merrick met her here on the stairs, and then afterwards, I believe, he recognised her at a dance. And there you are. If you knew Mrs. Vane-Merrick, you wouldn't be surprised. She's a very pretty woman,—a very attractive lady, I may say, very attractive indeed."

"And they're divorced now, are they?" said Venn, as casually as he could; "you said you had to arrange his divorce for him. I seem to remember hearing something about it,—probably read it in the papers. That must have been rather awkward for her brother?"

He hated himself for his curiosity, but his desire to know something more about her overcame his scruples.

"It was; very awkward indeed. We did our best to keep him out of it. Poor chap. As a matter of fact, I turned the whole thing over to Tracey, so as to spare the brother."

"But surely that kind of divorce is simple enough, always a put-up job? Merely a matter of an hotel-bill, and the evidence of a waiter and a housemaid?"

"It should be; it should be," said Block, evidently reluctant to volunteer information, but not at all reluctant to have it pressed out of him.

"Well, then, what about it?"

"It's quite understood, isn't it, that this must go no further? But if you read it in the papers at the time, which makes it public property, you'll remember that instead of letting her divorce him in the ordinary way, which is, as you say, simple enough as a rule, Vane-Merrick divorced her on the ground of adultery. Yes. She insisted on it. The only case of the sort I have ever known. Very quixotic of her, I must say. You see, she had a great belief in his political career, and she didn't want to imperil it in any way by damaging his moral reputation in the eyes of his constituents. Very sticky people, constituents. And Vane-Merrick, who is an ambitious man, with his eye on the Cabinet, accepted her suggestion. It's not for me to criticise him, naturally. Still, it did strike me as an out-of-the-way thing for a man to allow a woman to do. However, that's neither here nor there. There it was, and we had the nasty job of obtaining the necessary evidence against her."

"That can't have been difficult, surely, since she had agreed to it?"

"Well, do you know, it was. Very difficult. Having

behaved so well to start with, she went on to give us quite a lot of trouble in the end. It was as though she wanted to make fun of us all. It was as though the mischief seized her; as though she'd said, 'All right, I'll be *It;* now catch me if you can,'—you know the children's game. But we couldn't catch her, not for a long time. Finally . . ."

"Yes, finally?" said Venn, as Block paused.

"Really, you know, I'm being very indiscreet, very indiscreet indeed. If my old dad could hear me, he'd haul me properly over the coals. You mustn't think, Sir Venn, that I usually repeat my clients' affairs in this way."

"I wouldn't dream of thinking it, I promise you. I might as well assure you that I don't usually exhibit so much curiosity in the affairs of people I don't know," said Venn with an hypocrisy that was quite foreign to him, "only there seemed to be something about this case, well, rather out of the common, that excited my fancy."

"You may well say so. I thought so too, at the time. It was the first ticklish case I had to handle, after I'd taken over from my dad. Well, since I know it will go no further, I'll tell you. She baffled us at every turn. There seemed to be nothing in her life that we could get hold of. Of course there were always heaps of men round her,—I told you she was a very attractive woman,—but apparently they never got anything out of her, except to let themselves be made fools of, unless they were prepared to be just satisfied with the pleasure of her company, which I doubt. She's the sort of woman that men want more from than that. I'm ashamed to confess that we tried to catch her out through her servants,—a low trick, but what else could we do, since she wouldn't play into our hands?—but even there we drew a blank. The servants could report only that the children were allowed to run in and out freely as they pleased, whoever was there calling upon her."

"Oh, she has children, has she?"

"Three, or four, I forget now how many. That's a tragedy too: the eldest boy . . ." Mr. Block tapped his forehead significantly.

Venn shrank; it suddenly hurt him to think how that must have made her suffer. Still, because he wanted to know everything about her, however painful, he forced himself to say, "Wrong in the head?"

"Worse. Homicidal. At least, they suspect it. He isn't quite old enough yet to be sure. He's shut up now. Of course that made the case even more distressing, because, you see, it took some time before they realised what might be the matter with the child, paroxysms of rage and so on, and then she had to consult his father, and naturally they couldn't meet officially while the divorce proceedings were going on,—King's Proctor, and all that rubbish. Anyway, the other children are all right; jolly kids they are, too." Mr. Block, in love with a girl who would not make up her mind to marry him, sighed.

"Which of them has the children now?"

"Vane-Merrick, naturally, since she was technically the guilty party, but he behaves very decently about that; he lets her see them as much as she wants to. A friendly arrangement. No trouble about that."

"You were telling me, weren't you, how difficult you found it to obtain evidence against her?"

"Yes, and I hope I never have to handle such a job again; it's a nasty business, setting traps for a woman," said Block righteously, still thinking about his reluctant Ethel. "All the same, it was her own choice, and it was her own mischievousness that made it so difficult for us. In a way, she had only herself to blame. In the last resort, we had to put detectives on to her. Then we thought we'd got her. You see, we'd discovered through her servants that she disappeared for the whole afternoon and evening four times a week, and nobody knew where she went to. So we had her followed." He paused dramatically.

"And do you know where she went?" he added then. "You must remember that we all thought her no better than she should be, only just too clever for anybody to catch her tripping. Of course we thought she spent the time in some man's rooms. Not a bit of it. Our man followed her, and he found that she went either to a children's hospital, or to the lowest slums, or else prison-visiting. I don't know if you appreciate what that means, Sir Venn. It means that she went to places the police would hesitate to go into except in couples, and to talk to people that even a Salvation Army lass wouldn't be safe from. And, believe me, Mrs. Vane-Merrick doesn't look like a Salvation Army lass; quite the contrary. Yet when our man made enquiries about her, they told him that she could do anything with those down-and-outs; she made them laugh, you see, instead of talking goody-goody to them as most charitably-minded ladies do, and she looked pretty too, in her neatest clothes, instead of looking as grim as a church-warden's wife. She had her jokes with them, and she took their babies on her knee and never forgot how many teeth they had cut and whether they'd had croup or not. And as to the prison-visiting, they told our man that if they had to choose between sending the chaplain or Mrs. Vane-Merrick into the cell of the lowest tough, it would be Mrs. Vane-Merrick they would send."

"Then how on earth . . ." said Venn, strangely moved.

"How on earth did we get her in the end?" Block was quite wound-up by his own recital. "Well, that was queer. I suppose she got bored with her own game, and, having led us enough of a dance, decided one day that she wouldn't lead us a dance any longer. I'm convinced that she always meant to release Vane-Merrick with as little damage to himself as possible. I dare say she despised him a bit for having accepted the chance she offered him, and meant to have her joke on him in revenge, and who can blame her? but at the same time she really did believe in his career, or at any rate she knew that *he* believed in it, which comes to much the same thing in the eyes of a woman,—anyway, she ended by giving us the evidence we were looking for. It makes me laugh now, to remember the way she did it."

"?"

"Why, she sent me a note. She began by saying she couldn't bear to think of Miles,—meaning Vane-Merrick, —spending all that money on solicitors and detectives, not that she hadn't found the detective very useful, because he carried her parcels for her; you see, she used to take clothes and food and things to the poor, and it turned out to be quite true, because I had our man up and asked him about it; he looked rather sheepish at first, but then seeing that I wasn't blaming him he admitted that Mrs. Vane-Merrick had stopped and beckoned to him one day in the street and had asked him if he wasn't there for the purpose of shadowing her? Which, of course, there was no sense in denying. He'd been on her heels for a week already, and she must have known it. So then she said, *Well, if you've got to follow me anyhow, you might as well carry my parcels;*

I find them rather heavy. You see, she's the sort of woman any man would carry parcels for and gladly. After that, it appeared, they had gone out together every day in a friendly way, taking the same bus or underground or whatever it might be, pretending all the time that they didn't belong, till, having started on her heels, he had ended completely at her feet. Lovely feet they are, too; the neatest I ever saw. In fact, there was nothing he could say too good for her. He said he never enjoyed himself so much in his life. He said she made a joke out of everything, however solemn it was; she made him laugh more in a day, he said, than his wife had made him laugh in twenty years. Really, I do take off my hat to that woman. Our men aren't an impressionable lot as a rule."

"But what about the note?"

"Oh, the note. Yes. She suddenly sent me a note one day, telling me exactly where I could find her that night, in the most compromising situation possible. I can tell you, I was startled when that note came to me out of the blue, just when I was at my wits' ends how to catch her. Having tricked us and diddled us to her heart's content, she suddenly gave me the exact hour and the exact address, all as precise as you like. A most respectable hotel; the sort of hotel that never suspects anybody, or pretends not to. The sort of hotel that people use for those purposes upstairs, while the lounge downstairs is filled with God-fearing families up from the country for the winter sales."

Hallo, thought Venn, *has Block got some sense of humour after all? Or is he only bitter about the tricks he was forced to play on Mrs. Vane-Merrick, whom he obviously likes much better than he likes Vane-Merrick, his own client?*

"So you got your evidence at last," he said, prodding Block on.

"Yes, we got it." Block stopped dead; his rush of indiscretion had reached the end of its rope, pulling him up short. His sense of responsibility brought him up with a jerk just as he was about to reveal the true tit-bit of the whole story: the fact that the man she had been found with was no other than his own clerk Tracey. Of course he, Block, had been quite unaware of Tracey's intentions; he had been very angry with Tracey; and Tracey's identity had to be very carefully concealed under the mask of "a man unknown." It was a pity that he should have felt the obligation of stopping short of that funny additional twist about Tracey, an obligation which cheated him out of the pleasure of capping his own story. Le Breton was a good audience; it was a pity that le Breton, as an audience, could not be exploited to his fullest capacity. Still, there were limits. He sighed, and stopped.

"It's a curious history," said Venn, getting up to take his departure.

Mr. Block was not really very much surprised when he heard that Venn le Breton had married Mrs. Vane-Merrick.

II

Looking back, Venn never could decide whether he had had much difficulty in persuading her to marry him, or not. That was one of the many things which stung and tantalised him about her: she always eluded him. Mr. Block's phrase about her stuck in his mind, "*All right, I'll be It; now catch me if you can.*" And then, in a sense, he had caught her; officially, she became his. But, to do Venn justice, there was something in him which set very little value on the official aspect, but which cared a great deal for the underlying truth. He would, in fact, if given the choice, greatly have preferred to have her as a willing, loving mistress than as an elusive, dutiful wife.

She had the knack of giving him surprises, from the first. From the first, she always showed herself to him in a way that was never quite the way he had expected, yet her unexpectedness never did anything to destroy, but rather to enhance, his unphrased conception of her as a completed entity. Whatever she did, however disconcerting, made her not less like herself, but more so. Every time, it was as though she had shown him a new facet of herself, which, once shown, he recognised as a natural inevitable part of her, but which he had lacked the perception to imagine in advance. Thus, he had gone very wrong over the surroundings in which he thought to find her. Filled with the idea of an elegant young woman who frequented London ballrooms, he had visualised her as living in a small but intimate flat; he found her, on the contrary, in a large, rather bare, rather bleak house, deliberately impersonal; not in a feminine boudoir, but in a large drawing-room reflecting brown lakes of parquet floor; no carpet, no ornaments anywhere, no books, no trace that might reveal the impress of a personality. Moreover, she had her children with her. The servant who opened the door to him had looked very dubious: "Is Mrs. Vane-Merrick expecting you, sir?" He saw at a glance that she was the dragon type of servant, devoted, protective, hostile. She looked at him, whom she had never seen before and did not know even as a person who habitually telephoned. "Is Mrs. Vane-Merrick expecting you, sir?" she said, slightly intimidated by his assured manner; adding as an after-thought, "I'm not quite sure, sir, whether Mrs. Vane-Merrick is in or out." "Yes," he said, unpardonably, all the arrogance of his sovereignty over Storn lifting its head; "yes; if you will take up my name, I think you will find that Mrs. Vane-Merrick is expecting me."

Was she expecting him indeed? He wondered, as he waited downstairs in the hall. Had she indeed foreseen that he would call on her in her own house, the day after their meeting at Minna Lester's dance? He thought it probable. Would she receive him, or would she tell the servant to go downstairs again and say she was very sorry, but Mrs. Vane-Merrick was out? He waited, wondering. Again his preconceived idea of her was at fault, for he imagined that with feminine waywardness she would avoid receiving him; instead of that, the servant came downstairs again, rather resentful, to say would he please come upstairs into the drawing-room. He went up. He found her there with her children round her. She was sitting on the sofa playing some game with them; a lively little boy of perhaps two years old sat on her knee, a boy of perhaps four or five nestled on one side of her, and a little girl of the same age on the other. Twins, he thought. The group they made reminded him vaguely of some picture by Lawrence or Raeburn; the curly heads of the children, and her own curly head, rumpled now out of its ballroom sleekness, reminding him more of the wind-blown curls on Storn. She seemed to him too young to have so many children, nor could he forget the existence of the eldest boy, of whom Block had told him, and the suffering which that boy must have caused her; then suddenly he was seized by a jealous rage that these children, these so English, delectable children, with their straight limbs and their tousled heads, should have been begotten on her by another man. Suddenly, he hated her past, so much that he nearly took his leave for ever, in order not to become involved in her present. He foresaw too much pain and jealousy involved in any connexion between her life and his. For one instant he thought of turning his visit into a conventional visit paid by a young man on a woman who had attracted him briefly at an evening party. Why not leave it at that? Such a course was indubitably safer, but he then discovered that the safe course was not the course he preferred. He had been too well trained by his own temperament, and by Storn, always to choose the more cruel, more dangerous path.

The presence of her children made him shy until their friendliness won him over; their friendliness and her simplicity. She was natural and charming, today, laughing at the little boys, who were trying to stand on their heads, not very successfully; sitting on the floor with them in front of the fire and letting them play with the rings on her fingers while she talked to Venn. His pleasure in watching her was dimmed when a nurse arrived to take the children away. "Oh, is it time to go, Mummy?" "Yes, darlings, I'm afraid so." Venn noticed the instant obedience with which they scrambled up; he had expected a whine of protest, but all three came gravely up to him in turn, the boys to shake hands and the girl to drop a little curtsey. Yet in spite of the evident discipline which she had imposed on them there was no alarm in their gesture as they threw their arms round their mother and hugged and kissed her. They tumbled over each other like puppies in the effort to get nearest to her, the smallest boy pushing his way between his brother and sister, climbing on to her lap so that she might take him into her arms again, which she did, burying her face in his curls. "When will we see you again, Mummy?" "Not tomorrow, darlings; next day perhaps, if Daddy can spare you; don't forget to give him my love. You'll ask Mr. Vane-Merrick, Nannie, won't you?" she added, "and telephone to me in the morning." Venn had a sense of seeing into the intimacies of her life.

Then there was silence, as the children's voices died away down the stairs, and the front door banged behind them. Venn was watching her; she listened with a slightly wistful look, he thought; but with the shutting of the door her face cleared and she turned to him with her usual smile. "I'm sorry," she said; "other people's children are always a bore, but then, you see, I wasn't expecting you."

Now that he was alone with her his heart began to beat

harder, for he at last admitted to himself the purpose for which he had come. He now recognised quite deliberately that he had not stayed in London in order to see his solicitor. He had stayed in London in order to see Shirin Vane-Merrick again. It was a crazy folly, of course, but a wild recklessness possessed him, and in his hot-headed, impetuous way he would endure no restraint on the urgency of his own caprice. The beating of his heart oppressed him; he looked at her until he felt his eyeballs burn and a strange, cold fever took hold of his whole body. She was talking meanwhile; she was chattering and laughing; just mere nonsense, the sort of nonsense which would reveal nothing of herself, and which she had perfected into an art that would baffle and mislead the people who wanted to probe into her private secrets. Nor was she really ill at ease, for although she knew and recognised the expression in his eyes, she was on her guard and had sufficient confidence in her own defences. She had dealt with many men, and women too, and knew every move in this game which no longer even amused her. Nor could she feel, at the moment, that Venn was different from any other man; he was simply a man who, she knew, desired her and who must be kept away. What a waste of life! What a waste of energy! How foolish she had been to let him come in! But she had been so happy with her children, that his advent had caught her in a moment of light-hearted good-nature, and for some undefined reason she had wanted him to see the children too. Now she must get rid of him as quickly as possible; he would ask her to dine with him, probably,—the weariness of it all, and the monotony!—she would refuse, of course, for she wanted to stay at home and read; besides, she had promised Tracey to be at home all the evening, poor Tracey, that faithful dog-like bore, whom she had treated rather casually of late.

"Look here," Venn was saying, breaking into her chatter, "you don't know why I have come here. I want you to marry me." So vehemently was he impelled to say it, that he had no sense at all of the unusualness of his method. To him, it was as though a gale had suddenly arisen at sea.

She was not much surprised either. Her life had turned out so oddly and unexpectedly, that she could no longer be surprised by anything. It seemed no more surprising to her that Venn le Breton should now be asking her to marry him, than it had seemed surprising when Miles Vane-Merrick, that unknown young man, had made the same suggestion in the gallery of the Albert Hall. It seemed only as though she had expected him, Venn, to say it ever since she first went with him to Storn. As he said it, another line seemed to shoot upwards and fall into its ordained place on the vellum scroll of the pattern; it described an aerial curve as the curve of a rocket bursting into golden stars in the blackness of space, falling to earth again and leaving its trace in the inky path of the arabesque. Storn was the only thing she had ever allowed herself to care about; with an inner knowledge she now recognised, she had always known that Storn some day would be hers; Storn was hers at last.

"Are you quite sure you want to?" she asked, for under her secrecy and caution she was utterly honest.

"Quite sure," he replied, although until that moment he had not been sure at all; not consciously sure, only pushed along by something he did not understand.

"You can marry me if you like," she said without any

evasion, "but I warn you that you know very little about me, and that you may not like what you will come to know."

"I don't think I am in love with you," he said, considering her; "not what most people would call being in love."

She was amused by this, and raised her eyebrows, the spoilt and courted woman peeping out again.

"I don't think I even like you much," he continued; "I can't analyse what I feel about you; you alarm me, and I know we are running into danger; I only know that no one has ever woken me up or made me feel myself as you do. I can explain it no better than by saying it seems as though you were meant to come to me. Besides, I could never endure the idea of your going to anybody else, or giving to anybody else all that you might give to me. I have got to have you for my own, that's all I know."

"And supposing I refuse?" she asked, thinking that this was the oddest wooing she had ever experienced.

"You can't," he said with finality. "Besides, you've just agreed to marry me, and I fancy you would never agree to anything without meaning what you said, or go back on your word after you had given it."

"I don't want to deceive you in any way," she said; "if I am really going to marry you it is necessary that you should know I am not an easy person. I won't go into details, because I dislike discussing myself; I just want to warn you, that's all. I dare say you will find, as other people have found, that I am not entirely what I appear to be on the surface, and that I am a difficult person to love."

She hated saying this, she hated giving even that amount of revelation of herself, but her honesty compelled her.

She could trifle with people to almost any extent, but when she saw somebody intent and serious as Venn was intent and serious she lost all desire to trifle with them or to mislead them.

Venn, however, took up her phrase in a way she had not intended.

"*As other people have found?*" he quoted, and by his darkened looks she knew that he was retrospectively jealous.

"I don't think I like people very much," she said; "that makes one difficult, perhaps.—I know what you're thinking," she said; "you're thinking that I married,—yes, I did,—and you know, obviously, that it wasn't a success,—well, it wasn't. And you wonder how many other people there have been,—is that it?"

"I don't want to know; I'd rather not ask; I'd rather not be told."

"Listen," she said, "would it comfort you to be told that those things never really touched me at all?"

"What?" he said incredulously.

"Let's leave it at that," she said; "I've told you once and for all; I don't like saying these things, and I shall probably never discuss myself with you again so long as we live. This is probably the only serious conversation we shall ever have. I hope so. But now, since we've got to go through with it, ask me any questions you like, and either I'll answer you truthfully or not at all. If you ask me something I don't want to answer, I'll say so, but I won't tell you any lies."

How direct she is, he thought, *for such a feminine woman! She has all the charm of an excessive femininity, with none of its tiresomeness. She is perfect*, he thought; *she can be amusing and frivolous, yet dangerous depths are implicit in her; she calls out all the reality in me, yet her touch is so light and at every moment she seems so ready to bound away, that I am never sure where I am; at the same time I feel an absolute security. What will life with her be like,* he thought? *tantalising, difficult, never dull; but shall I ever catch her, hold her fully? Can I endure to own a woman I can never seize? Shall I ever be able to build up a picture of her mind, so that its landscape will no longer be strange to me?*

"I wish you had had no life hitherto," he said aloud.

"Wouldn't you find me very unfurnished?"

"If I had never let you go, when first you came to Storn," he said, "I could have furnished you myself."

She rested her eyes on him, with that same compassionate, almost maternal expression he had seen in them before, an expression which made him feel years younger than she. Again he wondered what she had been through and what she had learnt through the suffering she would never tell him about? He remembered the fragments Block had given him, to make up his broken picture, and suddenly began imagining her in detail; he saw Vane-Merrick bending to kiss her, taking her in his arms,—was she willing, or reluctant? did she yield herself softly, or reservedly submit?—he saw her lying back on her pillows, weak, happy, with her baby gathered into the crook of her arm; he saw her dressed for the street; he saw her lightly fencing with unknown men; he saw her, incongruous vision, mounting the stone steps of a prison. He saw her sitting before her dressing-table, smiling at her own reflection as she devised what new trick she might play on Vane-Merrick and his solicitors. But he could not follow her into the recesses of her mind; could not probe the private wound she had suffered through her eldest boy; and the exclusion angered him, in his possessiveness and exorbitance. "I don't even know the names of your children," he said, arrived at that point.

She accepted the apparent inconsequence without comment.

"Julian; Margaret; Nicholas," she replied, for she recognised the impossibility of evading the question; still, because they were part of her private life, she uttered their names only with an effort.

So, he thought, *she avoids any reference to the eldest boy.*

I can't tell him about Luke, she thought, *and yet I suppose I must. It isn't fair not to. But I can't say it; I'll tell him by letter.*

The same impulse to hurt her overcame him again, the same impulse which had seized him at the dance, making him want to carry her away as a prisoner to Storn and hurt her until he had her thoroughly broken. She was so cool, so self-possessed, so well in command of the situation; he felt that she was playing him, and remembering Lady Lester's light remark about her shallowness the devil tempted him to see whether he could not bring pain into her eyes. If he could do this, he felt, he would redeem himself from the sense of inferiority.

"I thought you had four children?" he said with deliberate cruelty.

She suddenly looked like a child herself; he noticed how she sat curled up in her corner of the sofa, plaiting a handkerchief in and out of her extraordinarily delicate fingers.

"He's an invalid, isn't he?" he continued, pressing home his victory.

Am I mad, he thought? *I shall lose her now; she is no tame kitten to submit meekly; she will fly out at me and send me packing.*

But she only said, "Yes, he's an invalid," in a small and quiet voice that left him wondering whether she had or had not guessed his intention.

"What are you thinking?" he said roughly.

"I was thinking," she said, getting up and moving over to the writing-table, "that if you really want to marry me you must . . ."

"Yes, must what?" he asked, following her.

"Throw away that tie," she said without turning round.

Venn's telegram made old Lady le Breton sit bolt upright in her chair at Storn: *Arriving Port Breton by usual train this evening with bride please send launch Venn.* Telegrams at Storn were telephoned from the mainland and taken down by a servant; therefore, having accepted the slip of paper from the salver presented to her by Graves the butler and having adjusted her spectacles to read the message, Lady le Breton realised immediately that Graves, however non-committal his demeanour, must be already acquainted with the news. It was significant, indeed, that Graves himself should appear with the salver, a duty usually delegated to the footman.

Graves stood respectfully aside while his mistress read the message; he stood aside in the attitude of a servant waiting to hear if there is any answer. By no flicker did he imply any knowledge of the message he had brought. But his wise little eyes noted the tightening of his mistress' hands on the arms of her chair.

"This came over the telephone, Graves?"

"Yes, m'lady. In the usual way."

Lady le Breton handed him back the slip.

"You can read the message, Graves, and you will order

the launch to meet Sir Venn. At what time exactly does the train arrive?"

"Five-thirty, m'lady."

"Then they will be here by six. They will want tea, Graves."

"On the terrace, m'lady? Yes, m'lady. And what rooms, do you think, m'lady, would Sir Venn wish prepared?"

Lady le Breton hesitated, her head whirling. Her one desire was to get rid of Graves and to collect her wits, but above all she must not allow him to see that Venn's telegram had come to her as a complete surprise.

"Sir Venn forgot to mention that in his letter," she said at last; "you had better tell Mrs. Hancox to prepare the West rooms, and if Sir Venn wishes it changed there will be time to do so."

Only when Graves had gone did she realise that she had made a slip; Graves, who sorted the letters every morning out of the postbag, must know perfectly well that she had had no word from Venn. Left alone, she let herself go in rage against him. It was just like the boy, she thought,—for she still called him the boy, although he was nearly twenty-eight,—to play this trick upon her, to humiliate her in front of her own servants. But for that one slip about the letter, she had carried it off well, no thanks to Venn! It made her much angrier to think she might have betrayed herself to Graves, than to think that Venn was now actually married. She passed the thought of his marriage by with scarcely any interest at all, dismissing it as a temporary irritation; no woman would stand Venn for long, she thought, nor would Venn stand any woman; she knew too well his irritability, his moroseness, his selfishness, and his perverse cruelty. Unless he had picked up some meek little creature, whom he could bully to his heart's content, that marriage of his was not destined for a long life. She gave it a year, at most. It was tiresome, certainly; there would be tears, scenes; Venn would grow more and more sullen, and that repellent, viciously cruel expression would disfigure his face; then there would be all the business of a divorce; but before very long it would all come to an end and she and Venn would go on together as before. That Venn's wife would interfere with her own position as mistress of Storn never entered her head; for one thing, Venn himself would never allow it. Their departments of government were far too strictly allotted, to offer any room for the intervention of a third, a stranger. There was only one function which Venn's wife might perform: to provide Storn with an heir. Old Lady le Breton cackled, forgetting her rage: what a miserable year the poor girl was going to spend!

All the same, she did wonder who Venn could possibly have found. His absence had been brief; so brief, that it was almost inconceivable he should have found somebody brand-new in those few days. She knew his impetuosity, and the hot-headed way he had of plunging through obstacles to obtain what he wanted; still, even Venn. . . . She was forced therefore to the conclusion that this marriage had been premeditated; but instead of making her angry, the insolence of his secrecy made her chuckle again: she quite respected Venn for having fooled her. Of his private life away from Storn she knew nothing and desired to know nothing: life outside of Storn held no interest and scarcely any real existence for her. If Venn had friends in London, he never spoke of them, and it was only as an address for letters that she knew so much as the name of his club. Occasionally during the summer a telegram would arrive, from some acquaintance or relation, proposing a visit to Storn; Minna Lester, for instance, was apt to descend on them once a year, bringing what Venn called "a packet of people" with her; but these telegrams invariably aroused a fit of temper in Venn, who demanded angrily whether he was never to be left in peace? and then he would refuse to send the launch for them, but would send a rowing-boat instead, especially if the sea were at all choppy, saying that he hoped the one experience would cure them of ever wanting to come to Storn again. Herein, he and his grandmother were in full agreement, for they both saw through the motive of these visits, and cynically appreciated the snobbish worldly value of boasting an acquaintance with the difficult and almost legendary Storn. Nothing but a storm at sea had ever induced them to retain any guest to spend a night on the island; and that, as Venn remarked, was more from a fear of losing their boat and their boatman than from any feeling of consideration for their guest.

Who, then, was this woman whom Venn was bringing back as his wife? Lady le Breton, inspired, picked up the morning's paper, which she had scarcely looked at, since the happenings of the world interested her not at all. Catalogues from shops she would study to any extent, writing to order the most recondite and unnecessary objects, patent foods having an especial appeal for her, but the daily paper left her undisturbed. Surely, however, Venn's marriage would have a little announcement to itself? She could find nothing. "Registry office, of course," she said to herself, throwing the paper down, and again she chuckled, thinking how the girl, whoever she might be, had already proved herself submissive to Venn's will in so far as she had forgone the allurement of an orthodox and social marriage for the more expeditious privacy of the registrar. No white veil and wedding march for Venn le Breton's bride! And Lady le Breton, who kept to her old-fashioned ideas about girls, judged her humility by the supposed sacrifice.

It would have surprised her to hear Shirin's own firmness on the subject.

"No," she said to Venn, who had suggested that perhaps she ought to take him to see her family, a suggestion which he made in the effort to please her, rather than from the least desire to hear it adopted; "no, you let me manage my affairs in my own way." He had already discovered the quiet obstinacy with which she did so. "I shall tell my father and nobody else, in fact I shall send a motor to bring him to the wedding. I hate weddings myself, but I dare say it will please him. I know I can trust him not to tell my mother until it is over; he will enjoy having the joke against her."

Shirin had told him nothing whatever about her family, save that her parents lived in Dulwich, but already he had come to the conclusion that there was no particular reason for this beyond her natural reticence. Moreover, it was not Venn's nature to trouble about such things; if Shirin volunteered any information, he listened; otherwise he asked no questions.

Still, he was unreasonably displeased at the suggestion that her father should be invited.

"Why should you particularly want your father?" he asked. "I thought we had agreed that no one should know about it till afterwards."

"He can witness our marriage."

"Anybody can witness it. One calls somebody in from the street."

"I'm sorry, Venn, I've decided to ask him."

"But if I ask you not to?"

"You needn't marry me, you know. I won't sue you for breach of promise."

He saw that she had hardened into an obstinacy he was later to know well. It was the first time she resisted him, and he did not like it, unaccustomed to being defeated. He scowled. All the same, he pulled himself together, feeling that it was unbecoming to quarrel with one's bride three days before one's marriage. There would be plenty of time to conquer her afterwards.

"Have it your own way," he said.

Seeing that she had won, she softened into generosity.

"You see, he's blind," she said, "so if he does consent to come you must be nice to him."

"Blind?" said Venn. "That does make a difference; I see now why you wanted to ask him. Why didn't you say so at once? Do you never give explanations? But why is he blind?"

"He lost his sight in Persia."

"Persia,—have you been to Persia too?"

"I was born there."

She was always giving him surprises; he liked her better, somehow, for having been born in Persia.

"Do you remember it?"

"Of course I remember it. I was five when we left."

"Tell me about it."

"Some day perhaps I will; not now. Didn't you say you had business to see to?"

"I must go to the solicitors," said Venn, making a face.

"Well, go, then," said Shirin, jumping up. She was always prompt to act. "Go along," she said impatiently, as he lingered, and laying a small hand against his chest, she pushed him.

"You don't care in the least if I go or stay?"

"Of course not," she replied, looking surprised; "I never pretended to be in love with you, did I?"

"Well, you are frank, anyhow," he said, rather taken aback by her candour; "tell me, Shirin, have you ever been in love with anybody?"

"Never mind," she laughed; "that's my business, not yours. By the way, if you are really going to your solicitors, you'll find that they know about your marriage already."

"What?" said Venn. "How should they know?"

"I told them."

"You told them?"

"Yes, last night. At least, I told Mr. Tracey, whom you will probably see. Mr. Block is away. You needn't worry, he will have been perfectly discreet."

"But why did you do that?" asked Venn, bewildered. He knew that Tracey had been concerned in her divorce, but he scarcely imagined that she would now have anything further to do with Vane-Merrick's solicitors. Her divorce was a subject that neither of them had mentioned.

"Ask him, and perhaps he'll tell you."

"Shirin, don't make mysteries."

"All right, I won't. He came to see me last night, after you had gone. In fact I thought you would probably run into him, here."

"You mean you were expecting him? You never told me."

"Why should I tell you? Tracey is one of my oldest friends."

"But we dined together, afterwards, and you never told me then either."

"My dear Venn, you will have to get used to not being told things."

"Are you never going to tell me anything?"

"Not unless I want to."

"Or unless I make you."

She laughed, that delicious laughter which attracted and tantalised him. "You'll never make me. Now go, and come back to fetch me for dinner. Don't keep me waiting; I suspect you of being very unpunctual." Although her tone was light, her eyes were caressing. *What would she be like,* he wondered, *if she really loved one? She would be very sweet to love. She would be unbelievably sweet, if she loved in return.*

"What should you do if I kept you waiting?" he asked, because he was reluctant to leave her.

"Go out with somebody else, of course, or by myself; I dare say I should soon meet somebody willing to give me dinner."

"The devil you would. You have a good opinion of yourself, haven't you?"

She shrugged. "Not particularly; just experience."

"Well, instead of putting your experience to the test, will you have luncheon with me as well?"

"I've already told you, Venn, I can't."

"Without giving me any reason why."

"That's another thing you will have to get used to: I never give reasons." This time, although she still spoke lightly, there was an underlying firmness in her tone, so that even he, who was not accustomed to being crossed, was silenced.

He was falling rapidly in love with her. She amused him by her many twists and turns; by the elusiveness which constantly cheated him. It amused him to spoil her, to see her frank and childish pleasure in lovely things. He gave her carte-blanche to buy whatever clothes she wanted, and, coming into her house in the evening, would watch her with delight as she laid out the purchases she had made during the day. "Venn, you are good to me," she would say. She handled silks and tissues with instinctive tenderness and skill.

"What a child you are," he said, watching.

"No; I'm a woman."

She was adorable in this mood. He brought her a sable cloak. It matched her hair, he said; and indeed there was an equivalence of light and darkness between the soft silky fur and her sleek brown curls.

"Oh, Venn!" was all she could say; "oh, *Venn!*"

He might have suspected another woman of what was vulgarly called marrying him for his money. But not Shirin. He knew that for all her pleasure she might spring away at any moment, leaving him. No wonder she found it difficult to get him out of the house.

At last he went. She gave a sigh of relief mixed with amusement: it was so characteristic of Venn to give no thought to the fact that owing to his intransigent behaviour he had turned the whole of her life upside-down in a way that would have flustered most women. A spoilt child, he could see nothing but the thing he wanted. She recognised the trait, from the little she had seen of him, years before: at Storn. Luckily she was not easily flustered, only prompt to get down to the business in hand and to settle it with the greatest dispatch possible. Her impending marriage was affecting her very little, but she had a good deal to put in order, and being extremely practical when she was not lost in her own private thoughts,—for she never did anything by halves,—she fretted at being delayed in her arrangements. The thought of marriage, the thought of Storn, which she would see again in three days' time, were put away at the back of her mind, since at the moment it was imperative that she should deal with the settling up of her present life. There were letters to be written, which she would post on leaving the registry office; then she must see about selling her house; and she must see Miles, she supposed, and come to some agreement with him about the children. That would be easy; she could always end by getting Miles to do what she wanted, but how he would laugh at her for marrying again! "Why," he would say, "that's the one thing you swore you would never do; you always said you were a born prostitute but no wife."

She sighed. Miles and she, although they had hurt one another bitterly, had always had a certain understanding of one another.

She would not bother about other people. Everybody concerned could learn of her marriage by letter, when once she was safely in the train; only she was afraid of forgetting someone; people made so little impression upon her, even those to whom she had given her body; they seemed very little more than an interrupting noise, a clamour disturbing the current of her true life; she was for ever surprised to find how readily they assumed that she took an interest in them; she was always misleading people, half intentionally, half unintentionally; she supposed that it must be the fault of her eyes, she had been told so often enough; men, if she looked at them, seemed to think that she appreciated them as no one had ever appreciated them before, and women told her their troubles at a first meeting; yet in fact they seemed to her no more real than marionettes making the expected gesture as one pulled the necessary string. She must certainly be very careful to forget no one who could possibly be hurt by her forgetfulness, for superficially she was quite kind-hearted; and so, being surprisingly methodical always, she sat down to make yet another list.

Lists she had already made in plenty; lists of what clothes she had to pack, what books to take; lists of things to say to the servants; a list of things to say to the children's nannie; now to these she added a list of people who must be apprised of her marriage. *Miles*, she wrote; and put an X before his name, meaning that she must see Miles and tell him verbally, not merely write to him; *Mother*, she wrote; *Paul; Roger. Henry*, she wrote abstractedly; *Cristina.* Thank God, she would soon be leaving all these people behind her. Her pencil stabbing the paper, she paused to wonder how often she would leave Storn and come to London to find these people once more clutching, surging round her. No oftener than she could help! and the bliss, the release of living for ever on Storn away from people made her head swim suddenly, so that she pushed her fingers through her hair regardless of its expensive order, making it stand out round her head in the old unruly curls. *Taffy*, she wrote, recalling herself to sense; she must not allow herself to think of Storn just yet; *Gerald;* no, she need not write to Gerald.

Tracey. Well, she had told Tracey. *My old hearthrug*, she called him; he had never made up his mind as to whether he liked being called an old hearthrug or not, but to so devoted a resignation had he schooled himself, that he responded gratefully to the compliment of any nickname, however inglorious, bestowed by her, from whom any recognition of existence, with a place in her life, was valuable. On the whole, it warmed him, even as an old hearthrug might be warmed by the fire, to hear himself called *my old hearthrug* in her voice. Of all the men who had loved her, whether for one evening or for years, Tracey had been the most faithful, the least exacting, the dullest, the most touching, and the most dependable. He had loved her in the hopeless humble way which can never conquer, but which gets the kind of reward it deserves in the end. He had got the reward of her affection when she had time to think about him at all, and he had got the consolation of knowing that she would turn to him, if to anyone, in trouble. (It was difficult enough to get her to turn even to him, so proud was she; and but for the chance of his being mixed up in her misfortunate marriage and divorce, he doubted whether he would ever have had the luck of rendering her any service. But when he came and expostulated with her over the bother she was giving his firm, wringing from her the admission that she wished neither to implicate any man nor to put herself under an obligation to any, then he urged his devotion and begged that he might for once put it to some practical use. Her divorce, he said; he quite realised that a nature as fastidious as hers shrank from the idea of asking any man to help her out; but why couldn't she call on him quite safely? it was irregular, of course, highly irregular, especially as he was employed by the very firm acting for Miles Vane-Merrick;

but never mind that, he said: devotion such as his could override all such professional considerations. They would never, he said, be found out; and finally he persuaded her. He was never quite sure that she had not accepted his suggestion as a joke, the ironical kind of joke that would most appeal to her; he felt only that his life had reached its fulfilment when he gained her consent. Contented with little, he knew that he could spend the rest of his life living on the memory of that one night with her, with its deluding sense of intimacy as he watched her put out her things on the dressing-table in the hotel bedroom, so sordid with its dusty plush, made gracious by her presence; she had moved about gaily, chattering to cover up her embarrassment, and he, confused, enraptured, had watched her, unaccustomed anyhow to the intimate grace of a woman's life, because, loving her, he had known no other woman; doubly confused because the woman in question was the woman he had loved at a distance since she was sixteen, without ever hoping to come nearer to her than in a seat at the theatre. He had loved her the more, in that queer situation, for being a little shy. "Tracey," she had said, coming up to him and hiding her face against his coat, "Tracey, I'm shy; make it all right." He had not known how to make it all right; all that he could do was to refrain from straining her to him and kissing her in the way which instinct suggested to him but which he was sure she would not like. As it was, he had only patted her shoulder, looking over the top of her head at the vast double bed. Then they had dined in the sitting-room, attended by a greasy little waiter with a remarkable gift for balancing an over-loaded tray on the palm of his hand; and they had had champagne, because Tracey knew that in these cases it was necessary to make an impression on the waiter, so that later on, when the waiter's evidence was taken, he would remember the couple clearly, but they had poured the champagne away in the bathroom during the waiter's absence, since Shirin never drank any wine at all, and Tracey dared not drink more than half a glass that night, lest it inflame his desires beyond endurance. "What a waste," Shirin had said; "I think we ought to send Miles the bill for this, don't you, Tracey?" and Tracey had been slightly shocked, as he often was by Shirin, though at the same time he admired her for daring to say things he would never have dared to say himself. Several times he nearly lost his head altogether, to look at her sitting opposite to him in her jacket of flowered silk, whose sleeves fell loosely back revealing her soft round arm; but very professionally, and again in order to produce a deeper impression, he only made her talk to the waiter, asking him about his way of life, how many rooms he had to serve on that floor, whether the work was not very tiring, whether he had a home of his own or not, and how often he was able to see his wife and children. Since it was Shirin's habit to talk to all stray acquaintances in that way, she found no difficulty in carrying out his instructions; indeed, she was relieved at being able to talk to the waiter instead of to Tracey, for at the back of her mind she was worrying over the peculiar embarrassment of dealing with the forthcoming night, although with Tracey she carried the situation off lightly. Tracey himself had made up his mind in advance: forced by the exigencies of the law to share a room with Shirin, he would spend the night on the sofa. He tried honestly to block out all other thoughts from his mind. But Shirin herself seemed determined to defeat his intention, for as she lay finally in bed she called him to her. "Don't worry about me," he said, not feeling like an old hearthrug at all, and trying not to look at her bare throat, her dark curls, her whole relaxed attitude; "I shall be quite all right on the sofa." "Nonsense Tracey," she had said then; "do you suppose I would allow you to do all this for me, and give you nothing in return?" She had never thought of him as a proud man, and his reply raised him in her eyes as his humility could never raise him: "Do you suppose," he said, "that I would allow you to sacrifice yourself from a sense of honour?"

She had written to him afterwards, thanking him, and adding, "*I may have refused things to lots of men, but I shall always think of you, Tracey dear, as the one and only man to whom I ever made advances, and who turned me down. It was chic of you: I love you for it.*" He had felt compensated then for the hours he had watched her asleep, in the slow London dawn.)

She had felt that Tracey deserved her confidence. Moreover, she knew that the announcement of her marriage would hurt him, and preferred that he should hear it verbally from her than in any other way. About her mother she had no scruples whatsoever, for she had long since outgrown all family ties except the affection she retained for her father. She knew well enough the hubbub that her mother would set up; the snobbishly embarrassing things she would say; it had been bad enough when Shirin had announced her engagement to Miles Vane-Merrick; it would be worse now that she was going to marry Venn le Breton. Firmly and quietly, she dismissed her mother from her conscience. With Tracey it was otherwise. Tracey was not a matter of conscience; he was a matter of heart. Tracey had been good to her, really good; and Shirin, ruthless enough to some, could be tender enough to others. She never hesitated for an instant between the two categories. Nor would she shirk the unpleasant task. Poor Tracey, he had looked so shocked and hurt when she told him; an expression of real dismay had come over his nice ugly face and into his nice trusting eyes. "Then I shall never see you?" he had stammered as his first reaction; but she had reassured him, saying that she would often be in London, partly on account of the children, partly on account of various occupations which she could not wholly abandon.

She did not specify what occupations, but he knew she meant her slums and prisons. Tracey and Cristina Rich were the only people to whom she had ever spoken of her slums and prisons, the only people admitted to a knowledge of that serious side to her character. And even Tracey had never known about it until Vane-Merrick's detective revealed to him how Mrs. Vane-Merrick spent her afternoons. He never forgot her blush when she learnt she had been discovered, a blush as though she had been taken in guilt.

Now she was wondering how she should arrange her life at Storn, for without some work of the kind she knew she never could be happy. But that, she thought, could be left to settle itself later, for she had no idea of the conditions down at Storn, nor did she know how seriously she would first have to contend to get her own way with Madame, old Lady le Breton. That Venn's grandmother was still alive she had already learnt from him, and a thrill of anticipation ran through her at the thought of renewed contact with that alarming but magical old woman. Wasn't it partly on Madame's account that she had agreed to marry Venn? For Shirin had cherished a special, secret feeling for Madame, ever since that day on Storn; it was more than a feeling, it was almost a worship, above all a desire to explore the mysteries which Lady le Breton might consciously or unconsciously teach her. She had remained grateful to Madame for ten years for having given her her first glimpse of beauty, energy, and courage. Madame had broken strongly coloured across the drabness and dreariness of life as she was accustomed to see it lived in her own family circle at Dulwich; Madame, that day, had given her an indication of what people and life and danger might be. She was quite ready, now in her maturity, to admit that morally Madame might stand gravely in need of justification; indeed she was sure that morally Madame was entirely discreditable; she might have done the meanest, unkindest things, certainly had; might have broken the heart of some devoted humble creature, might have done a variety of things which by all humane and moral standards should most be disapproved; still, Madame continued to hold her special position in Shirin's queer heart, as the person who had first shown her that damage could be repaired by one lovely smile; the person who had first shown her that beauty is the natural destroyer of evil. *Thus*, thought Shirin, *could Helen easily repair the ruin of Troy*.

The idea of living in the same house as the old woman, of penetrating again into that peculiar and overcrowded room, of listening for the rare and oracular revelation, of seeing again the flash of beauty, like lightning against the night of evil, excited her far more than the idea of sharing a life with Venn, whose existence she constantly found herself forgetting. But how would Madame receive her? As a negligible addition? As a young usurper of her name and privileges? Autocratic old women were traditionally not well disposed to welcome the intrusion of a young successor.

She need have had no fears, and indeed she had none, life and her own temperament having hurt her until she no longer dreaded anything but accepted with resignation whatever came along, always expecting the worst as a matter of course. She had no fear of Madame, for she felt that she and Madame understood one another; she had no fear, only a certain interest in seeing what battles would await her. At most, she hoped vaguely that there might be no battles, for she was tired of fighting, tired of playing always for her own hand in the loneliness and isolation which came of her own choice, but which she never could prevail upon herself to amend. There would be battles enough with Venn, she foresaw that, but, not caring for him, she knew that he never could really touch her; the old woman she did, strangely, care for, and knew that caring, as always, would render her unbearably vulnerable.

So persistently had Lady le Breton dwelt in her mind, rushing closer and closer during the few, the very few, days that preceded her marriage,—for Venn would hear of no delay, but swept her along with, as it seemed, increasing speed towards the culmination,—that Shirin began to contemplate almost with terror the moment when the old woman's physical presence would replace the remembered image. Had she imagined the whole thing? Had she imagined that day on Storn? that conversation so unlike any conversation she had ever held before or since? Looking out of the windows of the train she began to recognise the landmarks she had not seen for nearly ten years, and, knowing that in a few moments she would see the sea, she glanced across at Venn and saw that he too was staring out of the window with a rapt intensity. For an instant she was icily afraid of him. *My God*, she thought, *what have I done?* and then, because she had never lost the childish trick of sudden prayer, she prayed, *Oh God, save me from being too much hurt any more*. He was a stranger to her, so unfamiliar that she scarcely knew his features, but now she looked at him as it were for the first time, seeing him for the first time with an inward eye, so that he acquired a meaning for her where no meaning had been before; she saw his pale, curious, threatening eyes, his sensual and rather beautiful mouth, his cruel hands, his air of elegance and distinction, the outer envelope of his secret personality whose shape and aspect she would eventually learn to know. Six days ago, he had not been in her life at all; now she had acquired him, with all the complexity of an unknown human being; she was responsible for him, knowing that she was stronger than he and must shoulder the weight of his troubles, never allowing him to guess that she was doing it. At what price to herself she did not stop to reckon, for she was used to paying the price and paid it gladly, provided that no one knew or guessed the effort it cost her. Six days ago,—fantastic thought! and now she was entering into the intimacy of two unknown lives, with all their apparatus both external and internal; the lives of two beings, utter strangers to her, but whose fortunes she shared and whose name she bore. As though to convince herself of this reality, she looked at the dressing-case which Venn had given her, with the neat initials: S. le B. How curious a label was a name! so persistent, yet so insignificant; the fact that a new name was now affixed to her, which to most people would mean *her*, as a recognisable identity, in no way affected the fact that she was still the same continuous person, still the child who had lived in Dulwich and had thrown stones at her brothers in defence of the cove near Storn.

She pulled the dressing-case towards her, opened it, and looked at her photograph of Storn. That was the only possession she valued, the only possession she had retained through all the various mutations of her life. And as she looked at it she was suddenly carried back to her little bedroom at Dulwich; to the evening when she had washed the child's blood off her shirt, and had seen with horror the water turning pink in the basin.

The train rounding a corner, they came within sight of the sea. She looked at Venn, and saw his face light up. This, then, was what he had been expecting; this, which had made him stare out of the window with almost mystical intensity? She had known that Venn loved Storn, she had known that he loved the sea, but now for the first time she knew it not in words but with her inner knowledge, even as, ten minutes ago, she had for the first time really seen his face. The sea lay spread out calm and glittering, the sun already slightly lowering towards the west. One single sail made a dark triangle in the path of the sun. It was serene and beautiful, the coast running away from them in a curving line of broken rocks and little headlands, deserted, lonely, wild. "Oh, Venn," she said. She clasped her hands and leant forward; she could not help herself; all her childish memories came back to her; to her own surprise, she felt a rush of gratitude towards Venn for giving her a right to claim this beauty, this serenity, as now her own. She felt her trust in life revive, bringing with it a sense of being at a new beginning, and she smiled confidently at Venn, losing her momentary fear of him, but he replied with a glance so strange and so forbidding that, startled, she wondered what she had done amiss.

"What a perfect evening," she said; not the sort of remark she usually made, but an inexplicable nervousness prompted her to do so now.

"It won't last," he answered.

"What makes you say that?"

He pointed to a small black-purple cloud low down on the horizon.

"Thunder, I shouldn't be surprised.—We shall get there before it breaks," he added with sudden kindliness, thinking she might be alarmed.

"I don't mind thunder, Venn; I rather like it. Do you get bad storms on Storn?"

"Yes, they go round and round the island; they don't seem able to get away," he replied with relish. "Lucky you don't mind them. But you wouldn't enjoy crossing from Port Breton in an open launch in a rough sea, the currents are very tricky there anyhow, and it can be choppy enough to upset most people. However, as I say, the storm won't come up till later on. We shall have plenty of time to get across."

"I know you get storm-bound sometimes; the people at Port Breton used to tell us."

"Days on end, sometimes."

She wondered what it would be like, to be imprisoned on an island alone with Venn and his grandmother, without any possibility of escape.

His grandmother's greeting, however, reassured her. Lady le Breton had waited for them, pacing up and down the yew terrace with Venn's two Great Danes in attendance. The launch was already within sight, cutting its way across the water with a faint chugging of its engine, two figures discernible in it besides the dark blue figures of the two boatmen. Venn, she could see, was steering, and near him she saw the woman, but, although she peered through the telescope swivelling on its fixture on the parapet, she could identify no recognisable features; at most she could make out that the woman was hatless, her hair blown back by the breeze of their advance. "Young," she said to herself; "scarcely more than a girl; pretty, I should say; neat. Poor little devil." She turned to look at the now heaped and angry sky. "She'll be blown into her bed, her first night at Storn," she added grimly, for although the sea was still calm and the trees motionless, she knew as well as Venn what that scarlet sunset among the inky clouds portended. "It isn't from Venn," she added, "that she'll get any comfort."

The dogs were uneasy; as other dogs who recognise the significance of packing and luggage, so they, island-bred, had recognised the significance of the launch departing, and now with some sixth sense seemed aware of its return. Still stalking gravely, one on either side of Madame, they raised their muzzles and snuffed the air; at a given moment, she knew, they would bound away and be down at the harbour in time to meet the incoming boat. They had never yet been known to miscalculate the time, or to take the trouble thus to meet anyone but their master. "Yes, Olaf; yes, Sandra," she said, resting her hand on Olaf's huge head, "he's coming, but not alone." And, knowing their strength, she hoped Venn would not let them leap against the girl and possibly knock her down. That would be a bad introduction for Venn's wife under the eyes of the inquisitive, assembled village.

The launch was drawing nearer; she could now hear the sound of its engine quite plainly, and could distinguish Venn at the steering-wheel, beginning to take the curve which would bring them into the harbour. She could see the white wake of the little craft beginning to describe the curve as a pattern on the water. Soon they would be lost to sight under the shelter of the island, and then there would be a pause while they drew into the harbour, made fast, and landed: a pause prolonged while Venn introduced her to such village notables as the post-mistress, the publican, and old Dunn, the doyen of the fishing-fleet, all of whom would certainly be taking the evening air round the harbour by some remarkable coincidence as the launch bearing the Ranger and his bride arrived. Graves and the boatmen could be trusted to have spread the news by now. Lady le Breton grinned: how like Venn to have evaded the triumphal arches and the flags of welcome which the islanders would surely have hung out, given a proper warning! Then there would be another pause, while they climbed up the winding path,—and at that thought, seeing that the launch had disappeared from view, Lady le Breton began making her way slowly back towards the castle, where the rough steps from the village reached the upper level.

As she turned, the dogs left her; they leapt away as by common accord, and went with great bounds down the slope, more like brindled ponies than like dogs, ignoring the steps, taking the shortest way. Lady le Breton smiled to see them go. No command, she knew, would have held them back. Even now they must be leaping round Venn on the jetty, and he quieting them by hand and voice so that he might give his orders to the boatmen.

Standing at the head of the steps, shading her eyes with her hand,—for she wore no hat, only some black lace over her head, and the reflection off the red sea troubled her,—Lady le Breton listened. She heard voices; Venn's voice; then a peal of laughter. So she arrived with laughter, did she, the unknown girl? Good luck to her, that she might not depart with tears. And after a moment's listening, she heard laughter again, and thought she recognised a note that she had once heard; then she heard Venn's voice, calling to his dogs; and they came into sight. Venn first and then the girl, and a pang went through Lady le Breton, at last confronted by a physical presence, as she realised that here, however temporarily, was another Lady le Breton, and that she had seen her before.

Amazed, she said, "You?—But, my dear child, I've forgotten your name."

III

VENN, to his surprise and not wholly to his pleasure, found that his grandmother regarded Shirin as her own invention. "I always liked that child," she said to him with great firmness, "from the first day you brought her here. I saw through her, which was more than you had the sense to do." In fact she talked and behaved as though she herself had arranged the marriage. It was she, and not Venn, who took Shirin away into the castle; she who introduced her to Graves and the housekeeper; she who insisted on leading her up all the stairs to the great West bedroom. Under all her charm and courtesy, however, she remained the mistress and Shirin the guest,—a guest who had come for a long stay, possibly, and for whose comfort everything would be done, but still, quite firmly, a guest. At any moment Shirin expected to hear her say, "You will ask, my dear, won't you, for anything you want?"

The great bedroom with its groined ceiling, stone walls hung with tapestry, and oriel window overlooking the sea, fulfilled almost absurdly the Storn of Shirin's dreams. Like the back-cloth in a theatre hung the menacing sky, black and silver now, and swollen with the hurrying clouds. Three steps led up to the window, recessed at the back of a platform and three-sided window-seat. Shirin ran up the steps to look out. Lady le Breton watched her. "She looks like a bird," she thought, "beating against the glass."

Shirin had no such thought. In that moment she was transported by happiness; everything twisted and broken in her life was straightened and healed; Venn did not exist; nothing but Storn existed, and Storn was hers. She had no wish to control it, no wish to trespass on the privileges Madame had for so long enjoyed; she desired only the right to live there, to lose herself in its fantastic beauty, to wander unmolested, or to dream for hours in this embrasure above the sea, working her way through to some inward peace in which one might come at last to terms with life.

"So you have married Venn," said Lady le Breton.

Shirin turned to look at her. Leaning on her stick near the fireplace, the old woman wore her most enigmatic expression. She even nodded her head slightly, as though in communion with some secret thought. She was frail and lovely, ivory-pale under her black lace mantilla, her fine hands clasped over the crook of her stick, but beyond all her loveliness and charm lay something sinister, as though she retained all the time the full awareness that life held dangers from which no illusion would ever hold one secure.

Shirin, shaken out of her forgetful happiness, shivered. "Yes," she said gaily, without betraying herself, "I've married Venn."

"When?" asked Lady le Breton.

"When?" said Shirin. She laughed; it seemed so long ago. "This morning at ten," she said, "in London."

"He never warned me," said Lady le Breton, "but I

didn't mind: Venn is like that. And it is no good expecting people to be unlike themselves, is it? especially in unusual circumstances. I didn't blame you either, my child; I expect you thought Venn quite old enough to be left to deal with his own relations and to warn them of a detail such as his marriage. You will find, I dare say, that Venn is not old enough to be left to deal with anything except a sailing-boat and a seine full of fish. He thinks he is, and thinking so sometimes makes him behave in the most high-handed fashion. Luckily for him, and luckily for myself too, I have known him long enough to regard him always as a little boy who likes showing off. I don't know what your life has been, my child, since you came here years ago,—you look scarcely a day older, except that you seem to have smartened yourself up,—you were a tousled little scrap when I last saw you, and now you're a finished young woman,—but I dare say you have learnt enough not to take undue notice of little boys when they show off. A woman, fortunately, is always a great deal older than a man; that seems to be a compensation given to us to make up for our other disadvantages. It prevents us from taking too much notice of what they may do or say."

Is she trying to caution me against Venn? thought Shirin.

"I hope you like your room," said Lady le Breton in a conversational tone; "of course Venn said nothing about which room he wanted you to have, so I had to take the decision for myself."

"I think," said Shirin sincerely, "that it is the most beautiful room I have ever seen. But what is that little lattice high up in the wall?" she asked, pointing.

"Oh, that," said Lady le Breton. "That was put in by an ancestor of Venn's, whose room it was. He suffered from melancholia towards the end of his life; refused to see anyone for days on end, and had all his meals pushed in on a tray through that kind of a buttery-hatch you can see cut in the door. The one thing which could solace him was music, so he installed an organ in a little room next door; the lattice enabled him to hear it played. A very sensible idea, I always think."

"And does anyone ever play it now?" asked Shirin.

"Venn's secretary," said Lady le Breton; "a nasty little man, most inefficient, but a very fine musician. That's why Venn puts up with him, I believe, unless it's because of his ridiculous devotion to Venn." A note of ill-temper jarred her voice; it seemed that she would have said more, but turned the subject aside. "And now," she said suddenly becoming brisk, "we must do something about your things. Graves should have asked you for your keys. This room looks bare enough without any things about. The fire, too,—look at that. Really the servants are disgraceful. You see what I mean, Shirin: no unpacking done for you, and the fire not properly made up; you see what I mean?"

"But Graves, if Graves is the butler," said Shirin, "did ask me for my keys and I told him I would rather do my unpacking myself." She was amused by this abrupt change in Madame. Her mellow tone had become fussy and irritable; she tapped on the ground with her stick in an exasperated way. She paid no attention to Shirin's defence of Graves, beyond exclaiming that the old man was hopelessly past his work, and seizing the old-fashioned bell-rope she tugged it so vigorously that Shirin feared it would come down from its fastening into her hand.

An elderly housemaid appeared at the door.

"Annie! at last! why don't you answer the bell when I

ring it? Why have you not seen that the fire was kept up? It is freezing, in here. And why have you not unpacked her ladyship's luggage? Really, Annie, I should have thought you had been long enough at Storn to know your work properly by now. You must look after her ladyship as though she were myself. See, Annie, I am going to give her ladyship some of my pearls," and so saying, Lady le Breton took off the pearls she was wearing and passed them over Shirin's head. "You see, Annie," she said with pride at her own gesture, "her ladyship is like my own daughter-in-law. You must treat her as such."

Annie received this demonstration unmoved. She was evidently well accustomed to the moods of her mistress. She threw two fresh logs on the fire, and came towards Shirin with a pleasant smile, but a smile almost of complicity: "If I might have your keys, my lady?"

The storm grumbled round them as they sat at dinner, but Lady le Breton's personal ill-temper appeared to have passed away. She looked very distinguished tonight, in a great deal of black lace and ropes of pearls. Shirin thought that she and Madame and Venn made an odd trio. Venn was morose, crumbling his bread and keeping his eyes bent upon his plate. She had not seen him alone since their arrival.

Queer creature, she thought; most men, married that morning and bringing their bride to their home,—and such a home!—would have come to tap at her door before dinner. Not so Venn. He had let her go to her room with his grandmother, and had left her to find her way downstairs again alone. Shirin had no idea what he had been doing in the interval, or even of where his own room was, should she have wished to find him. She was not in the least offended, only amused; Venn, evidently, was not domesticated by temperament. She liked it better so. She was unaware that, finding his possessions transferred to the dressing-room of the West bedroom, he had flown into a rage, rung for his servant, and demanded to know by whose direction the change had taken place. On hearing that it was by his grandmother's orders, he commanded that his things should immediately be replaced in the room he had occupied all his life; sought his grandmother out, and engaged her in one of those scenes of abuse which punctuated their existence. Lady le Breton first mildly protested that she had thought it the natural thing to do; then taking fire herself at his violence, retaliated in kind; brought out every grievance she had ever nursed against him; and ended by threatening to leave Storn for ever, *but that I wouldn't abandon that poor girl to your mercy*. She thought then that he was going to strike her.

"That poor girl, please remember, is my wife."

"It looks like it," she sneered.

"You damned interfering old woman, will you leave us to manage our own affairs?"

"I know you too well, my boy, for that. Is the girl in love with you, may I ask?"

She saw that she had hit him.

"You had better ask her yourself, you seem to be hand in glove with her already."

"Jealous, Venn? Well, she might not tell me if I did ask her; she knows how to keep her own counsel. I fancy you've met your match, especially as she doesn't care for you."

"Who says she doesn't care for me?" he said, beside himself at her taunts. "Why else should she have married me?"

Lady le Breton's eyes narrowed.

"Why should she have married you? Do you really want to know? You blind idiot! For the sake of Storn, of course."

"Perhaps she told you that, did she? By God, if she told you that, she leaves Storn tomorrow."

"Do you really imagine that any woman would be such a fool as to say such a thing? To me, of all people? And do you imagine also that I haven't got eyes to observe with?—No, Venn," she said, sobered by his expression and regaining her self-control, "I promise you, the girl hasn't said a word."

Shirin of course knew nothing of all this. She observed only that Venn was extremely sullen and his grandmother extremely amiable at dinner, from which she deduced that they had had a battle in which the grandmother had come off the victor. She hoped sincerely, but without much conviction, that she herself had not been the occasion of the battle. It was the most freakish thing she had ever done, to be sitting between those two people, a stranger, yet in such close connexion; *I feel like Alice*, she thought, *between the Gryphon and the Mock Turtle*. Would she sit thus, she wondered, every night for the rest of her life? but because she was always lacking in any sense of permanence she shrugged the idea away. *Here today and gone tomorrow* had been her experience, a transient passage in which nothing but her own personality preserved any continuity. Since, however, with the top layer of herself she was able to observe and to appreciate the humour of the moment, she amused herself by noting the habits of her two hosts,—for she could not regard Venn in any other light,—habits which were the growth of years and which would shortly become so familiar to her also that she would cease to notice them any more. *What a lot of little pots and bottles Madame has in front of her*, she thought; *five different sorts of mustard, three different sorts of sauce, four little dishes of gherkins, olives, pimentos, anchovies; and how she occupies herself with them, pressing them on Venn who does not want them, and on me who do not want them either but accept in order to save trouble. Madame is either very greedy or very fidgety; probably both; in any case she is contriving to complicate life this evening in the most surprising way. Is she always like this, I wonder? She badgers Venn, who is evidently determined not to be won over. It amuses her to irritate him by pretending that nothing is the matter. What an odd twist, not going with the rest of her character in the least. But then people are never all of a piece. Venn is not all of a piece either; he is very young and uncertain of himself, though he does not know it; that is his charm. He is the most unaware person I have ever known. Any gust might blow him along and he would make no effort to resist it. Tonight he is angry about something, and is giving way completely to his anger*,—so she spoke to him, laughing, just in order to see how he would respond.

The eyes which he raised upon her startled her, so full of a lowering passion; then as they rested on her their expression changed; they travelled searchingly over her, dwelt on the waves of her hair, on her mouth, on the little hollow at the base of her throat, on the slight curve of her breast under the blue Chinese jacket. She knew then that he desired her, but whether in love or in hatred she could not decide. His scrutiny seemed interminable, but fortunately for Shirin the Great Danes had their habits too, and, rising now from the dark corner in which they had been lying, they stretched themselves at leisure and approached Venn with their slow majestic gait. They stood on either side of him, expectant, beating the leg of the table with their tails. "One scarcely knows which is made of wood," said Shirin, trying to make conversation, "the table or the tail."

At the sound of her voice both dogs turned their heads in her direction, and the great Olaf came to take his stand beside her. "Look, Venn," said Madame, "Olaf is deserting you for Shirin." She said it with more malice than conviviality. "And now Sandra," she continued; "you will have to look to your authority, Venn, or Shirin will steal your followers from you. Do you always exercise this fascination over dogs, Shirin? for upon my word I have never seen Olaf or Sandra pay the smallest attention to anyone when Venn was present. They tolerate me when he's away, but as soon as he returns I count for nothing. Look at Olaf now, Venn; that really is very extraordinary."

Olaf had lifted a huge paw and laid it on Shirin's knee, gazing upwards at her with melancholy eyes.

"He'll tear your clothes," said Venn, and ordered the dog roughly back to his corner. Olaf slunk away, but, after lying down with the stiff unwieldiness of his bony limbs,—*rather like a camel folding itself up*, thought Shirin, who could just remember the camels in Persia because they had frightened her as a child,—he lay with his nose between his paws and his eyes still fixed on Shirin. She knew that Venn had come within an inch of losing his temper. "I like your dogs," she said casually; "you must give me a dog of my own, Venn; I never wanted one in London. May I have one here?"

She's clever, thought Lady le Breton; *she has taken his measure.*

At last alone in her room, Shirin stood in the middle of the vast floor-space and looked round her. Her own familiar possessions were set out, as reassuring as friendly faces suddenly perceived in a crowd. There were her little travelling-clock and the silver box that contained her nail-scissors and her orange-sticks, things she had known ever since she broke away from home and married Miles Vane-Merrick. There was the bit of Persian embroidery, given to her by her father once as a birthday present, that covered her underclothes for the morrow. They were all disposed in unfamiliar surroundings, but still there they were, faithful humble servants that confirmed the sense of personal continuity, the only security she could cling to. They took her back to Dulwich, back to Port Breton, back to the tempestuous and painful years she had spent with Miles Vane-Merrick, back to the lonely, unsatisfactory, over-populated years she had spent since she left him.

Strangers amongst them were the things out of the dressing-case given her by Venn, the palest tortoise-shell with her new initials in gold. She knew what had prompted the gift: a jealous desire to obliterate all traces of her former life. She had seen him wince when his eyes fell on the initials S. V.-M.; and, because with lazy kindliness she had no wish to make him suffer unnecessarily, she had afterwards taken the trouble to eliminate all such of her possessions as might revive that distressing recollection. *How fortunate*, she thought now, *that I have never been in the habit of putting out photographs in my room, for I should certainly have had a photograph of the children, and nothing*, *not even the desire to spare Venn's feelings, would have made me conceal that.* The only photograph she had of her children, an enlarged snapshot, was in its usual place: in the note-case next to the photograph of Storn; locked up.

The mood of optimism and courage assailed her again: she could manage Venn. She could manage, and even love, and even make herself beloved by, old Lady le Breton. She would throw all her energies into making a success of this marriage. It should be the beginning of a new life. Never before had such a feeling of strength and confidence consciously inspired her, not even when she married Miles. She had gone into that adventure gaily, with relative irresponsibility; into this new adventure she was going equipped with a fuller knowledge, with no illusions as to the dangers she might be running, but with confidence in her own power to meet them. She would almost welcome difficulty, for the satisfaction of overcoming it. Where was the use of all those years of suffering, if they had failed to enrich her? for somewhere in the depths of her unorthodox and personal religion, she rejected the idea of wastage as something evil and unconstructive. Never before had she trusted in life, never believed in the possibility of personal happiness, until now when a strange flame rose in her, lighting her to the belief that in her hands life's cruel material might be turned to creative purposes. *I will, I will*, she thought, pressing her hands together as though she indeed moulded a lump of plastic clay between them.

So much was on her side! Her own experience, and this lovely Storn, her secret passion since childhood, given to her now by a sudden swirl in the pattern of her life. All the beauty and the magic of Storn seemed to pass into her will, raising it, multiplying it; like a faith, like an ecstasy, it transformed her, filling her with strength and purity and ardour, with a passion that transcended all material love. It was the spirit of Storn that she loved; its spirit of pride, and loneliness, and poetry.

How well, as though it divined her mood, it suited itself to her at this moment! The storm encircled the island with its full fury at last. She threw back the heavy curtains, and, curling herself up on the window-seat, stared out into the torn and angry night. Round the castle swept the wind, until she saw it almost as a presence personified, a Valkyrie with streaming hair and eyes of fire, the rain in its wake lashing the high window, and the sea below hurling itself against the rocks with the boom and roar of Atlantic breakers. Exultation filled her. Suddenly the night was split by lightning, and simultaneously the thunder crashed overhead, so that she saw the sea for an instant lit up, a black expanse tossing and flecked with wild white crests. The frenzied rain redoubled in intensity. She thought of the ships labouring at sea, and of the little boats rocking in the harbour, and of the pines straining and groaning in the wind. Had something been struck? There had been no interval between the flash and the thunder. Abruptly all the lights went out, and at the same moment she became aware that somebody had entered her room.

It was Venn.

She heard the key turn in the lock, and knew that he could see her silhouetted against the faint glimmer of the window. Then she was frightened, feeling trapped, but her strength returned to her at this first test, and putting out her hand towards him she said with the utmost gentleness, "Venn? I'm here."

He came noiselessly and sat down beside her, putting his arm round her shoulders so that she felt the caress of the soft silken garment he wore. Yielding, she moved a little closer to him, and together they gazed out, straining their eyes to pierce the night.

"How do you like this?" he whispered. "Are you afraid?"

"Venn, I love it; I love it; nothing could have happened that would have pleased me better.—Look, another flash."

She shivered slightly in his arms, but with rapture, not with fear.

"It is right over us," he said, as the thunder died away.

"Yes, right over us. Did you put out the lights?"

"No, they must have fused all over the house. It often happens in a storm like this. You can't get a light, even if you want one."

She knew that he was glad of this; she knew also that he would have preferred her to be frightened.

"I'm sorry I can't be frightened, Venn," she said with a low laugh, "but I can't pretend, even to please you."

"The lightning will give us all the light we want," he said; he tightened his hold on her, for her soft, low laughter had sent a quiver of desire through him.

"Hush!" she said, and he felt her body stiffen. "What was that?"

It came again: a strain of music, sombre, low.

"The organ!" she said, relaxing. "Oh, Venn, what a fantastic lover you are!" For the first time she voluntarily put her arms round his neck and drew him down, and for the first time he kissed her unresisting mouth.

"Why have you never kissed me till now?" she asked when he released her.

"I thought you did not want me to."

"Proud? But you were right: I didn't."

"Shirin, Shirin, are you always so cruelly truthful?"

"Why have you not come near me till now? Why did you avoid me? why didn't you come to my room before dinner?"

"Again, I thought you would not want me to.—Besides," he added in a tone she could not interpret, "I was talking to my grandmother."

"What a good reason," she laughed, "for staying away from your wife."

"It was," he said, getting up and moving away from her; "a very good reason indeed."

"Venn, don't be so grim; come back; have I said anything to offend you?"

"You're very sweet," he said, sadly and without irony, for she looked very small and her patience touched him; "you make me see how sweet you could be,—if you loved."

"No, Venn," she said, alarmed, "don't make that mistake; I'm not sweet at all, or tame; I warned you from the first that I was a difficult person to love. You don't know me yet; you may live to find that loving me is a whole-time job."

"Oh, you may joke," he said, smiling in spite of himself; her occasional funny little half-slang phrases always made him smile; "I wasn't talking about loving you; I said: if *you* loved.—Hell!" he exclaimed; "it tortures me to imagine what you must have given to other people."

"My silly Venn, I told you that other people had never really touched me at all."

"Oh yes, you told me, you told me . . . but how do I know you were telling me the truth? That's the sort of thing that women always say. You want me believe that you've always been cold; you're daring me to rouse you. What about those children of yours? conceived without passion, were they? Don't tell me you're not passionate; pretend as you may, you can't wholly disguise what lies underneath; one has only to look at you,—at your eyes, your mouth, the very way you move; of course you're a passionate woman, not sexually only, but in the way you feel, the way you think; even in your desire to keep yourself hidden. Why, you only keep yourself hidden so that you may some day have the more to give. But will it be given to me?"

"What a piece of analysis, Venn! Did you work all that out for yourself, or did your grandmother prompt you?"

He paused while another clap of thunder shook the house, drowning the sound of the organ, then without taking any notice of her words he went on.

"Besides, I know enough about you to imagine the kind of life you have led. People talk, you know. The only thing which has been held back from me is the names of your lovers, and I dare say I could have learnt those too, had I cared to ask. As it is, I see them without faces; just as bodies, owning you, possessing you. Are you going to tell me next that a cold woman gives herself, as you did, to one man after the other?"

"Your analysis is breaking down now," she said, still patient because she knew he was trying to goad her, "but I know nothing I can say will persuade you of my indifference. You see, it seemed to matter so little. For various reasons . . ." she hesitated, for she hated speaking of herself, and above all she could not bring herself to mention Luke, yet she must force herself to some degree of revelation unless she meant deliberately to betray that half-hour of solitude in which she had seen so clearly, so purely, that Storn might mean the clearing away of the old incomplete life and the opening of a finer, cleaner chapter; "for various reasons," she went on, "I had always been so unhappy that it seemed to matter little how I passed the time or what I did with my body. You can't realise, Venn, how little I felt that I belonged to this life at all. And if men wanted me, and were good to me, why should I refuse, when in reality I was giving them nothing? That was the only thing that troubled me: that I should give them nothing, in return for so much. Because,—I do ask you to believe this,—I never gave myself to any man who didn't sincerely love me. It wasn't a mere frivolous promiscuity on my part; it was more an indolent good-nature."

"Very obliging," he sneered.

"Don't, Venn; I am honestly trying to explain. If I had loved, or had pretended or even imagined that I loved, cheaply,—then, I agree with you, it would have mattered. As it was, it left me intact. I used to feel that I was scarcely there at all; I could abstract myself, and not notice. I used to look out of the window, half the time. And I was always truthful with them; I never led anyone to believe that I cared more than I did."

"That, at any rate, may be true: you have been truthful enough, as you call it, with me, God knows."

"I'm sorry if I hurt you," she said, "but I couldn't ever do otherwise than be truthful when truthfulness mattered. Isn't it better so? At least you know where you are."

"Yes, I know where I am, although I may not enjoy being there," he said wryly. He knew, even at that moment when he was importantly and dramatically moved, that he said it in a way that a novelist would epitomise as "wryly." *How very odd*, he thought suddenly, with his unexpected sensitiveness to words, *that word "wryly" must look in print to a foreigner ignorant of English!* Then, after that small excursion into a different, more abstract, and easier world, he returned to the world where he and Shirin, his wife, were beginning to live out their difficult relationship, complicated permanently by temperament and framed temporarily by storm. "And if you ever came to care for me," he asked curiously, "would you tell me even then?"

She was silent; the reply that rose to her lips seemed so harsh, so imperilling, so ill-timed in this hour of opportunity. She wanted to say with finality: *I shall never care for you, Venn. If you ask me why, I can't tell you, for I don't yet know. There are many reasons why I should love you: you have many qualities which appeal to me, and you lack many of the shortcomings which would put me against other men. Nor is it because you are cruel that I cannot love you. Your cruelty is a humour I could understand and forgive. There must be some obscure reason which I have not yet fathomed.* This was what she wanted to say, and what she felt she ought to say; at the same time, the temptation to soothe him, to bring him back, to bind him closely to her in the very hour when she had had that vision of her life at its new beginning, stopped her for an instant with her reply unuttered. Then her integrity triumphed, though she softened the wording of her reply a little; after all, she fully meant to build up some edifice with Venn, though the edifice she meant to build must arise only from foundations of the deepest honesty. She would not cheat him, but she would hurt him as little as possible.

"You would know it soon enough, if I loved you," she said, "but never count on my loving you, Venn. You think me passionate, and in my other feelings I may be so,—indeed, I suppose I do enjoy or suffer things out of all reasonable proportion,—but remember that in the matter of love I have never yet been aroused by a living soul. I have listened to the phrases of various people in love, and I noticed that they all used the same expressions, but I admit that I never really understood what they meant. I understood it with my mind, but I never responded to it with the real me. You can make it your business to catch me, if you like, but don't say I didn't warn you. For all you know, and for all I know, I may be utterly lacking in the capacity to love."

She had lightened her tone at the end, till it almost contradicted her words, filling them not with a caution but with the richest promise; the charm worked, as she knew it would work, and he was again beside her, glowing, urgent.

"You're talking nonsense, Shirin," he said; "wait till you're fifty before saying that you lack the capacity to love. You! you're as deep and as complex as the chords of that organ next door. In the meantime I'll try to overcome my damned jealousy. Or are you so much of a woman that you don't resent my jealousy?"

"I don't resent it; I only find it rather inconvenient," she laughed, joking, trying to turn his seriousness aside.

"So do I, I assure you. Shirin, some day, little by little, you'll let me into your past?" He did not notice that, sadly and gravely, she shook her head. "I think I would rather know," he went on; "I think facts would be preferable to imagination. I paint such unbearable pictures, to myself. . . . There," he said, checking himself, "I won't begin again. You have made it better already by what you said about never having been roused by a living soul,—not that I can quite believe it."

"But you must, you shall, believe that things always mattered to me much more than people. You must believe that, Venn, if we are to make a possible life for ourselves at all. You can't be humanly jealous of such things as the sea and the trees, the only things I ever cared for. Listen, Venn; I'm telling you the truth now,—I'll tell you that much; and in telling you that, I'm telling you a good deal; I'm telling you more than I ever told to anyone; I'm telling it to you now because I want you to understand how little cause for jealousy you have, humanly speaking."

"The sea and the trees?" he repeated, as though he were the hollow from which that particular echo could reverberate, for she had voiced his own particular loves. Then he saw what she really meant. "I suppose you mean Storn," he said.

She heard the note of jealous anger in his voice, and realised the danger but would not evade it. Her strength and confidence were still such, that she wanted an understanding between herself and Venn, and how could that understanding come into existence if she concealed the most vital love of her being? Besides, was it not he who had given Storn to her? She was so deeply and inarticulately grateful to him for that, that she could repay him with no reward other than perfect honesty.

"Ah, Storn!" she said, letting all her secrets go into her voice.

He drew away from her a little.

"Listen," he said, "one thing has got to be clearly understood between us: Storn is mine, not yours." He did not speak angrily, he did not even speak cruelly, but with a cold and final deliberateness. He was remembering his grandmother's words: *Why should she have married you? For the sake of Storn, of course!* Well, much as he loved her now in his queer way, much as he desired her, he would pinch out the shoot of any such idea at the start. There should be no false pretences of that kind; no nonsense about Storn, his Storn. Not even for Shirin would he abandon one scrap of his jealous hold on Storn.

She was silent; the readjustment she had to make wrenched her too abruptly to allow strength for speech. He had hurt her so mortally this time that her one idea emergent from the pain of her bewilderment was to prevent him from seeing that he had, in truth, killed her at the very moment when she was most warmly and generously alive. She felt no grudge against him; she merely wished he had not chosen that particular moment to knock her down. *Any other moment*, she thought, *but not just this moment! Anyhow*, she thought, as usual utterly and instantly uncompromising in her decisions, *he has done what he intended to do, once and for all: there will never be any question of my trespassing on any corner of Storn again. He need not fear. He shall never know what he has done to me. That's a thing I shall keep to myself till I die.*

"But of course Storn is yours, Venn," she said; "Storn is you, and you are Storn. Did you think I didn't realise that? If so, you thought wrongly. Put all such ideas out of your head. You will never find me a bother in that way. I'll do exactly what you want me to do in the way of being useful, I'll open bazaars and flower-shows for you in Port Breton once a week if you like, but beyond that I shall never infringe."

He grunted. As always, when he had given way to his devil, he could neither enjoy the consequences of his victory nor quiet his own conscience so as to pass forward unhampered to something else. Uneasy, trying to right himself, he moved closer towards her, following the line of his physical desire. She, experienced as she was, recognised the movement and shrank from it as she had often shrunk from such movements before. Then she remembered that Venn could not be relegated to quite the same category as other men, since she had allowed him to become officially married to her that morning, and then, as a woman, responded in part to his demand. *It is only polite*, she thought, *to respond; I owe it to him: he allows me to live on Storn; I am his wife*. But these words broke her; they were so empty; they were such a betrayal of the reality she had apprehended. They bore no relation to the vision she had had of Storn as her dark island of sanctuary and refuge, the vision which had lit her for an hour, gone now, blotted out for ever.

"Shirin!" Venn was saying. He held her fiercely, trying to forget his unhappiness. She let herself go soft against his shoulder, skilful, resigned. Why not? He had killed her; he was welcome to what remained. She could give him nothing of value now, but if he wanted the dross he could have it. Why not?

The storm and its splendour had passed over and the wind had died away. The organ, ironically, passed from the improvisations of the organist into the soul-rending chords of the *Liebestod*. Shirin stirred restlessly as she heard the deep passionate volume of sound begin, swelling out into the night as though it were a black and bellying sail, rounded by music instead of wind or by a body of wind solid with music; as though it were drawn upward from some underground cavern—Andromeda's Cave?—with the sea booming rhythmically at its mouth. She stirred; *I cannot bear this*, she thought; *it is too exquisite, too fantastic; it comes too close to everything I love; it stabs too directly against my most secret heart. How well Venn understands Storn! how well I understand Venn! how well he and I could unite in our understanding of Storn and all that Storn stands for, keeping our personal independence always inviolate, respecting one another's separateness all the time, leaving our understanding implicit, unexpressed! How perfect a lover he could be; and I, how perfect a mistress to him, but that some perversity has made it all go wrong as everything always goes wrong with me like the Princess fated from birth to prick her finger on the spindle; by what a narrow margin have we, Venn and I, missed the pure perfection offered us! That we have missed it, surely and for ever, is certain. We should not complain*, she thought, *for perfection is not to be exacted from earthly life. I always knew that. I always knew that perfection hid always just round the corner, ready to run away round another corner just as I came into sight and was about to seize it. I had the vision for an hour, and I ought to be grateful. To few people is so much vouchsafed. The vision I had was a true vision; it showed me the beauty that could be wrung out of life, but for that damnable bad fairy god-mother who put her curse on it at the start. Spirit of evil, spirit of cruelty, spirit of imperfection, splinter in the willing eager soul. Imperfection everywhere; why were we given the vision of perfection at all, only to recognise it as unattainable?*

"Shirin!" Venn was saying, holding her close, his hand cupping her breast.

Oh, the flesh, the flesh! she thought, responding to his passion; *how false, how false! how true, how true! Wretched us,* she thought, *deluding ourselves with this short-cut of sex through the jungle of personality. Do I want Venn to make love to me now? yes, I do, because my body is alight and my soul is alight also with that deep passionate music of the Liebestod* (for all this time the organ was pouring out the amorous, painful piling-up of wave upon wave of physical, spiritual desire, until she felt that at any moment it must crash down in the supreme fulfilment), *but he has killed me,* she thought; *I shall never live again.*

Lifting her up in his arms,—for she was very light,—he carried her across the beautiful room and threw her down on her bed.

"Take me, Venn," she said, lying there, thrown down; "take me; make me forget."

She put her arms round him. The organ next door piled itself up into the supreme, unendurable ecstasy of love and death.

PART III

THIRTY-SIX

I

LADY LESTER continued to give parties; in common with other people who give parties she grumbled about them periodically, saying what a bore they were, and what a waste of time, and why on earth did one do it? but still she continued to give them; it was difficult to see why, if she found them such a burden, since no obligation from outside imposed the practice upon her, but the fact remained: she continued to give them, and her friends, grumbling also, continued to attend them. Sometimes a logically-minded guest, taking her to task, would challenge her about her complaints. And then she would laugh, being at heart a good-natured woman, and would plead in justification that at least on one occasion her parties had been the means of uniting two completely happy people. "Yes, my dear," she said, addressing herself to Cristina Rich; "happy marriages are rare enough, as we all know, but I think I may say I made one when I introduced Shirin Vane-Merrick to Venn le Breton. If ever I did a good deed in my life, I did one then. I oughtn't to take much credit to myself, perhaps, since it was at no greater cost to myself than taking Venn across the room and introducing them to one another, and I couldn't foresee what would happen, could I? but all the same, when I saw in the paper five days later that they had married, I thought to myself, *There, now, that's my doing*, and I admit I felt proud, even if a bit doubtful. These sudden marriages, you know. . . . Even with Venn it surprised me, coming five days after meeting her for the first time, but Venn was always impulsive, and as for Shirin, well, none of us could tell what Shirin would do, could we? Look at the way she caught poor Miles,—no, perhaps I oughtn't to call him *poor Miles*. I dare say she gave him a good time while it lasted, and he deserved it, after that silly affair he had with poor Evelyn Jarrold,—I always believed she killed herself on his account,—and then his engagement to the Anquetil girl got broken off, you remember; so perhaps he deserved his four or five years' run with Shirin. But then she got rid of Miles, so of course I thought history might repeat itself with Venn, but it hasn't, has it, Cristina? they've been as happy as the day was long, ever since, haven't they? Very odd, too, for I should never have described Shirin as a domestic person. Too frivolous altogether; and Venn isn't easy, either, like all the le Bretons. I couldn't have believed she would stick to Venn as she has, down in that barbarous island of his,—I always call it his barbarous island, you know, Cristina, partly because it annoys him, and partly because it's true,—but he doesn't really mind, because he knows I like him and don't take any notice of his odd ways. I insist on going to stay there once a year, whether he likes it or not. I must say that he hasn't been quite so difficult since he married Shirin. I used to think Shirin rather an empty-headed little flirt, but upon my soul I've begun to think her rather a remarkable character, to manage Venn as she does. Don't you agree, Cristina?"

Cristina Rich replied somewhat shortly that she had

never been to Storn, and added mendaciously that she had scarcely set eyes on Shirin for nearly ten years. *I wish Minna wouldn't discuss Shirin,* she thought; *I know Shirin would hate it, especially with other people listening* (for at least six people were sitting round Lady Lester's tea-table); *I remember Shirin once saying how much she hated the vulgar inquisitive talk that people carried on about other people. Shirin herself never gossips: she seems to have too much respect for other people's privacy.*

"Now doesn't that prove my point?" exclaimed Lady Lester, looking triumphantly round. "Here's Cristina, who really knew Shirin as well as any of us could claim to know her (not that that ever amounted to much for any of us), saying that she has never been to Storn and has scarcely set eyes on Shirin ever since she married Venn. Doesn't that prove my point that Shirin has been so wrapped up in Venn and his odd ideas that she doesn't even want to see her old friends? Of course she comes to London from time to time to see her children,—the Vane-Merrick children, I mean,—but she's vanished again before any of us have had time to find her out. She never lets me know, and then when I discover by accident that she had been in London for a week, I find that she has already gone back to Storn. Goodness only knows what she does with herself on those occasions. Perhaps Cristina sees her. Do you, Cristina?"

"I've seen her once or twice," said Cristina, with whom Shirin stayed every time she came to London. But Cristina was as secret and reserved as Shirin herself.

"Once or twice! in ten years! Well, I always said Shirin was a queer fish," said Lady Lester, who far from saying anything of the sort had always been at pains to emphasise

Shirin's ordinariness. "So you've seen her in London, Cristina, have you? but you haven't seen her at Storn? I'm one up on you there, ha! ha! I can tell you, she's a marvel, down at that place. I don't know how she manages it, what with Venn so unaccountable, and his old grandmother, who is mine too, so domineering; but manage it she does, though she must have had to put up with a great deal; the people adore her, and what she has done in the way of health for that place is beyond telling, so the local doctor told me; and yet she always seems to keep herself in the background, never offending the old lady, who gets more tyrannical every year as she gets older, and never offending Venn either, who is very much the power in command. Of course the explanation is that he simply worships her. More tea, Cristina?"

Cristina said no, thank you, but Timmy Lester, chirping, put forward his cup.

"*Four* bits of sugar, Minna dear," he chirped, "not *three;* and now do go on,—it's *too* fascinating, hearing about Shirin. You know, I was *frantically* in love with Shirin years ago,—I promise you, I nearly threw myself under a train once, on her account, and if you don't believe me you can ask Dan Orlestone, who pulled me back *just* in time,—so do go on: I love hearing about our darling lost Shirin cracking the whip in the le Breton circus."

Cristina got up, saying she was very sorry, she had an appointment, and must hurry away.

As the door closed behind her, the tea-party sagged down in relief; now they could really talk: Cristina Rich, definite personality that she was, always imposed a slight check on easy gossip; they wondered why she ever came amongst them, raising her eyebrows without comment.

Had she been a novelist, they would have suspected her of hunting for copy. As it was, they knew nothing of her beyond the fact that she was said to be a sculptor of considerable talent, with a studio somewhere in St. John's Wood, to which none of them had ever been invited.

They had never seen the really brilliant caricatures which she kept in a portfolio, nor the little wax dolls modelled in their image, which amused Shirin so much every time she stayed at the studio.

Cristina left Lady Lester's house, angry; half-way home, her anger dissolved, and she laughed. It was really not worth while, getting angry with Minna Lester or her friends. Shirin had said so, years ago; Shirin had been right. Shirin was always right about such things; she had that rare gift, a sense of values. It was laughable to see how Minna Lester and her circle misjudged Shirin. Things were either supremely important to Shirin, or insignificantly unimportant. The chatter of Minna Lester and Minna Lester's friends came into the unimportant category. Cristina agreed with Shirin's estimate; she and Shirin shared the same sense of values. That was the thing that made them friends, difficult and mistrustful as they both were in matters of friendship. They agreed about essentials.

Cristina went home, feeling very close to Shirin, who was so different from that gabbling crowd, so reserved, so dignified, so proud, so secret under her external appearance of gaiety and light-heartedness. Cristina had privately compared her to the summer sea, dancing, sparkling on the surface, with dark depths beneath. She loved Shirin, and would have loved her more, had Shirin ever allowed anyone to come close to her, in the intimacy of love or friendship.

Nothing would induce her to force herself on Shirin; nothing would induce her to eavesdrop, or even to guess at the things Shirin kept concealed. She did, however, allow herself to wonder how much truth lay in Minna Lester's theory of the perfect marriage. Shirin never spoke about herself, and Cristina would have shrunk in horror from the idea of coaxing anybody's confidence, least of all Shirin's. So deep a respect had she, in fact, for other people's independence that she had sometimes caught herself turning away when a certain expression came into Shirin's eyes, a grave, abstracted look which hurt Cristina and on which she refused to spy. She refused to draw the conclusions implicit in that expression. If Shirin was unhappy, that was her own affair, until she chose to reveal it. Cristina felt instinctively that Shirin would never reveal anything of the sort. She sighed, loving Shirin, and feeling the hopelessness of attempting to help her in any way. There were some people who were impossible to help; Shirin was one of them; she would bear her own strain till she broke under it. Then it would be too late. Cristina sighed again, knowing how much comfort she could give to Shirin, if Shirin were only willing to receive it.

She reached her studio, and found a letter with the Port Breton postmark lying on the mat.

Shirin's letters were oddly always uncharacteristic of their writer. They were so untidy as to be almost illegible; so curt, as to be almost chilling, their coldness in strange contrast with Shirin's warm personal arrival; so ungrammatical, as to be almost illiterate; so ill-spelt, as to be almost unintelligible; their punctuation so erratic as to give rise to the most serious ambiguities. Yet every now and then a phrase jumped out, as it were involuntarily; a phrase of pure poetry, a phrase of pure Shirin.

Familiar writing-paper, large, creamy, with the insolently swagger address engraved in the single word: STORN.

Dear Cristina, she wrote, *will you come and be our secretry?* (sic) *Venn's secretary* (sic) *has just died. No one who played the organ like that could have lived long. I think he wore himself out. Perhaps Storn was too much for him. I know you are strong enough to stand Storn. That's why I ask you to come. Do come if you can, Cristina. I know you want a job. You can do your sculptour* (sic) *down here. You would have all your afternoons and evenings free and a big room to yourself for it. Do come if you can.—Shirin.*

P.S.—I do hope you'll come.

In that postscript Cristina read an appeal. Shirin wanted her. Without a moment's hesitation she sent off a telegram of acceptance.

Not until she was sitting in the train did Cristina realise that Shirin had never spoken to her about Storn. Not a word of description, not a word of enthusiasm for what passed by reputation as one of the most beautiful and romantic places in England. That allusion to being *strong enough to stand Storn,* in her letter, was the first hint she had ever dropped about the place. *How odd,* Cristina thought, amused; but then amended it to, *How like Shirin!* It took some time to realise that the personal note never entered into Shirin's conversation. *For such a chatterbox,* thought Cristina affectionately, *she avoids cheapening herself with remarkable skill.* And she tried to remember what she and Shirin talked about when they were together in London, for she had the impression that they never stopped talking, yet she could scarcely remember the stuff of which their conversations were composed. Perhaps they were scarcely to be described as conversations, but rather more like the gay and irrelevant singing of the bird to which Cristina privately compared Shirin. Cristina herself was rather grave by temperament, and inclined to be silent; she lived alone, solitary, and, on the whole, content; Shirin's arrivals into her lonely rooms were of the nature of sunlight and vivacity, lit by the irresponsibility of a child on holiday. *Yes*, she thought,—for she meant to devote the long hours of her journey to coördinating her scattered impressions of Shirin, with whom her life, it seemed, was to be closely bound up during the next years; perhaps for the whole of their future, who could tell?—*yes*, she thought, *whenever she has been blown in through my door she has brought life and gaiety with her; but how true or how false is that mood? how much pretence is there? how deep a tragedy beneath? The perfect marriage!* she thought, remembering Lady Lester; and suddenly it seemed silly to estimate Shirin in terms of a marriage, whether perfect or otherwise, for Shirin was not to be put into so simple a category; happiness or unhappiness, for Shirin, would come from the inner spirit, not from anything so obvious as a personal relationship. Personal relationships would never touch her as her own deep secrets would touch her, and which she would keep always silently to herself.

That's true, thought Cristina in the train, forcing herself to arrange her ideas clearly; a sculptor, she saw it in terms of blocking out the malleable clay, roughly, without detail as yet; *that's true*, she thought, *Shirin lives inside herself. What creed, what philosophy, what religion of life sustain her, I don't know. But I am sure that she herself knows. She is not an artist, she is not creative; she has been denied that outlet, which her temperament should demand and need; she is neither a creative nor an intellectual person; she is merely elemental, and, I suppose, suffers accordingly. By all the rules, she ought to be creative, and isn't. She has created children, though,* thought Cristina, barren herself, *and I suppose that that, to an elemental woman, must mean something? Yet it doesn't seem to mean much to Shirin. It seems to be a thing imposed upon her from outside, a mere function of the body, rather than a thing which has ever touched her inner life. Yet she loves babies. I went into the slums with her once, and I shall never forget the tenderness with which she handled those poor little suffering starved mites. All curly and lovely as she was, lighting up the poor squalid rooms, she suddenly took on the sleek divine compassion of the traditional Madonna. And it was obvious, how those wretched mothers trusted her. Their eyes became quite different, as they watched her. They knew she was practical as well as sympathetic. She could scold them, and did, about their mistakes; and they accepted her scolding without resentment. They saw she knew what she was talking about. The poor and the ignorant always know. . . . It was extraordinary, how she got them to tell her everything, without ever seeming to ask them questions. I never heard such revelations in all my experience; so terrible, that I could hardly bear to listen, yet Shirin took it all in, just nodding, and looking wise. There was nothing of the Lady Bountiful about Shirin; she managed to be severe and clinical and human, all in one. I had never seen that side of her before and it was a surprise to me. She never alluded to it again, afterwards. Naturally, she wouldn't. And then I saw her with her own children,—the children of her own body,—and, adorable as she was, sitting on the floor playing with them, she seemed as detached from them as she had been from those dirty pitiable children of the gutter,—as detached, and yet as tender, and as intelligent, but not really seeming to have any connexion with them at all. Mummy, they called her. It seemed so odd, that they should call her Mummy. It sounded so intimate, and so usual, yet so difficult to connect with Shirin, who is like a sea-gull flying over the summer sea, with aspiring wings outstretched.*

She comes up to London, she thought, *to see her children. The Vane-Merrick children. Now she has others,—the le Breton children: Dominic and Nerissa. I wonder which she loves most, the Vane-Merrick or the le Breton children? Does she love either, more than she loves the unknown children of the slums? the children of her own body, or the children of any woman's body, begotten in passion and born in pain? She loves Luke, I know; Luke, the tragedy of her life; Luke the failure, Luke the disaster, Luke the crazy boy. She loves Luke more than all the others. Perversely she loves him, more than she loves her other, sane, beautiful children,—not that she ever says so, but I see it on her face after she has been to visit him; she returns, as gay as ever, but she wears that abstracted look more often, and I notice that she avoids going out on the evening of that day. She avoids seeing even that poor dull adoring Tracey.*

Cristina wondered with detachment whether she was doing a wildly reckless thing in going to live at Storn. There was that ominous phrase in Shirin's letter, *I know you are strong enough to stand Storn.* Was she? Then she shrugged her shoulders; ever since she had run away from home at the age of eighteen, because her parents wanted to make a school-mistress of her instead of a sculptor, she had never led the cowardly cautious life. Tall and tawny, with a characteristic toss of the fine head, Shirin teased her, saying that anybody would recognise the born adventurer. "A bad lot, that's what you are, Cristina," she said, "with a dash of the buccaneer in you, as unscrupulous as you can be." People admired Cristina rather than loved her; she was indifferent to that; but knowing that Shirin liked her, she valued Shirin's liking beyond an easy popularity, and merely smiled when Shirin thus boxed her ears. (She said "liked," not "loved," for love was not a term lightly to be used in connexion with Shirin.) Reckless or not, she was on her way to Storn now for better or worse; and, looking out of the window much as Shirin herself had looked out, ten years previously, she appreciated the beauty of the coast and saw the dangers it might breed in human souls.

I shall be able to work, down here, she thought, meaning her sculpture; *if Storn doesn't kill me, that is,* she added. *As well it may,* she added again, looking at the breakers lazily smashing themselves against the rocks.

She had not been more than a few hours at Storn before she realised that something was seriously wrong. It was more than wrong; it was alarming. But for her natural adventurousness and her love for Shirin, she would have taken the next train back to London. Outwardly, everything seemed civilised and serene. Old Lady le Breton,—strange old woman!—obviously adored Shirin; Venn, equally obviously, adored Shirin also. Shirin was the mainspring of the place; she was carrying the whole on her shoulders. Cristina detected all that, in the few hours that elapsed between her arrival and dinner. She detected more than that: a few minutes' conversation with a garrulous Mrs. Jolly, whom Shirin introduced to her as the housekeeper, told her that Shirin was carrying the local population with all their troubles; her own observation told her that Shirin was also carrying Venn, Lady le Breton, and their relationship towards each other as well as their relationship towards herself; she was carrying her own children, Dominic and Nerissa; furthermore she was carrying something Cristina could not diagnose; she was carrying too much, and too bravely, for her frail strength. She looked ill; her eyes were unnaturally dark and large; her face was not only pale, but the lines of pain had drawn themselves round her mouth; *Shirin*, thought Cristina, profoundly worried, *is no longer so gloriously young and light as she was when I first knew her; she is thirty-six now at least,—yes, that's right, for I am forty, and she is four years younger than I.—Luke must be nearly eighteen by now, and Dominic is nine,—she has been married to Venn for ten years. She is a ripe woman, as lovely as ever, and even more desirable for the experiences by which she has been enriched; yet, for all her ripeness, she retains the same childish quality she always had; the same physical attraction; the same high spirits, ready to break out; what is Shirin?* she thought; *has she ever allowed anyone to know?*

Venn looked ill too; his body thin beyond all reason. Cristina, who had never seen Venn before, found herself unable to judge whether his extraordinary emaciation of body was his normal condition or not; *there's something the matter with that man*, she thought, *but if Shirin, who has far more medical knowledge than I have, doesn't see it, or pretends not to notice it, it isn't my business to interfere.*

Disaster, she thought, *is pending; there is too much strain here. What the strain is, I don't yet know; I won't spy on Shirin; I won't try to find out. If Shirin wants me to know, she will let me know. I respect her too much to eavesdrop. In the meantime, how fantastically beautiful Storn is! How well I understand Shirin never having said a word about Storn! If Storn were mine, how silent I should remain about it! I should come up to London, as she does, and keep Storn as a secret in the background of my life. Shirin is one of the few people who know how to keep both beauty and tragedy to themselves.*

The moon rose early that night, and Shirin allowed the children to stay up for dinner in honour of Cristina's arrival. She made it quite clear to them that a treat was intended, giving Cristina the full credit for this exceptional evening. Cristina got the impression that Shirin meant her to stand well, from the first, with the children; she meant Cristina's first evening at Storn to represent a definite treat. So, after dinner, when Cristina and Venn had wandered out onto the terrace, Venn smoking his cigar, Shirin came out after them with the children Dominic and Nerissa dancing round her, onto the terrace of fantastic yews. The children tugged at her hands; they were foxy little sprites, with pointed faces and reddish hair, not like their mother in the least, but like their father, sharp and pointed and thin. The boy especially was his father in miniature. *How odd*, thought Cristina, *that Shirin's children should always be so like their fathers, and not like her at all; that just endorses my theory, that she has no real connexion with her children beyond the physical fact of having conceived and borne them; she is the sea-gull really, the wild free spirit; not the mother or the wife, though she forces herself into that rôle because circumstances demand it of her. . . .* "Come along now," said Shirin to her children, gaily; "let's play 'It' in the pine-wood; Cristina can play too, if she likes, unless she'd rather go and unpack,—would you, Cristina?—and Daddy can play too,—he can be 'It' if he likes;" but the children said, No, Daddy isn't such a good "It" as Mummy; Mummy never gets caught, and we don't like being "It," it's too frightening;

we'd rather Mummy were "It" all the time. Do come, Cristina, they added, for they were simple friendly children and had taken a fancy to Cristina as grown-ups seldom took a fancy to her, so that she felt rather flattered and pleased, in spite of herself; "do come, Cristina," they said, calling her quite naturally by her Christian name, instead of saying Miss Rich; "come and play 'It'; you won't be as good at it as Mummy is, but that doesn't matter; and anyhow Daddy's the duffer always, so you needn't feel ashamed, and you won't have to put yourself into the position of being caught. Come on," they said, tugging at her hands, and letting go of Shirin's; "come and play."

She went to join in their game in the moonlight. It was very queer for her, to be thus precipitated into the intimate domestic life of her well-known Shirin and Shirin's unknown Venn and their unknown children and their unknown Storn. This, then, was the wildly reckless thing she had done? to break into the lives of a man and his wife and their children, on the dark strange island of their intimate existence?

They were dodging each other between the trees. The children were excited; wild; unskilful. They were especially excited at being up so late; puzzled as to why their mother, habitually strict, had relaxed her rules today. They rushed backwards and forwards, from tree-trunk to tree-trunk, trying to touch their mother, who slipped past them each time. They shrieked with excitement, loving her the more each time she eluded them. A mother whom one could catch was an ordinary mother; a mother who slipped away was a mother better worth catching, because more difficult to catch. As for Venn, he did as badly as the children. He couldn't touch Shirin at all. A sort of genius seemed to possess her in evading him. He nearly had his hands on her, twenty times, when with a curving of her body she swerved away. Cristina could see him getting angrier and angrier as she continued to elude him; yet although he grew angrier, she could see his desire to catch her grow.

She had rather liked Venn, for the readiness he showed to join in the children's game; having composed an imaginary picture of him, it surprised her to find him prepared to play naturally and even boyishly, on the best of terms with two small things; yet she also rather disliked him, for the zest he displayed in trying to catch Shirin. There was nothing boyish about that zest; it formed no part of his rather attractive, unexpected simplicity, but impressed her disagreeably as something sinister and unnaturally intense, according only too well with his reddish foxy colouring and the slinking meagre grace of his movements. *Weasel? ferret?* she wondered, watching him in pursuit of the soft body of Shirin. She could not make up her mind, whether she liked him for his unaffected simplicity towards his children, or feared him for some element in him to which she had not yet had time to give a name.

She had, indeed, walked rashly into a complex and concentrated situation.

Besides, there was old Lady le Breton. What element of mischief did she provide? She was a very old woman now. (Cristina realised with amusement that Shirin had never mentioned her; she had heard of Lady le Breton's existence only from Minna Lester, as a passing comment.) Lady le Breton came out to watch their game. She was a very old woman, nearly ninety, Cristina judged, but still alert and active, and still beautiful. Propelling herself on a stick, she made her way down to the moonlit pine-wood, and stood there, mocking at the efforts of her great-grandchildren to catch their mother and of her grandson to catch his wife. "You'll never do it," she chuckled. All her appreciation of Shirin was in that chuckle. "She's too quick for you," she taunted the children; "and as for your father, he hasn't a chance."

In the end, it was Cristina who caught Shirin. Trapped between two tree-trunks, with Venn and Cristina hemming her in, she slipped between them both and ran down to the sea. Avoiding the rocks and the little creeks overhung with box and myrtle, she ran out onto a stretch of white sand, with thin waves lipping at it, a long narrow stretch, white even in the daylight, but paler still in the light of the moon, and Shirin, pale in her summer frock, ran along it, —ran, as though she had forgotten that anyone came in pursuit; as though she ran for the pure pleasure of running, liberated, like a blanched deer on the free margin of the sea, like a skimming bird almost grazing the water. *A shame and a pity to seize her*, thought Cristina, tempted to let her go, but then a mischief possessed her; a mischief and the determination that if anyone were to catch Shirin it should be herself and not Venn. *She'd be safer with me*, she thought, blindly, half inspired by a desire to protect Shirin, half by a desire to annoy Venn, already guessing his mistrustful hostility towards herself; then it seemed to her that Shirin slackened her pace a little, offering herself to be overtaken, and next moment the soft, warm, supple, breathing body was in her arms, bending backwards, while the eyes of Shirin laughed up into her own. She could see the moon reflected in them, in two small luminous discs,—like a beauty-patch, like a *mouche*, only white not black,—queer, small, intense. Fey,—the word leapt into her mind, a word she had always mistrusted and misliked; a word whose misuse had exasperated her to the point of looking up its exact meaning in the dictionary, that cold repository of precision and erudition; she had looked it up, for she felt it to be one of those words that must be exactly or not used at all: "*Fey*," she had found in the dictionary; "*fated to die; at point of death; disordered in mind, like person about to die.*" *Was Shirin fey in that way?* she wondered; *was Shirin* "*disordered in mind, like person about to die*"? *Anyway*, she thought rapidly and briefly, *are persons about to die really disordered in mind? may they not be, rather, more lucid in mind than persons too smugly confident in their chance of continuing happily and successfully to live? than persons secure in the trust that life holds no sudden dangers, no crouched wild beasts, no dark secretive islands?* . . . But here her philosophy stopped short, for she was many things besides being an artist and a contemplator of life from the outside. The magic of the white beach and the moonlit sea was potent. She was holding,—she had almost forgotten it,—Shirin. Strange, that one should forget Shirin, while one's mind ran down paths trying to trace back the meaning of such a word as fey! She looked down again into the reflection of the moon in Shirin's eyes, cheating that recklessly laughing Shirin, unaware of any reflection there; cheating, for she could see things that Shirin couldn't see; she could see the reflection of the moon, in those two round luminous patches within the pupil of her eyes; she could see more than that, for she could see her own face reflected, tiny, minute, so bright was the light of the moon; cheating again, for Shirin could not know that her image was reflected in her eyes, as bright as by day; and had Shirin known, indeed, what could she have done about it? there it was, the reflection, but no one knew of it, only Cristina, who had caught her on the beach of white sand, the first evening she had spent at Storn.

II

So this is Storn, thought Cristina. She had been there a month only, but already felt as though she had never belonged to any life other than the life within this closed circle. She recognised the power of the place to keep itself absolutely self-contained and apart. It had put its spell and its magic on her from the first moment. She scarcely knew whether she loved or hated it,—a teasing quality of uncertainty it shared with its owner, for she still had not decided whether she liked or hated Venn. (Nor had she, incidentally, decided whether Shirin loved or hated him either.) But, whether she loved or hated, Storn had caught her; it held her now within the ring of its fatality. She was resigned. She had no fear for herself. Her only concern was how best to help Shirin.

Her own relationship with Shirin had changed its character since the days when Shirin had been in the habit of coming to stay with her in London, a charming, gay, amusing guest whose chatter remained always so very much on the surface, with no weakening into the usual intimacies of feminine self-revelation. Cristina realised now that their ten years of friendship,—a friendship so rigidly impersonal that most people would have called it acquaintance,—had laid the foundations of this new development;

had created a trustfulness which was due more to the things they had refrained from saying than to the things they had said; she realised that she knew Shirin far better than she had ever suspected, and that Shirin knew her; their very reticences had enabled them to take one another's measure. Cristina, being something of a gardener, knew well enough that certain plants may appear to remain stationary for years while they are really making roots underground, only to break into surprising vigour overhead at a given moment; *thus*, she thought, *has it been between Shirin and myself; the moment has come when the plant is about to shoot. It has already put forth green leaves; let us await the blossom and the fruit.* Mixing her metaphors, she thought also of an iceberg, nine-tenths invisible below water and only one-tenth showing above it; *of such proportions*, she thought, *has our friendship hitherto been.* And, lying newly awakened in her bed at Storn on a May morning, she wondered what, precisely, was about to burgeon from the rare and difficult plant which she and Shirin had set almost fortuitously in the soil as an unrooted cutting, years before?

The change in their relationship had been neither violent nor sensational. It had been, indeed, so quiet and secret as to be almost imperceptible even to their two selves. Cristina might well have questioned whether Shirin was aware of it at all. Only her divination of Shirin as a quivering sensitive person could have endorsed her conviction that Shirin knew quite as well as she herself knew what was going on; perhaps better, for she discovered,—another discovery,—that she could trust Shirin always to keep pace with her, if not, indeed, to out-run her. She wished she could go to Shirin and say, *Tell me, what is happening between us?* But of course she couldn't. Shirin was not a person to be forced or rushed. To try to catch Shirin would be like trying to close your hand over a bird on the ground.

Yet hadn't she once, in the moonlight on the beach, a month ago, caught Shirin, when neither Venn nor the children could succeed in catching her?

Yes, the change in our relationship, she thought, lying in bed newly awakened, while the early sun poured through her windows coming straight off the sea, *has been so subtle as to be almost imperceptible. It hasn't, really, created any greater intimacy as yet between us. Shirin has uttered no phrase she mightn't have uttered years ago. True, she and I have slid now into the intimacies of daily life; I go to her room in the morning and she dictates her letters to me; thereby I learn something,—no, everything,—of her official activities as Lady le Breton. How odd, to think of my wild bird tamed into a Lady le Breton! How does Shirin accommodate herself to that rôle? That she succeeds in doing so is evident. But it isn't my business to enquire into that. I must always remember that she is Lady le Breton and that I am her secretary. Still, it doesn't obscure the fact, as I suppose it ought to obscure it, that she is Shirin and I am Cristina; we were Shirin and Cristina long before we became Lady le Breton and Lady le Breton's secretary; and now it looks as though we should become Shirin and Cristina again, our real selves, more real than ever we were before. We became our real selves, for the first time, when I caught her into my arms beside the sea.*

Still, she thought, *intimacy is not ours; not yet, although it may lie just round the corner; I go into her room, and she looks up at me with her lovely smile; then we have our hour of business together, which lets me into one side of her life; then we meet again at luncheon and again at dinner, and the conversation runs easily over the little events of the day; but that is only familiarity, not intimacy, and Venn is always there, listening, checking; a third presence, critical, hostile. It is being admitted to the outward life of a person, not to the inward. I know that I have never yet been admitted to the inward life of Shirin; but do I,* she thought, *want to be admitted to it? yes!* she replied to her own thoughts, *I want it more than anything in the world, at present; I want the whole of Shirin, greedily; yet not for anything in the world would I steal her, unless she asked to be stolen; I respect Shirin more than anybody I know, and if she elects to keep herself as a secret to herself, I will be the last person on earth to seek her out.*

For all this, their relationship had changed its character. There was, for instance, the tacit understanding between them that Venn must be humoured. That might be the understanding of two women as against a man, but it was something more than that. It involved the unspoken admission that Venn was very difficult. Did that difficulty proceed from his nature, from ill-health, or from any maladjustment with Shirin? Cristina did not know. Outwardly, he had everything that a spoilt child could desire: Storn, wealth, position, relative youth, healthy children, and an adorable wife. That was how most people would have phrased it. Yet he was clearly a tortured man. Cristina wished she might be a little better informed. She did not even know whether he was a sick man or not; looking at his extraordinary thinness she sometimes believed he must be gnawed away by some insidious disease; at other times she thought his spirit consumed him, so that his long nervous fingers played uneasily with a paper-cutter as he talked, and in his restlessness he would get up and stroll unnecessarily over to the window, tracing with his finger the pattern of the panes. Outwardly his manners were charming; no one could be more charming than Venn when he chose; and in his knowledge of nature, and more especially of the sea, and in his simple love of his children, and in his easy manner with his dependents, Cristina found him attractive, indeed lovable. At such times, and in such a mood, she had seen Shirin herself look at him with, as it were, a wistful love; at other times, when he said sharp, veiled, and bitter things, always under the mask of his perfect manners, she had seen Shirin look at him with an indefinably sad compassion. He, for his part, let his eyes rest on Shirin sometimes with an expression that Cristina could only call hungry; he looked at her sometimes as though he loved her so much that it dragged the soul out of him, sometimes as though he hated her so much that he could scarcely keep his fingers off her throat. It was only by such accidental glances that Cristina could judge at all what went on between them in private; what their relations really were. And even in such judgment she was hampered by her determination never to eavesdrop on Shirin.

Of one thing she was certain: that here was no common question of a so-called happy or unhappy marriage, but of a very deep drama playing itself out in the struggle between two human souls.

Then there was Storn. That beautiful and fantasic but, as she began to believe, diabolical island took the part of a third actor as surely as though it had been a living thing. *It amuses itself*, thought Cristina, *by provoking them, now with its loveliness, now with its savagery. It plays deliberately upon their nerves.* And then she came to one of the problems which perplexed her most: What did Shirin feel about Storn? By all the rules, she should have passionately loved it. Shirin being Shirin, its solitude, secrecy, and concentration should have won and held her love and understanding, where a shallower and vainer woman would have fretted and rebelled. But Shirin was not one of those who crave for a worldly exciting life. She and Storn, it would have seemed, were made for one another, mystically, fatalistically, as some lovers are. Yet something seemed to have gone wrong. Shirin's attitude towards Storn was not one of hatred, not one of dislike, not one of boredom, but merely one of indifference. Cristina could not understand this at all. *That Shirin, of all people*, she thought, *should have been offered this possession for her own, and should have remained untouched, detached, indifferent! That's incomprehensible. There must be some reason somewhere, if only I could find it.*

And Venn, she thought, finding a new puzzle, *is himself so like Storn, so intimately at the heart of nature and the sea, so bound up with their moods; so curiously pure, too, as though he flamed with purity and single-heartedness, like the pine-trunks and the water and the castle itself flaming in the setting sun; cruel too, and merciless, hurting himself even as the sea hurts the coasts of Storn by breaking against them; well*, she concluded, *if Shirin doesn't love both Storn and Venn with all the passion of her nature the reasons must be intricately mixed up, somehow; but how and why, is at present beyond my power to fathom.*

Venn, in the meantime, made himself agreeable to her personally. He never gave her any outward justification for her unpleasant conviction that he resented her presence in his home. Why, indeed, should he have resented it? They needed a secretary, and Cristina certainly made herself as useful and as unobtrusive as possible. She even tried to tame her own fine, tawny, independent appearance to a tidiness she considered more suitable for her job, discarding her favourite gaudy colours of bronze and orange until the evening, when she thought she might allow herself to become a private individual again. Shirin noticed, and teased her: *What's happened to the autumn tints, Cristina?* But Cristina, although she smiled, stuck to her policy. There was a certain severity in Venn, which she would not risk offending. And so far he had had no fault to find with her.

She had, as it happened, little work to do for him, beyond a few daily letters. As the owner of Storn and of a great estate on the mainland, he was naturally well provided with such things as estate-offices already furnished with their own staff. Shirin, on the other hand, whose work was concerned chiefly with local charities and organisations, kept Cristina fairly busily employed. She was surprised to discover how business-like Shirin was; how clear-headed; how prompt and right and firm in her decisions. For someone so intensely and misleadingly feminine (though at the same time, she observed with amusement, Shirin was prepared to use her femininity quite cynically in order to gain her own ends) Shirin displayed a tireless sense of duty, a reliability, an absence of fuss or confusion, which made Cristina remember Lady Lester's comment: *Upon my soul I've begun to think Shirin rather a remarkable character.* With less surprise did she discover Shirin's general popularity. It amused her to see Shirin, gay, lovely, and deliciously dressed, doing exactly what she liked with all the grim and critical committee-ladies, although they had no idea that she was doing it, or with the fisher-people who looked to her for advice on every subject, whether domestic, economic, parental, or medical. "I sometimes think," said the local doctor ruefully to Cristina, "that they wouldn't take any of my doses at all if Lady le Breton didn't sanction them." Shirin certainly had no hesitation about speaking her mind, and Cristina sometimes shivered, thinking that for once she was really going too far, but she soon found out that there was nothing they would not accept. "It's funny," said Mrs. Jolly to Cristina; "they're a hard, proud people down here,—I can say that, Miss, for I don't belong down here myself,—I was bred to quite another way of life, if you'll believe it,—they're a hard, proud people, and they don't like foreigners, but with that way of hers she has got them all eating out of her hand like a pony coming for sugar." Mrs. Jolly's pride in Shirin was unbounded. She had nursed both Dominic and Nerissa in the past, and had now risen to the dignity of black poplin and a bunch of keys as the housekeeper. "There's none like her," she added, "the poor lamb." Cristina wondered why she said *poor lamb;* but although Mrs. Jolly was obviously bursting with the desire to talk, she let the opening go.

Whether Venn resented or appreciated the hold Shirin had achieved over his people and his neighbours, was another among the several things Cristina could not decide.

Venn himself, in his better hours, she must admit, possessed not only personal attraction but also attractive qualities. His personal attraction was easily explained by his innate distinction; by his physical elegance,—Venn could wear the shabbiest jersey and the most disreputable pair of trousers and yet look better dressed than the most expensive young man in Bond Street, an asset which Dominic had inherited;—by his lazy but dangerous charm of manner, with the fieriness always behind it; by his nervous and restrained virility. *That*, thought Cristina, sharply and carefully analytical, *is the accidental Venn. He was born like that, and has had no say in the matter. He has had his physical grace imposed upon him, even as I have had my six foot of height and my noble nose, which I hate, imposed upon me.* But his attractive qualities could not so easily be explained away. She saw those qualities in what she called his better hours: when he was at his simplest and most natural self; when he taught Dominic and Nerissa how to fish, for instance; or when he predicted the weather likely to come up from the Atlantic; or when he took her, Cristina, out sailing as he now frequently did, having discovered that she was, apparently, fearless, and, incontrovertibly, a good sailor. In the hours when he took her sailing she liked him best. (He had a lovely little Red-wing, very slender, with scarlet sails.) He was at his best in a boat. He sat at his ease, in a small boat, in the same way as a good rider sits at ease in the saddle: the same rhythmical understanding existed between him and his boat, as between a good rider and his horse. Cristina liked him very much then, when his foxy head outlined itself against the sky, and his nervous hand lay sensitively ready on the sheet, waiting to luff; the hand she feared and mistrusted when it played with the paper-cutter or followed the pattern of the window-panes. She then liked the practical Venn very much; she felt that she was seeing the true man, and wondered why Shirin could not have loved him, as by all the rules she ought to have loved him. He told her things, too, about the tides and the weather, imparting the information not as a thing learnt, but as an inborn, inherited, traditional part of knowledge, imparting it casually, as incidental on the course they were setting or on the weather they might expect. She liked him then.

Out at sea, in a small boat, he was quite different from the Venn who ruled Storn, quarrelled with his grandmother, and seemed torn between love and exasperation with Shirin. He became a natural, happy creature, as natural as one of his own fishermen plying his daily craft. An odd friendship had thus been established between them; she knew that on those occasions, impersonally, Venn liked her as much as she liked him. He liked her, as a companion, because she was neither afraid nor seasick, and because she loved the sea.

Then came an occasion when Venn's good and bad hours got themselves curiously mixed up. They had had a difficult luncheon that day; Dominic had been fractious, he had tapped his knife against his plate until his father lost his temper with him, and old Lady le Breton had subtly turned the blame for everything onto Shirin. (Cristina could never quite explain this trait in the old woman: that she loved Shirin, almost savagely, was evident; yet she lost no opportunity of inciting Venn against her, whenever he was in one of his most difficult moods.) And then, after luncheon, as they strolled on the terrace, Venn asked Cristina casually if she would care for a sail. "I don't suggest Shirin coming," he said, with one of his strange, vicious looks, "because it might come on to blow, and Shirin having been brought up in Dulwich doesn't really care for the sea except when it's fit for holiday makers." Cristina saw Shirin's eyes, and they hurt her so much that she looked away. It was not right that she should see Shirin wounded and in pain. *But how can Venn*, she thought, *insult her so deliberately and meanly, sneering at her about Dulwich?* She very nearly refused his invitation, but for Shirin's sake controlled herself and went.

Venn had been right: it did come on to blow. Even the boatmen down by the harbour tried to persuade him not to go out; "It'll come up nasty in a couple of hours, Sir Venn." But Venn merely turned towards Cristina: "Would you rather not come?" She took it as a challenge, though not precisely as a challenge whether she dared to go sailing or not, and answered it by jumping into the boat.

For an hour they sailed on calm waters, tacking in the lazy breeze. Cristina noticed that he set his course away from the mainland, standing out to sea. This meant that should a squall arise he could not, at a pinch, make the easy harbour of Port Breton, but must bring them back into the difficult little harbour of Storn itself, after rounding the rocky point of the island where the currents were known to be foul and treacherous, with submerged reefs onto which a small boat might easily be blown. Still she said nothing, although she knew as well as he the danger they were courting, but because she had an idea that he was deliberately taking her into danger she remained silent, pretending not to notice. Only after an hour, seeing that the wind freshened, that the sea was getting up, that clouds were gathering on the horizon, and that Venn still held on, sailing due west, she laughed and said, "Are you taking me to America, Venn?"

He looked at her then with much the same strange, vicious look as he had turned on Shirin.

"Should you mind if I were?"

"Well," she said, lightly, "I know Columbus crossed the Atlantic in a ninety-ton boat, but, after all, the Red-wing is many tons short of that. Besides, what will Shirin say if I'm not there to take down her letters tomorrow morning?"

"I see," he said; "I see; you think she'd notice your absence, though not mine?"

Cristina did not know how to answer this; she felt as though she had suddenly been blown onto one of the submerged reefs of Storn. It was a remark to which one could not possibly return the conventionally polite answer; it was a remark which suddenly showed her the horrifying unreason of Venn's potential jealousy.

She tried to turn it off lightly; it seemed the only thing to do.

"Well, as you know, Shirin is an amazingly practical person," she said, "and practical people resent any upset to their time-table. I wasn't flattering myself that I counted to her as anything more personal than the hands of the clock."

She saw then with relief that he had no more intention of discussing Shirin than she had herself. His remark had cracked out merely as a flash of ill-temper. But although he said no more,—did not even take up her comment about Shirin being amazingly practical,—she knew that his temper had not yet faded away. She knew this, by the way he unexpectedly swung the boat into the wind, making her heel over so that she shipped water, nearly throwing Cristina off her balance and anyway filling her shoes with the quick rush of sea. (A foolish false pride had prevented her from putting on oil-skins or gum-boots.) He was sailing now, not close-hauled, but with his sheet perilously strained. The little boat lay right over at an angle which even Cristina with her short experience recognised as risky; getting the full strength of the breeze, they were cutting through the water at an uncomfortable angle and at a maximum pace. They shipped more water at every dip into a wave; the boat was beginning to fill; and Cristina, taking the can out of the locker where she knew it was kept, silently began to bale.

"I say," said Venn, solicitous, seeing this, "you aren't getting wet, are you?"

Cristina thought this funny; *Venn's perfect manners!* she thought; *he would gladly drown me, and himself too, if necessary, but in the meantime his perfect manners will make him assume concern at my getting my feet wet!*

"Well," she said, baling, "you don't want your boat full of water, do you?"

He respected her for her pluck and her common sense, both. He liked Cristina, personally; he couldn't help liking her, she was so straight and real and honest. So fine, too, with her tawny appearance and her big limbs; her large gestures, her large generosity, her love of bright colours, her coltish way of striding about, her impatient way of pushing her hair back, her strong square hands, her direct speech,—*all rather Wagnerian,* thought Venn; *all rather heroic and over life-size; all on a big scale; no feminine charm at all,* he thought, having a preference for small, soft, dimpled, obedient women, such as he had imagined Shirin to be, until he discovered the recalcitrant independence which he never could conquer; *Cristina has no feminine charm at all,* he thought, *but she has a certain magnificence of her own; she makes me think of Lady Macbeth, who should have borne sons only; she makes me think of brown leaves, driven before an autumn gale.* But at the back of his mind, in spite of his admiration, he feared Cristina; he feared that she might achieve an ascendancy over Shirin such as he himself had never been able to achieve. He knew himself to be a weakling; he knew how he clung to Shirin, to her strength; he knew how he depended on her, how terrified he was that she would, some day, desert him; he knew he would go to pieces without her, like a plant deprived of its stake; he would die without her, he would have nothing left to keep him up. And so he feared Cristina, because she might so easily take from him the one thing he had coveted, and had never been able to win,—the love of Shirin. A weakling, he could not endure the thought that another person might discover the treasure for whose exploitation he had himself been insufficient.

So he sailed on, into the rising sea, for that was the one thing he could do better than Shirin, better than Cristina, who sat there, unmoved, steadily baling. He knew that what he was doing was highly dangerous; indeed, insane. He knew that the boatmen must be watching him, saying *what the devil has come over the Ranger?* He hoped only that they would not pursue him with the launch. For he wanted, definitely, to see if he could frighten Cristina. Not caring about his own risk at all, he wanted to assert his superiority over her. He wanted to take an oblique revenge on her for the many times he had come into Shirin's room and had found them there together, happy, confident, and at ease; the many times he had come in, and had been hurt by their sudden silence, as though they had been talking of things he should not hear and could not understand; he had been hurt by the way they fell silent, looking up at him with polite enquiry as to what he wanted or what brought him there; and then he had always made an excuse and had gone away quickly, hurt right down into the wells of his heart. He knew quite well that he had never caught Shirin. That phrase of young Block's had stuck in his mind, significant as certain chance phrases are, charged with a truth their utterers never wholly intended, but which their hearers remember long years afterwards, when life has begun to fall into its pattern and stretches away into its true perspective. *It was as though the mischief seized her*, young Block had said, *and as though she's said: All right, I'll be It; now catch me if you can*. He had been playing at It with Shirin for ten years now, and had never caught her yet. But Cristina had caught her on the first night, and it seemed to him, thwarted as he was, that Cristina had held her ever since. He divined,—he might be mistaken, of course,—a closeness between her and Cristina such as he himself had never attained, even though he and she shared Dominic and Nerissa, and shared their common life on Storn, and shared the myriad common daily things that make up a life between husband and wife. He had been jealous of men, of course,—passingly jealous of any man who looked on his Shirin with desire, as any man might look on a charming woman, especially so charming a woman as Shirin,—but then his jealousy had been assuaged by his legal possession of her, his wife, his woman, whom no man had a right to touch. This jealousy of Cristina was a different thing, less frank, more dangerous; he was full of suspicion; he suspected their feminine cohesiveness against him; he suspected their understanding, their intimacy; he suspected Shirin,—but how wrongly!—of making confidences to Cristina, of telling her things she had never told to him, things about her first marriage, things about her past, things about her present. Had Shirin, for instance, told Cristina how he had beaten her recently? losing his temper because she refused to make some admission he wanted her to make; hitting her with his clenched fist while she crouched down in her bed, making no defence but only trying to protect her head with her arm; had she told Cristina that? (There had been a certain satisfaction, too, at the moment, in hitting her with his fist; it was always an experience to hurt her soft flesh instead of caressing it, though afterwards he might suffer an anguish of remorse, increased by the fact that from beginning to end she uttered no protest, no complaint.) Had she told Cristina these things? Had she told Cristina how, on the first night of their marriage, he had killed her soul in killing her love for Storn? Had she told Cristina how, for the past ten years, she had lived beside him like a person dead inside, dutiful indeed, and good to him whenever he suffered mentally or physically,—how good she had been! how competently she had nursed him whenever he was ill, harsh and bracing to him when his wave was high, unbelievably kind when ill, injured, or depressed, he went down into the trough! how she alone had the power of lifting his dark moods! of amusing him, interesting him, stimulating him, she, the only recipient of his difficult confidence, the only person to know his doubts, fears, despondencies, the only person whose strength he leant on! And had she told Cristina how he had requited her, with thought-out insults, with inexplicable harshness, even when she herself was ill, with a straining of her strength until he had sometimes wondered at what point she would begin to break?

But she had never broken, she had never complained; she had defended herself only by shutting herself completely away, so that he knew her no better now than he had known her at the time of his reckless marriage. That was at the bottom of his trouble; that was the secret of his unkindness: she had been good to him, as a nurse might have been good, but she had never loved him. If only she had loved him as he had loved her! Then, then indeed, they might have abandoned themselves to a perfection of communion in the island which now by its very beauty added only to the irony of his failure. For was it not by killing her love for Storn that he had killed her potential love for himself?

Cristina could not but admire the way he was sailing his boat; not having the key to his thoughts,—though she plainly saw that something outside himself possessed him, —she could observe only that he sailed with genius, sensitive to every gust of wind, to every threatening wave. *Most men*, she thought, *would have upset us long ago. Heaven help us*, she thought, *if he does upset us, for neither of us could swim back to the island now in such a sea. Well*, she thought, being practical, *I suppose we could cling on to the upturned boat, and the boatmen from Storn would come to look for us before long. Shirin herself will be worried and will send the launch after us. Even if she doesn't worry about me, she will worry about Venn. I fancy that Venn, to her, is always a sick child, needing to be watched. And although she doesn't appear to care much about her own healthy children, except disinterestedly and as a matter of duty, she cares deeply about sick children, as I well know and have seen for myself; she cares for them with an instinct perhaps deeper and more widely humane than the elementary maternal instinct, which possesses and flatters and ignorantly spoils.* (*Perhaps*, she thought, *that's why she really loves Luke best; why Luke, of all her children, is the only one who has left any real impression on her soul.*)

Venn knew that he ought to turn back. He had known it for some time past. He knew that the sea was getting up, beyond the capacity of his little lovely delicate boat, which he loved much as he loved Shirin, testing them both to the utmost, and always wondering just how far he could trust either of them. At the moment, he was wondering whether he could trust his boat to accept a Dutchman's gybe and whether he could trust Shirin to accept without a fuss the danger into which he had deliberately run her friend Cristina. *If the boat survives the gybe*, he thought, *then Shirin will accept the danger into which I have run Cristina. If the boat upsets in the gybe, then I shall know that Shirin minds about Cristina. I shall know that Cristina really caught Shirin, that night, as I have never caught her.*

The boat, for all Venn's symbolism, refused to behave symbolically: without any upsetting, she came round perfectly though perilously, and resumed her reversed course towards Storn. Cristina, too, unwarned, recovered her balance in a manner that earned Venn's respect as well as his resentment. She remained calm; she said only, "Dear me, Venn, were you trying to tip us both into the sea?"

Shirin met them as they landed. The last few minutes were difficult ones, for the waves were dashing high over the stones of the breakwater at the entrance to the harbour. The launch, manned by two boatmen in oil-skins, was tossing in readiness at the steps of the jetty. Shirin, looking very white but controlling herself in front of the boatmen, said, "I was just wondering whether to send the launch after you, Venn." The boatmen stood by, grinning; they had appreciated the Ranger's handling of his boat. It was not until they reached the yew terrace, climbing laboriously against the wind that cuffed them in great squalls and beat them back, that Shirin spoke again. "You must come and change at once, Cristina," she said then, much as she might have spoken to Dominic or Nerissa; she ignored Venn, standing beside them.

Remembering his outburst in the boat, Cristina saw the danger.

"We must both change," she said, trying to include Venn.

"Venn can look after himself," said Shirin. "Come, Cristina."

She had not reproached him, but her voice of ice was more deadly than any reproaches. Cristina felt almost sorry for him. She could imagine the effect of that coldness on a man incurably in love; she could imagine, moreover, how that unapproachable and tantalising coldness would keep an exasperated love for ever. She began, almost, to understand why Venn said cruel things, as the only way of touching Shirin at all. If he could not possess her, he could at least hurt her. Cristina saw him going away, alone, towards his own room, like a dog in disgrace.

"Shirin, don't worry about me; go with Venn, if you go with anybody."

"Go with Venn? when he might have drowned you?"

Cristina was astounded by the sudden passion in her voice and eyes. Was this the inscrutable, mocking Shirin, who never allowed anything of her personal feelings to appear for an instant? She must pretend not to have noticed.

"My dear Shirin!" she said. "He didn't mean to."

"Didn't he?" said Shirin. "Didn't he? Are you so sure?"

She said no more, but in that moment her white and tragic face spoke of possibilities beyond the reach of words. *Lord!* thought the startled Cristina, *what odd fate removed this child of a respectable middle-class home in Dulwich into this charmed dangerous circle of Storn? Is she one of those, in whose existence I firmly believe, born for drama? And if so, what is the drama going to be? Venn's? hers? or mine?*

At this point they saw old Lady le Breton approaching them down the passage. Cristina always shuddered slightly when she caught sight of the old woman approaching thus at a distance. Propelling herself with her stick, all black lace and distinction, she advanced very slowly, almost surreptitiously, and no one ever knew on what mission she was bent. It might be, to spy on one of the servants in the hope of finding out whether they had or had not done something they were supposed to do or not to do; it might be, to come unaware on Shirin, either in love or malice; it might be, to enter a room where Shirin and Venn sat together, and to pause unseen in the doorway overhearing their talk; it might be, to examine the letters on the hall-table when she thought nobody was looking,—Cristina wondered whether she ever took them away to steam them open, especially Shirin's?—it might be, again, that she went on a mission of pure charity and kindliness; no one could ever be certain, with Madame, just as one could never be certain what mood she was going to be in, whether devilish or wise and charming.

She met them in the passage now, and chuckled to see Cristina dripping.

"So he's brought her back safe, the scamp, has he?" she said to Shirin; and then, turning to Cristina: "You'd have been flattered, my dear, to see the fuss Shirin was in, all on your account. Oh yes, all on yours. She didn't give a thought to her poor husband, did you, Shirin? It was all *Venn had no right to take Cristina out on such a day.* Well, my dear, all I can say is, I hope you didn't let Venn see you were frightened. It doesn't do to let Venn see when you're frightened: he enjoys it too well, doesn't he, Shirin? Shirin could tell you that, if she ever told anybody anything. Well, run along and change, my dear, and then let Shirin look after you. She'll give you hot toddy and a hot bath too, if you're not careful. Put you into it herself, I dare say. She's a managing sort of person, as anybody in the village will tell you. As for Venn, he can take care of himself; he's used to it. Had to get used to it. Shirin doesn't approve of wives who run about with soup and hot bottles for their husbands, do you, Shirin? Quite right too, I expect; it never pays to coddle a man too much. Run along, run along." She hobbled off on her course.

Shirin opened the door into Cristina's room.

"Now, Cristina," she said briskly, "joke or no joke, Madame is right: you must have a hot bath, and I'll get you the toddy."

"Shirin," said Cristina, suddenly bold, "why are you crying?"

"I am not crying; I don't know what you mean."

"But you are; I can see; there are tears in your eyes. You weren't really anxious about Venn, were you? It was quite all right; it was rather exciting, but rather fun too. I enjoyed it; so did Venn, I'm sure. You know how clever he is with a boat; he was really brilliant today. But it was quite safe really. We weren't in any danger for a single moment. In fact, I wished Dominic and Nerissa were with us; they would have loved it.—Shirin, don't cry; he's quite safe, you know; you can always trust Venn with a boat; after today, I would trust him anywhere."

She ran on, trying to give Shirin time to recover herself,

and going into the bathroom she took off her wet clothes, wrapping herself in a dressing-gown instead. But even when she returned into the room she found Shirin still in no mood to grasp at an easy evasion.

"I wasn't worrying about him, Cristina; I was worrying about you. If Venn likes to take risks for himself, that's his business. It's true that I told Madame he had no right to take you out on such a day,—more fool I, for of course she'll hold it against me for ever after. I don't mind that. What I minded was the injustice. . . ." She stopped and turned away.

"Yes?" said Cristina gently; "the injustice? Go on."

Shirin must speak, she thought; *if she doesn't speak now she never will.*

"It doesn't matter," Shirin said wearily; "what does anything matter? I was a fool to mind. I thought I had got over minding things, long ago. It was only the injustice of suggesting that I had never looked after Venn when he needed me. I have, Cristina; I swear to you that I have; very often when I was ill myself, and I never let them know I was ill; I've sat up with him night after night, when he wouldn't allow anyone into his room but me."

"My darling, I don't doubt it."

The unexpected endearment broke Shirin down completely; she sobbed with her face hidden in her hands. Cristina, looking down on the brown childish curls, the fragile burying hands, and the shaking shoulders, felt herself helplessly and impotently moved. This sudden release and revelation of a secret, disciplined nature was a thing she did not know how to cope with. She was afraid of saying too much, and of scaring Shirin away,—her wild bird.

"Don't tell me anything you may regret, Shirin."

"Oh, Cristina, you are good to me."

The pathos of that phrase twisted Cristina's heart: that Shirin, the spoiled, the courted, the flattered, the independent, should be so grateful for a little ordinary kindness and understanding! What had she suffered, in loneliness, all these years?

"I think," said Shirin, looking up but turning her head away again immediately because she knew her eyes were wet, "that we have both probably been rather more frightened than we know. Those things weaken one. They make one emotional, which is always a great mistake, isn't it? The moment one lets oneself go at all, one says things better kept to oneself. I'm sorry, Cristina; I don't usually behave in this way. And please don't think that I intended to criticise either Venn or Madame; they have both been extraordinarily long-suffering and patient with me; I know I am very trying sometimes, as you'll probably discover. Please don't think I was blaming either of them. And anyhow, it won't be for very long."

Cristina was startled.

"What on earth do you mean, Shirin: it won't be for very long?"

Fey! she thought, remembering; *fated to die; at point of death; disordered in mind, like person about to die*. But Shirin wasn't disordered in mind; she hadn't lost her self-control, even now, when fright had shaken her. It must be rather a remarkable thing, Shirin's self-control; an ordered discipline of years; a harsh and painful discipline; an almost religious discipline; a discipline imposed by will and philosophy on a nature passionate and abnormally sensitive and too tightly controlled.

"Shirin," she said, concerned, "is anything wrong with you? are you ill?"

Shirin laughed at that; she laughed almost naturally.

"Cristina, I love your practical common sense. No, I'm not ill. Nor organically.—I just know."

"Know what?"

"Oh, well, certain things. Never mind. It isn't very important."

"But it *is* important, Shirin, if it affects you."

"Me! What am I? You know I don't matter, any more than you matter, or than Venn matters.—What an odd word 'matter' is, isn't it, when one says it several times over? When one has said it often enough, it ceases to have any meaning at all, any more than matter in the real sense of the term has any meaning today."

"Shirin, what an unexpected person you are; I never knew you thought about things like that."

"Didn't you? No, I suppose you wouldn't. Forget about it, Cristina. You see, you are more fortunate than I; you have your sculpture as a way of expressing yourself. That provides an outlet, a safety-valve. You're creative, and I am just nothing at all. I just live. I think I probably still live too acutely. That is the whole difference between being creative and just living. If I were a sculptor, as you are, I could thumb my life in soft wet clay; I could see life as a whole; I could put it once and for all into a single image. That would be satisfactory. That is a thing I have never been able to do."

"And yet you seem to have such strength, Shirin, I always feel it in you; like a deep well, as though you had made up your mind long ago and had got your values right and had arranged your own particular philosophy.

Unlike most people, who drift so long as things are easy, and then find themselves with no armour when they have to meet their troubles."

Shirin looked dubious; this came rather too close to her innermost self. She was not going to tell Cristina, not even Cristina, of the detachment she had by austere and diligent practice achieved. She was not going to tell anybody of the private mysticism which now at last enabled her to accept the wounds of life. Nor was she going to tell Cristina what she meant by the phrase she had let slip: *It won't be for very long*. She regretted that lapse, despising herself for her own weakness. She thanked her own creed that her moments of weakness should be so infrequently betrayed; even Venn could seldom provoke her into such shortcomings now. Very soon, she would be quite safe; immune; she would cease to feel; she would have killed herself even more effectively than Venn had killed her when he demolished her love for Storn; she would have destroyed the human thing in herself, that felt and suffered. That was the consummation devoutly to be wished.

She made no reply to Cristina's remark about her inner strength. If she had found strength at all,—which, tired, she sometimes doubted,—that strength was her own treasure, her own accomplishment, not to be cheapened by talking it over with anybody. True, Cristina was not anybody; not merely anybody; Cristina was, for her, in some odd way, different from anybody else; but even so, Cristina must survive a long probation before being admitted even to the outskirts of the secret life. She had not yet determined whether Cristina should ever thus be admitted. She, at present, only guessed at the possibilities inherent in such an admission of another being, since, in her life hitherto, she had known neither love nor friendship, having fought against them both and resolutely refused them. She knew only that if she once let Cristina through the gates at all, Cristina would then be allowed to run freely up and down the streets of her most secret city, looking into all the houses and into all the rooms of all the houses, for she, Shirin, was not a person to do things by halves. Either Cristina should be kept outside as Venn had been kept outside, or she should have free admission. But even in her loneliness she was not sure that she wanted anyone, even Cristina, who was different from anybody else, to have that.

All the same, she could not let Cristina go.

Cristina, however, was talking of going.

"Shirin," she said, "you must see, I can't stay here if Venn resents me. For your own sake you mustn't ask me to stay. I don't want to complicate matters between you and Venn. I see, forgive me for saying so, that they are complicated enough already. Don't ask me to stay here and make matters worse."

"Cristina, you don't mean that? You don't mean that you'd leave me now? Don't you realise the difference you are making to my life? Don't you realise the difference that you may make? Cristina, for God's sake say that you won't leave me now."

Cristina looked at her in terror. What was coming out of all this? Panic-struck and pleading, with widened eyes, Shirin was clutching her desperately in an implicit confession of dependence.

"Of course," she said, "if you feel like that about it, I won't go. I'll stay as long as you want me. I'll stay till I die, if you really want me."

III

It was easy enough to promise to stay at Storn; it was not so easy to keep the promise. Nothing but her loyalty and her now passionate devotion to Shirin would have induced Cristina to remain. She knew that Venn hated her; she knew that Madame, subtly, delighted in fostering the ill-feeling between them. And it was not in Cristina's nature to remain where someone wished her gone. Just as little was it in her nature to spend her life in an atmosphere of concealed hostility. An uncompromising person, she liked clear, open relationships, or else, impatiently, preferred to break them; yet here she was committed to relationships which were neither clear nor open. She must preserve an appearance of freindliness with Venn, just as he, outwardly, preserved an appearance of friendliness with her; and towards Madame she must act with deference and respect, when she really longed for nothing but to tell the old woman exactly what she thought of her. She was, in fact, committed to a way of life which went against her every instinct, and that, to a proud and independent spirit, was no small pill to swallow. Cristina felt it sometimes as big as a cannon-ball. What complicated it more, was the fact that she could not really dislike either Venn or Lady le Breton. She felt that they were just damned souls, gone wrong; and although her innate respect for the dignity of human beings precluded her from so patronising a sentiment as pity, her equally innate appreciation as an artist forced her to find them both extremely interesting. Even in wrath and indignation, she could still find them fascinating. Though she sometimes wanted to murder them both, she could still find fascination in the study of beings so contradictory, so devilish, and so odd. Even when they tormented Shirin, although she had to bite her lips into silence, she could still study them dispassionately. And this she felt to be wrong. It made the relationship even less clear, less open, than it already was.

She wondered sometimes whether she were really lessening herself by remaining, even though her motive for remaining was by no means a lessening thing.

For Shirin wanted her; and so long as Shirin wanted her, which she began to believe would be for ever, then she must stay. She must put her pride and independence aside.

"Cristina," said Shirin one day, "you ought to sculpt Venn."

Shirin was in high spirits that morning, Cristina didn't know why; her laughter had rippled all down the yew terrace. These sudden high spirits of Shirin always touched Cristina's heart: they showed her as a happy child; as a child that might have been happy, given the chance. (But would Shirin ever have been permanently happy? *Only in flashes*, thought Cristina; *but so deliciously happy then as to make up for all the rest.*)

"I should love to sculpt Venn," said Cristina, looking at Venn, "but I expect Venn would hate to be sculpted."

"Don't you believe it!" laughed Shirin; "on the contrary, he'd be flattered,—wouldn't you, Venn? You can't imagine, Cristina, how vain Venn really is. Just you prepare a lovely wet lump of clay, and you'll find him sitting still for hours, posing. Won't she, Venn?"

"Only if you will come and talk to us," said Venn, who was in a good temper too, that morning.

They were all three in a good temper; Shirin's gaiety had infected them. This was Venn at his nicest; he looked at Shirin with adoration. *Oh*, thought Cristina, *how happy they might have been!*

He was interesting as a model, the narrowness and thinness of his head offering an almost anatomical study. Cristina had long since realised that with different colouring he would have been good-looking. As it was, his sandiness made him plain; his sandiness which added to the rodent-like appearance she so much feared and disliked; also the meanness of the pale, small eyes. But his bones were interesting to her as a sculptor, so small and brittle-looking, and scarcely covered by the flesh, as though a single blow could smash them in. Transparent was the word most people would have used about him; but Cristina was tempted to say phosphorescent instead. His transparency amounted almost to an inner light; electric, even as the animal desire which streamed from him was electric. His being so inarticulate increased this sensing of electricity, of radiation. (*Dear me*, thought Cristina, *how inaccurate my scientific terminology is! yet I know what I mean. He doesn't talk, but he lives. Shirin doesn't talk, but she lives also.*)

This close examination made her realise with renewed perception how taut and nervous he was, and how much he must suffer from his temperament. When Shirin was in the room he watched her all the time; it was unpleasant to see him, it was like seeing an animal waiting to spring. But of course there were times when Shirin had to leave them; when, brisk and business-like, she came and went, carrying papers, sometimes accompanied by one of the children, always competent, never fussy, a little too hard perhaps, but so quick and reliable that Cristina could well understand why everybody always turned to her for everything. Her competence revealed itself even in the way she would catch Dominic by the shoulders and twitch his tie straight. When she treated Venn in the same manner, familiarly possessive, he would let her do as she liked with him in willing slavery. It was really pathetic to see the look of happy gratitude that overspread his face at such moments, or when she chaffed him when he was at what Cristina called his nicest. He looked then as though he drew all his sustenance from her careless kindness. But Cristina always had the impression that Shirin was never really careless; that she was always on her guard, because she must be; that she was always, really, keeping him at arm's length. She would be as kind to him as she could afford to be, partly because it was in her nature to manage people in the charming tyrannical way of a pretty woman, but she would never lose her head, be unwise, say or do more than she meant, get carried away. And it seemed wicked to Cristina that Shirin should have had to school herself to this lesson; Shirin, who could have loved so generously, so sweetly; so loyally, so passionately, so completely; who could have held the head of her beloved so warmly against her breast.

So Shirin was not constantly with them; and Cristina, no less than Venn, felt that some light and life had gone out of the room when she left it. Not that this troubled

Cristina very much: she was too much absorbed in her work. An artist, nothing counted for her when she was working, not even Shirin. Her departures worried Cristina only in so far as they affected her model; his face seemed to sag; it lost the alertness which might, it was true, be only the unpleasant alertness of the crouched insatiate animal, but which at least gave it life and expression. His face went dead when Shirin was not there. It became sullen; fallow.

Worse than these temporary absences, she suddenly went away for three days to London. She came into Cristina's studio when they were working, and said she must go. It was quite unexpected, and Venn looked as though she had hit him. Then the stunned look was replaced by a look of rage; still he said nothing, only glared at her. He asked no question, and she gave no explanation; she only said, "I'm sorry to interrupt you, Cristina, but could you come and help me to make a few arrangements? Venn, I'm afraid your sitting for this afternoon must be called off. I must go by the night train, and I haven't much time. Could you order the launch for me at six?"

Even to Cristina she gave no explanation, only a few business-like directions. Cristina had never seen her so shut away into herself. For the first time she felt genuinely sorry for Venn, now that she was sharing his exclusion; she saw how the iciness of Shirin's withdrawal could hurt. She almost longed to plead with Shirin not to avoid a moment alone with him, as she was obviously avoiding it, and as he equally obviously was seeking it, hanging round her on any pretext. But she dared not. Nor could she really find it in her heart to criticise Shirin, who was so clearly strung up to the limits of her self-control. Only at one moment did Shirin betray herself at all: "I hope," she said with sudden anxiety, "that Venn has ordered the launch."

"Of course he has, Shirin; you asked him to."

Shirin glanced at her; Cristina had never seen such an expression of cynicism in her eyes before.

"My dear Cristina, you don't imagine that my asking Venn to do something is any reason why he should do it? It might work quite the other way. Especially as he doesn't want me to go."

"Then," said Cristina, who felt that she could serve Shirin best by being practical, "why don't you let me go and order it for you?"

"No. It's Venn's launch," said Shirin, "and Venn's boatmen. You know quite well that I never give orders of that sort, here."

"But, Shirin!"

"I can't, I won't," said Shirin with finality; "Cristina, you mustn't argue with me over that."

"All the same, Shirin, you don't want to miss this train."

"How do you know I don't want to miss it?"

"Well, do you?"

"No, I don't."

"Then . . ."

"*No.*"

Cristina saw that she had better leave the subject, even while she privately resolved that she would make enquiries of her own about the launch.

"Don't fuss about anything while you're away, Shirin," she said; "I'll look after the children and see to it that Nerissa doesn't go to bed too late."

For she knew that Venn sometimes kept the children up too late, just in order to annoy Shirin. He enjoyed currying favour with them, at her expense. He enjoyed playing the indulgent and irresponsible father, in opposition to her as the stern and judicious mother. He did this, partly because he sincerely loved the children, but partly and principally also because he wanted to score off Shirin.

Then she saw that she had said quite the wrong thing. A look almost of hatred sprang into Shirin's eyes.

"I don't worry about the children, I assure you," she said coldly; "they're all right. Nerissa could stay up all night, for all the harm it would do her. It might even do her a great deal of good to be thoroughly tired out for once; she might discover then that life isn't always as safe and sheltered as she thinks."

Cristina realised then that Shirin had been sent for on account of Luke. Nothing else could have produced such bitterness in her voice, at the mention of the le Breton children.

"All right," she said, "I'll let them fall into the sea and get drowned."

"Cristina, don't tease. I can't stand it now.—No, you're right to tease. Thank you.—Yes, Venn?"

Venn came in.

"Not gone yet?" he said, looking round at the disorder of the room, where tissue-paper, shoe-trees, and underclothes lay scattered about. He looked round at them, half as though he hated Shirin and these evidences of her femininity, half as though he could not bear to let her go.

"How could I have gone? it's only half-past five. By the way, Venn, did you order the launch?"

"Of course I ordered it."

She looked at him very searchingly, then seemed satisfied that he was speaking the truth.

"Venn, I'm sorry to bother you," she said shyly and reluctantly, "but could you let me have some money? I haven't any left."

Cristina knew already that Venn allowed Shirin no money at all; it was, she imagined, one of the ways he had found to annoy and humiliate her; he paid her bills, and paid them generously, for he liked to see her well dressed, a delight to his eyes and a credit to his name, but when she needed personal pocket-money or cash for petty expenses she was compelled to ask him for every penny. Nor did he ever make it easy for her.

"I gave you ten pounds last time you went to London. That wasn't so very long ago."

"Venn, it was four months ago, and you know it. Besides, the ticket alone costs six pounds, as you won't let me travel third."

"And this time," he said, looking at her cruelly, "you will need a sleeper, as you are going by the night train."

Cristina saw Shirin clench her hands.

"You couldn't have waited till tomorrow morning, I suppose," he continued, nagging.

"No, I couldn't have waited," she replied, very quietly and restrainedly, "but I don't want a sleeper, thank you. I don't want to put you to unnecessary expense."

Unluckily, Mrs. Jolly at that moment came into the room. Venn hated Mrs. Jolly, irrationally, with all the hatred in his nature. He hated her because he knew she saw through him; despised him; accorded him nothing but a sneeringly conventional respect. He hated her because of her devotion to Shirin and because of her intimacy with Shirin, whom she had nursed in illness and whose babies she had seen born. He hated her because on such occasions she had had the right to forbid him the room, and had exercised that right with unconcealed pleasure. He hated her because he suspected her, correctly, of guessing things that no one but himself and Shirin should know. He endured her presence in his house only because Shirin had declared, with a decision that really alarmed him, that if Jolly went she would go also. And he knew that she meant it. Shirin seldom made a stand, but when she made one she did not make it lightly. So he had given way, and Jolly, crudely triumphant, had remained. He had never forgiven her the victory.

It was indeed unlucky that Mrs. Jolly should come in at that precise moment.

She came in, concerned and bustling.

"What's this I hear, that you're going to London, my lamb? And all in a hurry, like that? Well now, I've come to see what I can do for you. MacPherson was coming along to finish your packing, but I said no; I never did like that skinny Scotchness; no, I said, I've packed for her often enough, and . . ."

She had caught sight of Venn.

"Beg pardon, Sir Venn; I didn't see that you'd come to help too."

"I didn't know you had taken the place of her ladyship's maid, Mrs. Jolly; I thought you were the housekeeper."

Venn's voice cut like an east wind. But Mrs. Jolly, unlike Madame, took no conscious pleasure in making matters more difficult for Shirin.

"Now don't you be cross with me, Sir Venn," she said

comfortably; "you know well enough that her ladyship's been my baby for years, even before you knew her, and even before you thought of your own babies at all, which are mine too, in a sense. So what's more natural than that I should come to look after her, when she's flustered and in trouble?"

It was well meant, but scarcely tactful.

"In trouble? Mrs. Jolly, I think you forget yourself. Her ladyship is going to London to order some clothes."

This was too much for Jolly; she laughed frankly, scornfully.

"Tell me another, Sir Venn!" She turned to Shirin. "It's those wretched children of yours again, isn't it, my lamb?"

"Jolly, Jolly, for pity's sake!" said Shirin.

"Well, and why shouldn't I speak?" said Mrs. Jolly; "I never was not accustomed to speaking my mind, as you well know. . . ."

"Yes, yes, we know, Jolly," said Shirin hastily, "but if you love me don't speak it now! Look, I'm in a hurry, and rather late; so just stay and help me to pack, if you think MacPherson won't mind,—which she will, but it can't be helped,—and you, Venn, get me my money, and I'll meet you downstairs in five minutes' time."

"You can ask Mrs. Jolly to lend you the money,—the money you want in order to go and see another man's brats."

He left the room. Cristina, left behind much to her own embarrassment, was really horrified. She had not previously realised that Venn could lose his temper so far as to insult Shirin in the presence of a servant. Fortunately Mrs. Jolly could in no way be considered as an ordinary servant.

Although Cristina looked at Shirin in dismay to see how Shirin would take it, it was not Shirin but Mrs. Jolly who dealt instantly and rightly with the situation.

"Now how much do you want, my love?" she said briskly, scrabbling to pick up the long black skirt which she had long ago adopted as befitting her dignity as a housekeeper.

Cristina admired Mrs. Jolly then; she had had her doubts; had reserved her judgment; but now she became Jolly's loyal ally for ever. Jolly might fail in tact when the ice was merely thin, but as soon as the ice actually broke and Shirin stood in danger of drowning, she was capable of coming at once without any fuss to effect a quiet rescue.

"Could you manage ten pounds, Jolly?"

"A hundred, if you want it, honey."

"You don't mean to tell me, Jolly, that you've got a hundred pounds hidden in your stocking?"

"Never you mind what I mean to tell you or not to tell you; just you tell me what you want, and you shall have it."

"Ten, then, please, Jolly."

When Shirin said *hidden in your stocking*, Cristina thought that she was joking, but Mrs. Jolly pulled up her skirt and extracted a packet from the top of her large black cotton leg.

"It isn't everyone I would trust as I am trusting you, Miss," she said, nodding significantly towards Cristina. "There are those as have seen the bump, but I always tell them it's varicose veins."

"It shall always be varicose veins for me too, Mrs. Jolly."

"I'm sure, Miss. Else I wouldn't do it."

She gave Shirin two five-pound notes, and restored the others to their hiding-place, secured by a wide elastic band.

"I'll give it you back the day after tomorrow, Jolly."

"Yes,—he'll be in a better humour then, no doubt. It's only your going away upsets him. You mustn't take too much notice. People do get upset, and though it seems unreasonable to everybody else it seems reasonable enough to them. That's what makes him as contrary as a monkey with a sore bottom."

"Jolly, really you shouldn't say these things."

"Too late to stop me now, dearie; you should have thought of that before; besides, you never say anything yourself, so somebody has to say them for you. And somehow that somebody has always been me. Miss Rich won't take it amiss, I'm sure?" she added, winking at Cristina.

Cristina saw that she was blundering and joking, on purpose to save Shirin. She saw also that Shirin, strung up as she was, welcomed Jolly's comic turn: Jolly playing the part of the clown coming in to distract the attention after too dangerous an act upon the trapezes. No one else could have relaxed the tension for Shirin as Jolly had relaxed it. Cristina began to understand the relation between them; having frequently wondered how Shirin could endure the familiarities of this unorthodox woman, she now began to see that Mrs. Jolly was probably the only person who in her warm, common, human way had ever forced herself through the door of Shirin's reserve.

Venn, however, did not share Shirin's weakness for Mrs. Jolly. Venn, after Shirin had gone, was very difficult to deal with. Cristina found it difficult to preserve her loyalty to Shirin and yet to keep on good terms with Venn.

She found it difficult, for instance, to listen dispassionately to Venn's remarks about Mrs. Jolly after Shirin's departure, although she shrewdly realised that such remarks were made chiefly to relieve his other feelings. She felt that a certain disloyalty to Shirin was involved in listening to them at all, yet how could she serve Shirin better than by remaining on good terms with Venn? And Venn, during those two days, was in a peculiar mood which made him more expansive than usual, as though he must allow a few bubbles of his feelings to rise to the surface from the depths beneath.

"I can't think how Shirin stands that old woman," he said; "can you?"

That *can you* appealed directly for Cristina's support. But Cristina was cautious.

"I suppose she has been very useful to Shirin in the past," she said; "trustworthy with the children, and all that."

Venn grunted sceptically.

"There's something in Shirin which likes people who toady her," he said. As Cristina did not answer, he went on, provocatively trying to justify his contention, "Look how few friends she has,—none at all, in fact, except possibly yourself. She has never seemed to understand friendship or to want it. Most women do, don't they? They like confidences and intimacies, don't they? they like discussing their hearts and their bodies and their marriages, with other women. ("Oh, Venn," Cristina interjected, laughing, "what a very conventional, prejudiced point of view!" *How raw he is*, she thought, *and how unwise.*) Well," he said, slightly abashed, "that's what one is always given to understand. It certainly isn't true of Shirin. She sheers off any ordinary friendship and chooses a creature like that old tart instead."

"Old tart, Venn?"

"Yes, of course; didn't you know that Jolly was an ex-prostitute? Of course she is; ten years of respectability have scarcely sufficed to wash the paint off her face or the dye out of her hair. She used to have hair as yellow as a sponge, but now thank God she's let it go grey. She hasn't changed her morals with her hair, though. I gather that her conduct in Port Breton on her off-days isn't exemplary, even now."

"But, Venn, how sporting of her, at her age. She must be sixty-five if she's a day."

Venn looked amused at that; he was human somewhere, however warped he might be. He felt a sudden comradeship with Cristina, rather as though she were a man.

"Still," he said, reverting to his grievances, "I can't see how Shirin stands her,—Shirin of all people, who shies away from familiarities like a pony shying away from a bit of paper on the road. Of course the truth of the matter is," he said, working himself up, "that Jolly has always been more than half in love with Shirin, and Shirin likes that; she's always been accustomed to it, and she couldn't do without it, even from a sordid old creature like Jolly."

He stopped suddenly and shot a startled, challenging glance at Cristina. It was an awkward moment. Such oblique references were awkward in the extreme. Cristina wondered how much he really meant, or how much the remark and the glance had been accidental; due to chance. Fortunately he appeared to feel the awkwardness as acutely as she did, for he stopped the subject short.

"Well, I shall go and bathe," he said, getting up.

Cristina did not relish this type of conversation at all. It increased her discomfort. She longed for Shirin's return.

Mrs. Jolly, who also took advantage of Shirin's absence to seek out Cristina, proved herself a far kinder critic of Venn than Venn had proved of Mrs. Jolly. She might hate Venn with a deep hatred, but still she was able to understand him and fairly to size him up. In her large generous understanding she was even able to appreciate his good qualities: "You mustn't judge him as he is these days, Miss," she said; "he always gets wild when she goes away. Everybody knows it, here, and gives him a wide berth. You see, he knows all too well what she's doing. Oh, nothing wrong. I don't mean that. Poor lamb, she's played straight by him ever since she married him,—and he, I swear, has played straight by her. Give the devil his due. There hasn't been any other woman in his life, nor any man in hers; but on his side it was love that kept him straight, and on hers it was duty. There's all the difference, isn't there, Miss? I saw a lovely picture once, called 'Twixt Love and Duty; they showed it in Port Breton; but that's neither here nor there; that's not what I was talking about. I was talking about what she did when she went to London. I don't know how much you know about her, Miss, but I can tell you she goes as innocent as you please. I know she went and stayed with you, Miss, before you came down here, so I expect you know a good deal. Still, one never knows everything about a person even though they stay under your roof and let you see their comings and goings, does one? It all depends on how much they mean you to know; and Shirin was never one to let anybody know anything. One just finds out, little by little; one puts the bits together and makes a picture. Well, the Ranger doesn't like it, and who's to blame him? It can't be pleasant to feel your wife has thoughts of her own and has borne children to another man. I fancy he tried to forget about it mostly, but when she goes away like this of course it all starts up in his mind. And then he's like a wild beast prowling round. Upon my word, I've felt sorry for him sometimes. I don't suppose his own nature is any more pleasure to him than it is to other people."

Cristina was not sure that she ought to listen to all this. But Mrs. Jolly was off again. Cristina compared her volubility with that of Minna Lester; *they both gabble on in much the same way*, she thought, *with the only difference that their phraseology isn't quite the same, and that Jolly hits the nail plumb every time whereas Minna misses it with an infallibility all her own.*

She smiled to imagine Minna Lester's sentiments if she could hear her own conversation, which she thought so smart and shrewd, compared with the conversation of the ex-prostitute whom Cristina so greatly preferred.

"Oh, she hasn't had an easy time, poor child," Jolly was saying. "I say *poor child*, for she does seem a child, doesn't she, Miss, with her curly head and her pretty little hands? You'd never think she was a grown woman, with six children and two husbands and at least twenty committees and a packet of worries. Sometimes when I've come in and found her curled up on the window-seat, looking out across the sea for all the world as I've seen a bird tired out after hours when nobody has come to open the window and let it go, I've thought to myself, *You're just a poor child, you are, for all your six children and your good sense and your laughing about the house and your doing everything for everybody and your keeping things going for the Ranger and for that old witch of a Madame, God rot her soul.*"

"Mrs. Jolly!" said Cristina, startled by this last outburst.

"I shouldn't have said that, Miss, should I? No, I shouldn't; it wasn't my place. I hope I know my place as well as another; I've had time to learn it, in these ten years. No, I shouldn't have said *rot her soul.* I don't mean it either, not wholly, and I know you won't hold it against me, Miss. Madame has her faults as we all have, but I'll admit there's something in Madame that keeps one loving her however black one may go against her in the intervals. She's an experience, she is, is Madame. Written down on paper she might seem bad, but there's something about her that twiddles one round again every time just when one thinks one has made one's mind up once and for all to the worst. Every now and again I've had a first-class row with Madame, and she's said things I thought I never could forgive,—and it wasn't only for Shirin's sake that I held my tongue; it was on account of Madame, too, cross though she made me; I knew that at any moment she would stop maddening me by her unjustice and would look at me with that smile that can just twist itself round one's inside and make one go all soft and no-how. That's a thing that Madame and Shirin have got in common: they can do what they like with one. It doesn't seem fair, Miss, does it? It seems as though the blesséd God had given them some advantage over other people. The pictures may call it by some special name, sex-appeal or what-not; but to me it's more than that; it's just a thing some women have and other women haven't. Anyhow, when they do have it, they can get away with anything. And it isn't just the thing that makes men want to go to bed with you,—if you'll excuse me, Miss. It's something deeper than that; it's a sort of importance; the sort of thing that makes you think of the stars and of things you can't quite understand. It seems to have a sort of truth in it, which is more than any truth we know.—I don't know, Miss, I'm sure. It's a thing that makes me realise that though Madame can be as wicked as you please, there's some part inside her which is anything but wicked. All the same, there have been times when she has led that poor child a life. I sometimes wonder how long she'll stand it, between the two of them, Madame and Venn. Shirin isn't one to say anything, but it's my idea that one day they'll wake up and find she isn't there."

"How do you mean, Mrs. Jolly, not there?"

But Mrs. Jolly only shook her head lugubriously.

Shirin returned when she had promised; she returned in unnaturally wild spirits, and cried out that they must all three go down and bathe. "I want to wash London off me," she said; "I want to wash its grime off my body and its racket out of my system. Come with me, Cristina, while I get my things."

Is she trying to avoid being alone with Venn?

"What you really want," said Cristina as they reached Shirin's room, "is not so much to wash London out of your system, as to wash something else out of your soul."

She wondered how she dared to be so bold.

"How do you know that?" said Shirin, stopping. She looked feverish, and extremely pretty in her London clothes.

"Hadn't you better tell me about it? Is it a good plan, always to suppress everything?"

"Cristina, you've never asked me questions before."

"No, but I am asking you questions now. Go on; tell me. You went to see Luke, didn't you?"

She had not intended to say any of these things, but inspiration gave her courage; it gave her the strength, too, to force Shirin. She was dominating and compelling Shirin, who suddenly gave way.

"All right, I'll tell you. Yes, I went to see Luke. Miles wrote and asked me to come. He . . . he's worse, Cristina. He's really dangerous now, and it has become necessary to move him to another home where he can have better supervision. You see, he is nearly eighteen now, and very big and strong. So Miles, who has always been very kind and considerate to me about Luke, asked me to come and approve the arrangements he was making."

"But why was it so urgent?"

"Because Miles himself was going abroad," said Shirin wearily. "He was very nice to me, he really was. We went to see Luke together."

She shuddered and put her hands over her face.

"It's almost more than I can bear," she said in a low voice.

Then she said, "No, that's nonsense. Of course I can bear it. I can bear anything. Cristina, it is quite extraordinary for me to be telling you about this. Do you realise that I have never mentioned Luke to a soul except, of course, Miles? I used to come back to Storn after seeing him and keep it all to myself. What I minded most was that it gave me such dreadful nightmares for weeks afterwards. Nobody knew, nobody cared. It was rather lonely, sometimes. But now I'm telling you that too. You can't imagine how strange it seems to have someone to talk to."

"Why did you never tell me anything about it when you were staying with me in London?"

"I couldn't, Cristina; I'm not made that way. Besides, you mightn't have understood; you might have said I was being weak about it; cowardly. I couldn't risk it, you see."

Good God, thought Cristina, *what things have people said to her to make her shrink from them like that? For all her gaiety she's like a wretched child with its arm ready to ward off a blow.*

"You won't feel like that again?" she said.

"You're so good to me, Cristina." (Again that pathetic phrase!) "You're strong and gentle. I'll try to make myself talk to you. But you must help. You must be very firm and bullying."

She was laughing now; she looked quite different; the strain had gone out of her face; she looked relaxed.

"We're keeping Venn waiting," she said, jumping up and snatching her things.

"I must get my things too, if we're going to bathe."

"I'll come with you."

Linked by a new understanding they went happily towards Cristina's room.

"Tell me about the bust,—is it finished?"

"Yes, it's finished."

"Oh, Cristina, how exciting. Shall I like it? Where is it?"

"It's in the studio. I'm not sure whether you will like it or not. You can go and look at it while I get my things."

The bust stood where the evening sun fell on it. Shirin experienced a little shock on finding herself alone with this strange, silent presentment of Venn. For it was looking at her with an expression she knew so well and dreaded so profoundly. How had Cristina caught it? A real and inner vision must have inspired her. She had seen all the viciousness, all the cruelty, all the hunger of Venn's unsatisfied nature. It was brilliant; it was damning.

Cristina came in.

"Well?"

"Cristina, it is horrible."

"It is true."

They looked at one another.

"How did you know? It's a work of genius, a devilish work of genius. What does Venn himself think of it?"

Cristina laughed.

"He was rather funny about it; I liked him; you know when Venn suddenly gives way to his sense of humour? Well, he just looked at it in silence, and then said that if he really looked like that he wouldn't care to meet himself alone in a narrow lane at dusk."

"Yes, that is the nice side of Venn. And Madame, has she seen it?"

"Madame," said Cristina grimly, "took some pleasure in telling Venn that I had evidently managed to size him up."

The evening sun slanted low and warm on the sea, and after bathing they lay drying themselves on the rocks. They were not talking much. Shirin, in her black bathing-dress, made Venn think of the seal he had once imagined her to be: half-seal, half-woman, lying on the rocks of his Storn, on the edge of the sea. How unfamiliar she had been to him when he had had that fancy; how familiar to him now! And how little she had changed; it seemed to him that she looked no older than when he had found her at Minna Lester's party. Would she never lose that softly childish look?

She appeared unconscious of his scrutiny; she had found a little pool in a scoop of the rock and was arranging a pattern of shells and sea-weed round it. *She plays*, thought Cristina, *as naturally as a child*, *putting all her intentness into her game*, *yet what horrors are stored at the back of her mind?* Venn, watching her, had much the same thoughts, but in him they took a jealous, not a compassionate form: he was wondering whether she had seen Vane-Merrick and what they had said to one another; whether they had met in the old intimacy of a man and a woman who have shared a life and who have certain bonds that keep them permanently together; whether they had discussed problems and made old allusions from which he, Venn, would certainly be excluded. He would not ask Shirin and she would not tell him. They had long since agreed, after many storms, that the only hope of peace lay in a complete avoidance of such topics. But it infuriated him to feel that she had that separate life, away from him; his exorbitance could not endure it. He could not endure to think that she had smiled and talked intimately with Miles Vane-Merrick; he could not endure to think that she had brought back a fresh store of experiences and impressions which he would never share.

He let his eyes dwell voluptuously on the soft roundness of her arms and shoulders; a few gleaming drops of water stayed on them, slowly evaporating; he knew that if he kissed her now, she would taste of the sea. He wanted to take her in his arms, to lie with her on the sunny rock, to contrast the softness of their bodies with the hardness of the rock. But Cristina's presence frustrated him. It seemed to him that Cristina was always there, always keeping him away from Shirin, and that Shirin herself prevented

Cristina from leaving them alone together. Nor had the bust inspired him with any fresh liking for Cristina. It was not pleasant to see oneself so completely uncovered.

But as though Cristina read his thoughts, she got up and wandered away. Shirin called after her:

"Where are you going, Cristina?"

"Just for a stroll; I'm getting cold. I shall go back by the other path."

It was not true; she was doing it to please Venn. After all, it was natural enough that he should want Shirin to himself for a little. In saying that she would go back by the other path, she would hint to him that she should not return. And out here, on this lovely evening, in the amiable relaxation that comes after bathing, he surely could not be anything but kind to Shirin?

"Can't you bear to let her out of your sight, then?" said Venn in a low, angry voice.

Shirin knew better than to answer such remarks.

"Look, Venn," she said, tugging at his elbow, "look at my pool,—isn't it pretty? Roll over and look. It ought to have an inhabitant, don't you think? In a minute I'll go down and catch a tiny crab. But look at it first. I picked up all the shells while you were swimming. I never knew there could be such lovely shells as there are at Storn."

"Storn,—much you care about Storn."

"Venn!" she said reproachfully. She was familiar with this mood whenever she returned from London, and knew she must coax him round. Besides, she really did want him to look at her pool.

"Are you tired?" he asked unexpectedly.

"Tired? No. Why?" she said, although actually she was dead tired both in body and in spirit, and desired nothing more than to forget it. But she would never have admitted being tired to Venn, though she might, *now*, she realised with a thrill of surprise, have admitted it to Cristina.

"Well, London is tiring, isn't it? And I expect you went to bed very late. Did you see Minna?"

"No, I hadn't time.—Venn, do please let us forget about London, shall we? I like my shells better than all the shops in Bond Street. Come over here; be nice; tell me their names. And then we'll go and get a crab."

Unable to resist her, he rolled himself over to where she was lying, poking at her shells with a delicate finger. The drops of water still stood on her bare arm.

Cristina wandered for some way along the beach. She again thought how extraordinary it was that Storn, this magical possession which would have turned the heads of most women, should leave Shirin apparently so indifferent. For that was an enigma to which she had not as yet obtained the key.

It was the kind of evening which made one reluctant to return indoors. Cristina shivered at the thought of sitting at dinner with Madame, Venn, and Shirin. It produced a sensation of stuffiness, overcharged and difficult, in opposition to this large peace, this serenity, this golden light upon the sea. Still, she supposed she must climb the hill towards the castle soon. In the meantime, she was thankful to be out of it for the moment; she was even thankful to be away from Shirin. It gave her time to think about Shirin and about their relationship which was moving now so rapidly, and which she must make it her business to shape. She could not selfishly leave the shaping of it to Shirin's competence. In some ways, she knew herself to be stronger than Shirin. The moment had come when she must act as the stronger of the two. Shirin had had quite enough in her life of acting stronger than other people. Shirin was tired. Recalcitrant though she might and would prove to be, she must be forced for once to hand over the responsibility to another person.

It would be a curious contest between them.

Perhaps she had made a mistake after all in leaving those two alone together. True, she had hinted to Venn that she would not return to disturb them. But it had been a hint only; she had made no definite promise. So instead of climbing the path towards the castle she retraced her steps along the sand to the rock where they had all been lying. The rock was deserted; they had disappeared. Clambering up, she stood looking down into Shirin's little pool. It touched her heart, as a mother might be touched by the silent evidence of her child's toys and recent presence. But because Cristina was too firm a person ever to allow her love to become clouded by sentimentality, and because she desired her love for Shirin above all things to remain pure, clear-sighted, useful, she smiled at herself for her fancies and continued her path along the shore. There was a cave along here, called Andromeda's Cave, —she had never enquired why so called; a cave with a high narrow mouth opening on to a creek of the sea. Venn usually kept a dinghy there, so that he could get out unobserved by the fishermen in the harbour. At sunset, Cristina knew, the warm rays entered the cave almost horizontally, throwing a peculiar rosy-golden light into the cave and on to its black inner wall. At such an hour, the cave held a peculiar magic and beauty. She reckoned that she had just enough time to glance in at the perfect hour, even though such a glancing meant following a difficult path with a final wading through the shallow water of the creek to reach the mouth of the cave.

The water of the creek splashed coolly round her ankles. It rose almost to her knees as she advanced. But she had come this way so often, that she felt confident it would not suddenly deepen. She plunged forward in the security of complete safety. However crammed with danger her personal relationships on Storn might be, the way to Andromeda's Cave at least held no peril. She went forward without dread. Now she had reached the opening of the cave. She waded, helping herself with her hand propping her against the cliff. The sun struck warm on her back and shoulders. She tasted the relief of being momentarily removed from Venn and Shirin, in the remote beauty that the dark island alone could offer.

Then she came into the cave, still splashing through the water. The sun's rays struck, as she had foreseen, the back wall of the cave. Warm and rosy-golden as she had anticipated, they struck also like lances against the naked body of Shirin chained against the rock. Arms outstretched, as of one crucified, Shirin stood there on a ledge, lashed and bound to the iron rings provided for Venn's boats. And Venn himself, crouching, ready to spring, watched her, with a switch in his hands.

PART IV

FORTY-SIX

I

CRISTINA never knew whether either of them had seen her. Even now, ten years afterwards, it remained the one question she could never put to Shirin. For all the absolute intimacy, trust, and confidence which now existed between them, partly mystical in its character, neither of them by hint or allusion had ever referred to that day. Yet they were as closely united as it is possible for two human beings to be. The curious mystical current which ran between them increased their closeness by rendering them independent of the usual cruder means of communication; it was scarcely necessary for them to speak, they knew each other too well, knew each other with a deep inner response that transcended touch or words.

Shirin had changed. She no longer had that fleeting look of a poor waif ready to ward off a blow, but seemed rather to be leaning quietly against an inward happiness and security, as though outward events could not touch her because of the secret refuge within.

There had been struggles between them: Shirin was not easy to love, nor was her love easy to conquer,—as Venn and others had found to their cost. Savage independence and fey detachment shied away from love or friendship. Just as she had found herself unable to love men, so had she eluded friendship with women, mistrusting both, and preferring her private life to either. It had not been easy for her to yield; not easy to step down from her pinnacle of gay indifference; not easy to admit another inhabitant into her dim sanctuary of concealment. Anyone less firm, subtle, and aware than Cristina would have given up in despair. But Cristina had insisted, as one who has once had a vision. She had insisted on not allowing Shirin to escape, as she was constantly trying to escape. She had her reward, when she saw for herself how much Shirin had changed. She had it in a smaller degree, when people observed to her *how much Shirin has changed, why is it?* but what other people thought was of as little consequence to Cristina as to Shirin herself. The only thing they were concerned with was the innermost truth. That was the thing they both knew, and kept private to themselves.

Looking back, Cristina found it difficult to understand by what methods she had truly and finally caught Shirin. By chance glances, partly, when their eyes met and they said nothing; by queer spasmodic conversations, which discovered Shirin's self-evolved creed and philosophy. By these she had been confirmed in her intuition of Shirin as, essentially, the purest spirit she had ever known. Shirin might have led a life abhorrent to the church-going virtuous; it had left her untouched. Cristina realised now that this purity and incorruptibility was precisely the quality in Shirin which had goaded Venn in his thwarted love to outrage.

She understood Venn better too. She saw how the bullying and domination of his grandfather and of Madame over the orphan boy knowing himself the eventual heir to authority and great possessions, had produced in him a self-belittlement and a corresponding desire for domination,—a desire he had never been able to gratify towards Shirin. Over others he had been able to exercise domination, but over Shirin, the person over whom he most desired it, never. And so it had turned out that towards the people over whom he had been able naturally and legitimately to exercise domination he had proved a kindly and friendly master; but towards Shirin, who had resisted him, a devil and a sadist, morally and physically.

Yet she must be kind to him, because without her he would go all to pieces.

"I could kill him, if I were put to it," she said to Cristina once, "but I couldn't be merely unkind to him. He's an unhappy person; and he depends on me."

Cristina protested. "It would be better for Venn," she said, "better for his character, if you indulged him less; if you stood out for yourself a little more."

She spoke thus in no mischief-making mood; she spoke simply because she thought Shirin more worth while than Venn. (Yet Venn was not wholly un-worth while. She knew that. It was very confusing. She wished she could whole-heartedly hate Venn. But she couldn't. Her inability to do so made her understand Shirin's inability to do so either. Venn had his simple, charming, endearing moments which, when they came, made one forgive him all his unhappy faults.)

A remark of Shirin's had led her to this understanding.

"He's made like that; he can't help himself," she had said, answering Cristina's indignation on some occasion with her clear, profound simplicity,—a simplicity which, the wheel coming full cycle, was born of her complexity.

Cristina saw then that people could not help themselves, not beyond a certain point. She learnt a permanent lesson. Intransigent as she was, and loyal beyond reason, life suddenly widened for her at Shirin's remark, as though a pebble tossed carelessly into water had spread out into ever-widening rings. New possibilities opened; possibilities of tolerance and understanding. *He's made like that; he can't help himself.* Surely that was a truly Christian and imaginative doctrine? And from there she proceeded to a fresh appreciation of Shirin's tolerant, hard-won wisdom; she observed henceforth how Shirin (for all her mocking) never really criticised anybody; how she never exacted from anybody anything more than came within their capacity to give. Yet her standards were high. It took Cristina several years to learn how to accord Shirin's tolerance with her exactingness. It took her several years to learn that Shirin demanded the highest standards only from people she cared for,—and, so far as Cristina could make out, she herself and possibly poor humble Tracey were the only people to be filed under that difficult and exclusive heading.

"What should you do if I failed you?" Cristina asked her curiously.

"Failed me?"

"Well, if I did something you disapproved of."

"I should cease to love you," Shirin gravely replied.

"At once? Without giving me a second chance?"

"There would be no second chances for you. You would simply have destroyed my idea of you, and so you would cease to exist."

"Shirin, you are pretty ruthless, aren't you? Wouldn't you say, *She's made like that, she can't help herself?*"

"Not about you. You know I love you more than anything in the world, you know you're the only person on whom I have ever allowed myself to depend,—that's why."

"Yet you are tolerant enough to other people,—exasperatingly tolerant, sometimes; I often wish you were more capable of moral indignation."

"Well, I'm not," said Shirin laughing; "you must put up with me as I am; I'm irremediable."

At least Cristina knew that she could always get a firm and prompt reply. Shirin, although she seldom spoke of her own theories, unless directly challenged, seemed to have examined and to have made up her mind on all the major issues. There was nothing slovenly, cowardly, or unconsidered about her attitude to life. Cristina discovered greater and greater depths; she discovered a profoundly serious and thoughtful person.

Chance lines of poetry came into her head:

There is no danger for the man who knows
What life and death is. . . .

Shirin knew; therefore there could be no real danger for Shirin.

"Have you always been so decided?" she asked her. "Did you never go through the usual floundering phase of confusion and unawareness and indecision?"

She expected Shirin to say, *Not after I was twenty,* but she said, "Not after I was twelve."

"My darling, you must have been a very precocious child."

"I suppose I was." Shirin, who had at first appeared inclined to say more, stopped.

"Tell me about it. Tell me why."

"Cristina, I've never told these things to anyone in my life."

"All the more reason why you should tell them to me now."

Shirin looked doubtful.

"Is it? You know the things one keeps very secretly locked away? well, it damages them to be spoken of."

"But not to me, Shirin; telling me is almost like telling yourself, now, isn't it?"

"Yes, *now*," said Shirin, raising her eyes in one of the luminous, generous looks that put a dagger straight into Cristina's heart.

"Tell me, then."

"I suppose it was due to my father mostly," said Shirin; "you see, he was blind, and nobody really understood him or bothered about him except me. They all thought him a mean, mingy, peevish little man. And in a way he was. Mother got on his nerves, although he never said so, even to me; he was much too loyal, and also much too conventional; his loyalty and his conventionality made him dishonest towards himself. But he couldn't help it," she said with a smile, for the phrase had become a joke between them, "he was made like that.—Yes, in ordinary daily life at home I suppose he must have appeared as a rather thin, peevish, irritable little man. He nursed lots of grievances; he thought for instance that he had been badly treated by his Company, —whether rightly or wrongly, I can't judge; I know nothing about it, except what I heard him and Mother say, and Mother was always egging him on to indignation; he always contradicted her, but I believe that somewhere in his heart he agreed;—and he was always worrying because we were so poor. Constant poverty, you know, Cristina, wears people down more surely than anything unless they are big enough to rise above it. And Father wasn't big. He was blind; he was poor; he had three children to support; he had a wife who got on his nerves, although he wouldn't admit it; and all those things taken together were too much for him to stand. But underneath his grievances and his worries there was another Father, whom I loved. He had imagination, Cristina. He wasn't big, but he had imagination. He had a funny fairy-story side to his mind. You see, he had spent so many years of his life in Persia, and it had left a mark on him. He used to tell me about it. I don't remember Persia very well myself, because I was only five when we left, but I feel I know it intimately through Father's eyes. He wasn't blind then. And he managed somehow to give me an impression of light and freedom and beauty which I have never lost. I used to sit on the arm of his chair and listen to him by the hour."

"Did your mother like that?"

"She never knew. If she came in by chance, or if one of the boys came in, we used to pretend we were talking about something else. We became very clever at changing the conversation. No, Mother never knew. She wasn't the kind of person who could be allowed to know. Father and I had a funny private life of our own. We kept it quite separate from the daily life of worries and irritations; I think perhaps it was a help to him; it certainly made the whole difference to me."

"It probably made the whole difference to him too,"

said Cristina, visualising Shirin, aged twelve, perched on the arm of her father's chair.

"Yes, I expect it did," said Shirin frankly, for an assumed diffidence was incompatible with her self-searching honesty; "I expect he liked having one person he could really talk to, more especially as I was a child and he probably thought I didn't understand half of what he was saying. So he could talk quite freely, as though he were talking or thinking to himself. But I did understand. I understood even more than he meant me to understand. He taught me to realise that he wasn't really a peevish little man at all. He taught me that people aren't necessarily as mingy as they seem, whatever they may appear to be on the surface. He taught me that even a blind, repudiated clerk living in Dulwich may have had a vision once. And somehow or other he managed to convey that vision to me. Perhaps it had become clearer to him because of his subsequent blindness; I don't know. I only know that he and I could escape to Persia whenever we were left alone together. We could always get back to that lovely light and those lovely solitudes. Oh yes, Cristina, I owe more to Father than he ever owed to me."

Cristina realised then that her tenderness towards Venn in his illnesses was directly attributable to her early responsibility in the care of her father. But she made no comment.

"It's so odd," Shirin continued dreamily, "how people pass through one's life and out of it, who have once been important in it. Father; Mother,—but she never counted much; my brothers,—I was quite fond of Paul in a way, and Roger I might really have loved, if I'd known him better; he was a wild, difficult person, but for some reason or other we never came close; I always liked him in a distant unrealised kind of way, and I think he liked me too, but I was younger than he was, and then we drifted apart before the gap in our ages had had time to close up; he went his way, and I went mine."

"You married," said Cristina.

"Yes,—I married," said Shirin, as though she had forgotten it; "yes,—there was Miles too. Another person who passed through my life. Like the Wisdom of Solomon, *As when a bird hath flown through the air, there is no token of her way to be found.*"

"But surely Miles," she said, wondering at her own boldness, "surely Miles left more than a passing mark on your life?"

"No, I don't think so," said Shirin. "He hurt me, and I hurt him, but I wouldn't say that he had scarred me. Perhaps because I've never wholly lost my affection for him,—he's a very attractive person,—so no bitterness has been left behind. Besides, I never loved him."

"You left Miles; why did you never leave Venn?"

Shirin hesitated.

"Venn needed me more," she said then; "Miles was always perfectly self-sufficient."

"He loved you," said Cristina, "didn't he?"

"Oh Lord, yes," said Shirin wearily, "he loved me, —also in his way."

By such conversations did their intimacy advance. And again, they came very close together over Venn and the difficulty of Cristina remaining at Storn. On many and many an occasion, especially at first, she revolted and said she must go. It was impossible for her, she said, to remain planted in a man's house when he certainly hated and resented her. "You can't ask it of me, Shirin," she would say, after some subtly disquieting incident; "you can't, you can't; it's more than anybody's pride would stand." But then Shirin would fall into a mood of such passionate despair, that she always relented in the end. These moods of Shirin's terrified her; such reckless, unreasoning misery, such indifference to life, such desire for death, such conviction that death would put an early end and bring her to a welcome peace. Again and again she said, "Go then, if you must; in any case, it won't be for very long." Or she would say, "I never in my life asked anyone to sacrifice themselves for me as I am asking you, Cristina." So of course Cristina stayed. How could even pride allow her to do otherwise?

She had been there ten years. In a sense, she was as much a part of Storn as Shirin herself; *yes, just about as much*, she thought, *and just about as little, for Storn adopts no one, and we are both really strangers here. Foreigners, as they say.* Even the children knew it, for she had frequently heard Dominic say, "But then, Mummy, of course you're not really a le Breton; you don't really belong here at all." Venn, she noticed, always looked secretly pleased when his son made these innocently cruel remarks.

(She could not wholly like Dominic,—the young Ranger. Handsome, intelligent, now at nineteen, she had watched him grow up from childhood to young manhood with increasing apprehension. He had all his father's easy charm, but he also had his father's devil within him. She wondered what he, in his turn, would do to Shirin. Dominic was Storn again, incarnate, even as Venn was Storn incarnate.)

And old Lady le Breton would not die. She hung on to life as though to spite the younger generations. Cristina rather admired her for it. Years ago, she had determined to live until her hundredth birthday, and by sheer force of will had achieved her ambition. Now,—for it had become a game with her to set a future date always ahead of her, whether Christmas or Easter or what-not,—she had determined to live long enough to see Dominic's coming-of-age. None of them doubted that she would succeed in doing so. They had begun to regard her as immortal.

Meanwhile they could watch Venn getting daily thinner and iller, till it was no longer possible to disguise from themselves or from him that something serious must be the matter. Shirin insisted on his seeing a London doctor, and, not trusting him to go alone, firmly accompanied him to Harley Street. His behaviour puzzled her so much that she came to the conclusion he must be afraid; he seemed feverish and nervous, and even more irascible than usual, yet he would tell her nothing of what he was thinking and feeling, but merely grumbled at her incessantly for this enforced and, according to him, absurdly unnecessary visit. Then to her surprise he suddenly reappeared in the waiting-room, saying that the examination was over but that an appointment prevented him from staying to hear what the doctor had to say,—she must go in and hear it in his place,—he would meet her in an hour's time at their hotel,—and so saying he snatched up his hat and left the house. Shirin, who had heard nothing of any appointment, saw the tall meagre figure get into a taxi and drive off.

"Well!" she said to herself; and went in to see the doctor.

There was no doubt about it, the doctor said, after looking shrewdly at Shirin and contrasting her composure with the agitation of his patient; no doubt at all: his lungs were very seriously affected. Sir Venn must be warned to take no risks. Any illness,—say a chill, turning to bronchitis or even to pneumonia,—might be attended with the most serious consequences. In fact, Sir Venn ought to go away at once. Davos, or Banchory if he preferred it. Sir Venn lived near the sea, the doctor understood? in fact on an island? damp? relaxing? The worst thing possible! "You must get him away at once, Lady le Breton."

Shirin was appalled: Venn would never leave Storn. She could not imagine Venn as a confessed invalid, huddling miserably among other invalids in an alien sanatorium. Venn, she thought, would prefer to die on Storn than to drag out a few extra years elsewhere. She put some questions to the doctor, surprising him by her medical knowledge, and forcing him to an exact statement of the position. She did not reveal to him her fear that Venn would never consent to leave Storn, but, keeping her head, quietly possessed herself of all the information he would condescend to give her. And he, conscious of her charm, appreciative of her calm good sense, answered her with a greater frankness than was his usual custom.

She was appalled again when she saw how Venn

received the news she had to give him. She had been prepared for an obstinate incredulity, for a scornful repudiation of the diagnosis, for an indignant rejection of the idea of exile; she had not been prepared for the degrading hysteria to which he instantly gave way. She had seen frightened men before; that was nothing new to her; she was shocked only because she had never associated Venn with possible cowardice. Whatever his faults might be,—and she thought she knew them all,—she had never considered cowardice as a possible element amongst them. Venn whom she knew as a skilled and audacious sailor, a venturous swimmer, a daring rider! Yet he clung to her now, sobbing, hysterical, all self-respect gone; he would not, could not, die, he said; he would not leave Storn; he could not go into the blackness of death without Shirin; he must be saved somehow or other, he said; he was only forty-eight, not old enough to die; if Madame could live to over a hundred, why shouldn't he? surely he had a better right to life than that superfluous old woman? he would not and could not be allowed to die, he said again; she, Shirin, must do something about it, must work a miracle, must care for him, restore him to health; if only she had loved him, he said, accusingly, he would not be in this plight now; it was she who had driven him into it; it was she who must save him. She must not abandon him, he said; she must stand by him, however much she hated him and desired his death; naturally she must desire his death, for he had never done anything but make her miserable; but however much she hated him she must stand by him now, he said; she must not force him away from Storn; if she forced him away from Storn she would kill him surely; she must take him back to Storn and let him remain there, coaxing him back to health; and anyway, he said, the doctor was probably mistaken, making heavy weather as doctors always did; she, Shirin, probably knew more about it than any doctor; she knew him better than any doctor, better than anyone else in the world; in fact she was the only person who had ever known him at all; she was his life, his all; he would not die, he would not leave her behind him in a world where he could no longer control her doings; he would haunt her if she let him die, he said; he would put a curse on her, so that her children should turn against her. Dominic should turn against her, he said, keeping her out of Storn even as he, Venn, had kept her out of Storn, so that her life should never be fulfilled but thwarted to the end, even as his own life had been warped and thwarted by her indifference; and not only Dominic should make her suffer but Luke, he said, the other man's son, should escape from his confinement and run amok, murderous and at large, bringing disgrace upon her, so that she should feel it shame to have brought such a child into the world.

Then he turned again and clung to her, saying that he didn't mean a word of it; that he loved her and her only; that he would not hurt her for all the world, but some demon impelled him to it; he couldn't understand why. She would be good to him now, wouldn't she, as she had always been good? He quite understood, he said, that she had never been able to love him; but she had always been good to him, long-suffering, patient; she would continue to be good, wouldn't she, now that he was really in trouble? She wouldn't count his devilry against him, now that she had the chance of paying him out?

All this, and more, poured from him in the unfriendly strangeness of the hotel bedroom. He knelt on the floor beside her chair, laying his head on her knee, while, mortally tired herself and disgusted, she forced herself to stroke his hair and to soothe him. Could he possibly have been drinking, she wondered? for this complete loss of self-control and self-respect was excessive, even for Venn; but he never drank, so she dismissed the suspicion. They would go back to Storn at once, she said, and would defer the discussion of their future plans until they got there.

For the first time in her life she was thankful to get back to Storn. Venn seemed to recover himself as the train drew nearer and nearer to Port Breton, till, steering the launch across, he became quite the old Venn again, chaffing the boatmen and asking them for news of the fishing-haul. But unfortunately as they rounded the point of the island they saw Dominic emerge on horseback naked from the sea and kick his horse into a gallop along the sands. Often as they had seen this happen before, the sight of his son's strong young body made Venn darken; Shirin, who knew him so well, could read his thoughts; youth, health, for others; but for himself nothing but illness, exile, and death. She shuddered at the thought of exile alone with him. What would she be called upon to bear? Was it possible that she would be torn away from Cristina? even from Storn? Her courage almost failed her; she discovered that somewhere, suppressed, repressed, she still loved Storn with all her early passion. And without Cristina she felt she could not live. Yet how could she desert Venn,—poor Venn, so frightened, so humiliated, so dependent upon her?

But Venn refused stubbornly to go. He would rather die on Storn, he said, than live anywhere else. Did she, Shirin, really imagine that he would leave her alone on Storn with the woman Cristina who had ruined their lives? Shirin refrained from saying that at the time of Cristina's arrival there had not been much left to ruin; she was very patient with him these days. "But, Venn," she said, "do you for your part imagine that I would let you go alone? of course I should come with you, and Cristina would stay behind."

Perverse, Venn would not have it. She was only longing for him to die, he said, so that she might live at Storn with Cristina and override Dominic till the boy was crushed and nothing. Cristina would enjoy helping her to do that. He said many wild things, to which Shirin tried not to listen. She denied nothing; it seemed scarcely worth while. They led a miserable existence, with Venn growing more and more querulous, and brooding over his hatred of Cristina.

She and Shirin discussed again the question of whether she should leave.

"You see, Shirin, it was just possible for me to stay when he was relatively well; now, I feel that I may be making him worse; you know how bad it is, in consumption, to have anything weighing on your mind."

Shirin only looked at her with those widened, frightened eyes. And Cristina promised again, as she had promised dozens of times before.

It was becoming clear, however, that Venn was growing worse. The damp summer was turning into the damper autumn, and even he was compelled to admit that the winter would offer him few hopeful prospects. He seemed torn between his terror of death and his determination to cling to his native land. He was haunted also by the thought of what Shirin, left a widow, would do with her life. Intensely pitying, she tried every means of comfort, even to teasing him when everything else failed: "Really, Venn, the only system that would suit you is suttee." "Yes," he said, with sudden savagery, as though inspired by a new idea; "it is."

She wondered then, with complete indifference, whether she had put it into his head to murder her.

It was finally decided that they should go. They would go at the beginning of November and would spend the whole winter at Davos. Old Lady le Breton chuckled when she heard of this arrangement; extreme old age had increased her mischievousness rather than diminished it, for, her activities being necessarily curtailed, she had very little else to think about. "You'll enjoy that, won't you, my girl?" she said to Shirin in Venn's presence, "a nice quiet time alone with dear Venn, and some nice interesting young men, I dare say, doing winter sports. And what about Cristina? is she going to stay and keep me and Dominic company?"

Cristina said no, she was returning to London.

"Ah, till next spring, I suppose, when Shirin comes back," said Lady le Breton pointedly.

A particularly rough and stormy autumn set in. The lower parts of the island were practically inaccessible, lashed by the breakers crashing against the cliffs and amongst the rocks. Yet nothing would keep Venn indoors, no arguments, persuasions, or common sense. A devil of restlessness and misery drove him always down to the sea. It was as though he wanted to make the most of Storn, never expecting to see it again. Shirin gave up her attempts to restrain him. She herself was clinging in desperation to these last days, heart-broken at the thought of leaving her one comfort, Cristina; reserving all her courage for her patience with Venn, all her endurance to accept silently his incessant taunts. She was even sorrier for him than for herself; her heart was wrung by the bitterness underlying his gibes. "I shall never come back," he said, "but you'll come back,—to Storn and to Cristina." He said this sort of thing over and over again, whenever he found himself alone with her; he said it so often, that she realised it represented no transitory mood, but a fixed obsession.

Cristina was good to him too; she humoured him, trying to make things easier for Shirin; she endured his veiled insults, partly for the sake of Shirin, who was dearer to her than anything on earth, but partly also for Venn's own sake, whom she recognised now as a profoundly unhappy and frightened soul.

They did not see much of him during those last weeks; as though aware of being scarcely fit for human company, he kept away by himself. A sick animal, he sought solitude, frequently not reappearing until dinner. Whether he spent the day out of doors, or in his boat, or shut into his own room, they did not always know. On stormy days they would sometimes meet him, returning, his oilskins streaming with spray and rain. Daily, they expected him to grow feverish with a cold or a chill, but the elements seemed to have no power to touch him; he had been too well hardened to exposure, all his life.

Is he trying to kill himself by his foolhardiness? thought Shirin; *what is he brewing in his mind?* She was convinced that he was brewing something.

Old Lady le Breton was convinced of it too. "What mischief is Venn cooking now?" she asked Shirin. Shirin replied that she thought Venn was naturally distressed by his illness and by the idea of leaving Storn. "Ah, you're a sweet liar," said Madame; "you know very well that Venn's disease can do queer things to the brain. It hasn't taken the form of genius in him, but what interests me is, what form *is* it taking in him? We'll know before he leaves Storn. If once you can get him safe away from Storn, he'll be all right. So long as he remains on Storn he's in danger."

Madame's terribly percipient sagacity did nothing to reassure Shirin.

Then he seemed to turn towards Cristina. He was forever talking to Cristina about what she should do with Shirin were he to die. "You might take her round the world," he said; "you'd both like that; Shirin always wanted to go to China, but she could never get me away from Storn. She wanted to go back to Persia too, but again she couldn't get me away from Storn. She'll be much happier when she's free of my selfishness."

It was so unlike Venn to talk like this that Cristina ventured on a reply.

"Aren't you talking rather nonsense, Venn?" she said. "Instead of talking so much about dying, why don't you think that when you come back cured you might let Shirin go away sometimes by herself? You say she always wanted to travel but that you were reluctant to go with her. . . ."

"And now, I suppose," he interrupted, his eyes narrowing, "you suggest that she might safely go with you?"

Cristina saw the danger.

"Not necessarily with me," she said easily; "she could go with Nerissa. Nerissa is nearly eighteen, she would enjoy seeing something of the world. It would do her good; she knows nothing but Storn. There's no reason why Shirin should go with me." She felt hypocritical as she said it, for she knew that Shirin would never voluntarily leave her, any more than she would voluntarily leave Shirin.

Venn knew it too; he was not easy to deceive.

"On the whole," he said reflectively, with the unpleasantly suave note that sometimes came into his voice, "perhaps she'd be safer with you than with Nerissa. Nerissa is very young and, so far as one can judge, innocent. But you at least could see if Shirin were running into any danger, and I know you'd be the first to whisk her out of it."

Cristina pondered over this sentence; it was proffered in the friendliest, most confiding tone, but she mistrusted its possibly complicated insinuations.

She mistrusted Venn's new friendliness too. She did not want to show her mistrust openly, partly because, being a generous person, she preferred to give him all the benefit of believing that a real concern for Shirin's future might inspire his solicitude, partly because, for Shirin's sake, she wanted to explore the tortuosities at the back of his mind so far as was compatible with her creed of never eavesdropping on the unsuspicious. For even these ten years had never wholly taught her to regard Venn as a mean and subtle enemy. She divined something in Venn, finer and more tragic than mere meanness, cruelty, and subtlety. Condemning her mistrust, therefore, as an ignominious suspicion, she forced herself to respond to his overtures, accepting his invitations to play a game of chess with him or to go for walks with him in the roughest weather. The perplexing thing was, that she could never dislike Venn wholly, any more than he could wholly dislike her. She thought, *It's a confusing thing, not to be able to dislike one's mortal foe.* She preferred the walks to the chess. Into the chess he put too much intensity, unavowed, of personal malice, grinning too delightedly when he could snap "Check!" or could thwart her pawn hastening to acquire a crown. She thought that perhaps the very fact of being enclosed within four walls, as he necessarily was when they played chess after dinner, made him more covertly hostile, more furtively symbolical of himself, than when he took her for walks in the open stormy air. There was something nastily furtive about him, something sly and vicious, when he played chess within doors. But when he took her for walks he was different; she dreaded him still, but differently; she felt him to be sinister, then, in a different way. He seemed, then, to be more of an open enemy; sinister still, but with a difference; the difference between indoors and out of doors. To a person like Venn, that meant a great difference; he had never been an indoors person; his life had been lived on the sea or closely near it. And, remembering the day ten years ago, when he had nearly drowned her, she respected and acknowledged the enemy Venn of the open sea and the open air. That was an enemy she could understand. The enemy who played chess with her, under the mask of companionship, was the enemy she could neither respect nor like.

Once, on one of their walks, he blundered against her on the edge of a cliff.

"Here, sorry, steady!" he said, reaching out his hand. "Don't fall over. It wouldn't look well, would it, if you were to fall over while walking with me? I might be accused of your death at the inquest."

She was sure, then, that the danger threatened herself and not Shirin.

"Shirin," said Venn, coming into Shirin's room, "dinner is ready; have you seen Cristina?"

"Not since luncheon," said Shirin, looking up from her letters, startled; "why? where is she?"

"How should I know?" said Venn. "She came out with me after luncheon. We went in separate boats. I thought she must have returned. I thought she would be with you. She is with you, usually, isn't she, at this time? Doesn't she take down your letters, or something?"

He spoke in nervous haste; his tone and his words were both false; he knew quite well that Shirin, orderly and punctual as she was, never dictated letters at that hour.

"Venn," said Shirin, springing up, "where is Cristina?"

She stared at him, trying to read the truth in his eyes.

"How should I know?" said Venn again, shrugging and turning away; "am I my sister's keeper?"

Shirin went out. She was convinced that something was wrong; she knew it from Venn's manner. It was an unnatural manner, a manner which conveyed the impression that he had finally done something he was half ashamed of, half proud of. She knew also that he was withholding some information within his power to give if he chose. But he would not choose. He would remain silent and defiant. Therefore she left him and went out and found and questioned the servants.

None of them, they said, had seen Miss Rich since luncheon. They had seen her then, setting out with Sir Venn. Sir Venn and she had been seen, going down towards the sea; they had gone along the yew-terrace, and then down the path through the pines. That was as much as the house-servants could tell Shirin. They gave her even that poor amount of information in a scared way, as though they guessed that the hounds of suspicion were afoot, and feared to be implicated and pursued. Even in her distress, Shirin found time to be touched by the frightened misgivings of her servants. They touched her, even as the universal ignorant suffering of humanity had always touched her.

But she could not waste time on her servants' anxieties. Practical as she was, she knew when a matter was urgent, and acted accordingly. She would think of the servants later; would reassure them,—when Cristina was found. In the meantime she sent for the head boatman, a thing she had never done before in all her years at Storn.

He came, surprised, deferential, sullen. He liked Shirin, who had saved the life of his baby when it developed croup; he liked Shirin, who came and chaffed his wife and left her in a better temper for a week after the visit; he liked Shirin, as all the village people liked her, foreigner though she might be; but still his loyalty remained fixed upon the Ranger. He would not admit for a moment that the Ranger could have taken Miss Rich into peril.

"The Ranger knows what he's doing," he said obstinately; "he knows as much about boats as we do."

"But, Joseph," said Shirin, "don't you understand? Miss Rich is missing. Sir Venn hasn't seen her. They went in separate boats." Even in her distress she must protect Venn. "They went in separate boats," she said again; "Sir Venn hasn't seen her. Sir Venn has come back, but not Miss Rich. And now it's dark. Do you think it possible, Joseph, that something has happened to her?"

"Well, it might be; it might," said Joseph slowly. "They were making for the Gull Rock, last time we saw them. The Gull Rock is a nasty place, with these tides. But the Ranger knows, the Ranger knows. You can trust him, my lady; he wouldn't let anybody come to harm. Don't you worry. And anyhow you've got the Ranger back safe. Don't you worry."

"I won't worry, Joseph," she said, seeing that she could get nothing out of him; "I'll go and tell Sir Venn what you say. I dare say he'll come and talk to you himself. If he wants anything done, you'll do it, won't you, Joseph? I know we could trust you to do anything, couldn't we, Joseph? Sir Venn would want to go with you himself, I expect. . . ."

Joseph thought that her ladyship seemed unnaturally agitated. He was used to people remaining out at sea late at night. Dominic, the boy, the young Ranger, often stayed out as late, but never had her ladyship sent down to the village in quest of him, Joseph. Never had she shown herself in this state of anxiety. He was sorry now that he had reminded her that the Gull Rock was such a nasty place, with these tides. Still, that which was said could not be unsaid, he reflected as he took his way back down towards the village.

Cristina's boat was discovered bobbing about near the Gull Rock. Her body was washed up near Andromeda's Cave two days later.

II

THEIR preparations for departure went forward. Venn, as the last person who had seen Cristina alive, had to attend the inquest. The coroner was extremely sympathetic. A local man, he expressed the deepest sympathy with Sir Venn le Breton in this very painful case. It was most unfortunate, he said, and a matter for sincere condolence, that a lady residing under Sir Venn's roof should have lost her life in this way on a pleasure trip. It was obvious, he said, that Sir Venn and Miss Rich had gone out together as they had gone dozens of times before; that they had landed on the Gull Rock; and that Sir Venn, having business to attend to at home, had returned alone, confident that Miss Rich would shortly follow him. There was no reason why he should not have left her; the sea was calm that day, and although the tides in the vicinity of the Gull Rock were known to be tricky, owing to a slight race in the narrowness of the channel, Miss Rich had had plenty of experience both of managing a boat and of the waters round Storn. He would like to make it clear that Sir Venn was absolutely exonerated from blame or any possible suggestion of negligence. What had happened after Sir Venn's departure, no one could say. It was possible that Miss Rich had lost her footing and fallen, rendering herself unconscious by striking her head in her fall. But that would not explain the fact that the boat was found floating free, with her coat and camera in it. That fact seemed to point more to the conclusion that she had already left the rock and had started on her homeward journey when the accident occurred. Perhaps she had reached overboard to retrieve something from the water and had lost her balance,—who could tell? She was known to be a strong swimmer, but it must be remembered that her clothes would have encumbered her. Again, she might have struck her head on a submerged rock as she went over; the Court would remember that contusions had been discovered on the right temple. The coroner talked on and on; it was not often that he had the opportunity of dealing with so mysterious and sensational a case. He flattered himself that he had conducted it extremely well. At any rate his deference and consideration towards Sir Venn had been, throughout, remarkable and beyond reproach.

There were those, however, who were less satisfied than the coroner with the coroner's verdict.

His grandmother caught Venn alone.

"Happy now, are you?" she said, wagging her old head at him; "happy in being sure that if you can't have Shirin yourself, nobody else shall have her? Well, I don't blame you, not altogether, if you're satisfied to live beside a thing you've killed even more effectively than you killed Cristina,—than Cristina was killed, I mean. At least, I suppose I mean that, don't I? No, I don't blame you. I understand you; we've got the same blood, you and I. I can understand doing the same thing myself, if I hated anybody sufficiently. After all, people used to do these things quite often and freely once, when they lived more according to nature and cared less about civilisation with its judges and its gallows. No, that's not a nice word, is it? I see you don't like it, but it wouldn't have made much difference to you, if you've got to die anyhow. Still, it'll be nicer for you to die respectably of a hæmorrhage in your bed, and certainly nicer for Dominic, who has to carry on with your name. It's much better for everybody all round that you should have got out of it so easily and lightly. Think how awkward it would have been for the poor coroner, for instance, if he had had to return a different verdict. I dare say even Shirin herself prefers it,—if Shirin has got enough life left in her to know what she prefers or doesn't prefer, which I doubt. But don't delude yourself too much, my boy. The day will come when Shirin comes to life again, and then all I can say is, Heaven help you.—Not that I much want you to be helped, though," she added drily, "either by Heaven or anything else. I think you've deserved all you'll get. I told you I didn't really blame you, but at the same time I can't quite forgive you for killing Shirin twice over. I love that child, and I see what you've done to her, not only now but for the past twenty years. I would have minded less, and so would she, if you'd killed her body. But it isn't her body you've killed.—Look out for yourself, Venn, if her spirit ever comes to life again."

Venn did not enjoy this conversation. Nor did he enjoy meeting Mrs. Jolly in the passage. She would stop, as though civilly to let him pass, but as he passed she stared. He shrugged them both away, both his grandmother and Mrs. Jolly. Neither words nor looks should hurt him.

There remained Shirin. He knew what Shirin believed.

She was utterly cold and silent, going about her life as though only her physical presence were there. The impression which Venn had so often received, that she was not really in the room at all, was heightened now and more constant. This disquieted him; he could ignore the looks of Mrs. Jolly, he could dismiss the words of Madame,—though they returned to him sometimes in the sleepless nights,—but Shirin's absent coldness he could neither ignore nor dismiss. Shirin was too essential to him, too vital, to be ignored or dismissed; she was, in fact, his life, in so far as he had any life apart from Storn. Besides, he was frightened now as to what she might do to him. Morally and physically, he was frightened as to what she might do to him. One could not hurt a person as he had hurt Shirin, without expecting some retribution some day.

The parson at Port Breton, where in order to give a good example they always went to church on Sundays when the weather was not too rough, unfortunately chose as the text for his sermon, *Cast thy bread upon the waters and thou shalt find it after many days*. Only, in Venn's case, it was the wrong sort of bread which he was about to find again.

He took to following her everywhere. He had a very good excuse for doing so, since their arrangements for going abroad were going forward. Excusably he could follow her, asking her coöperation on this or that. She answered him always, never impatient with him, never irritable, never anything but cold, helpful, and polite. He could not get near her in any way; he could not unfreeze her; she gave her answers like an automaton, a dead thing. Although he knew what she believed, he could not tell what she was thinking. And although in a way nothing of her was there except her physical presence, yet in another way her spiritual presence alone was dominant, so that he felt that if her spirit appeared to him stripped of its familiar coverings, he would recognise it now, for it seemed suddenly to have grown in stature, to tower above him, and to be preparing to annihilate him under the ruins of its fall.

These fancies grew upon him, so that he feared Shirin and fawned upon her, uneasiness added to that thwarted sense of her unapproachability. The increase which he divined in the power and stature of her spirit oppressed and disquieted him so greatly that often he was on the point of crying out to her that she should reveal herself, do what she would with him, and let him go. At times, again, he felt that he could no longer live near her; that in self-defence he must escape; that, puny, he was a mortal living under the shadow of a giant. Her spirit was all the more terrible for being dead.

Cringe and propitiate as he might, he had occasional revolts when he attempted again to bully and to taunt. He did so in a mixture of timidity and daring, as one who provokes a wild animal, half hoping for the snarl. Many years had passed since by these methods he could obtain even a wince of pain from Shirin; but now he felt her indifference to be the outcome of her real deadness, and not of her self-control. He could even make references to Cristina without provoking any response. Seeing this, he ventured further and further. But still she made no sign, only towered above him a little higher and in a colder silence.

Shirin herself, had Venn but known it, had no more idea than he of what might happen. Like him, she was aware only of the tall, strange, strong power which had shot up within her. What it would make her do, she could not imagine. She did not ask. She was aware only of its blind instinctive force; knew only that it had some connexion with the curiously mystical current that had run between her and Cristina. Very dimly and vaguely she thought it might have something to do with her own approaching death,—a fact of which she had for years been superstitiously persuaded. But somehow things did not seem to be working out as she had apprehended, since it was Cristina and not she herself who had died. It was, then, impossible to foresee the eventual pattern? its scrolls and curves and arabesques would always follow their own unexpected fancy, however clearly one could observe, in retrospect, the genesis of the line? impossible to predict the eventual synthesis towards which one's life was working? possible only to live according to the apparent discontinuity of day-by-day, the grammar of life a series of anacoluthons, the picture of life a painting by pointilliste methods, unintelligible in detail, intelligible only when one could stand back and grasp the finished whole from a distance? So it seemed. Firmness and philosophy could help during the steady, detailed, monotonous stretches of time when nothing happened, nothing more than daily life, the daily round, the common task, insensibly building up the design; it was only when life began to rush and to take charge, that firmness and philosophy failed; something bigger took their place, something bigger and more alarming because inexplicable; something which transcended a settled and considered knowledge and was stronger than it. At such times, instinct turned intellect into a contemptible and pretentious thing. The inner knowledge, at those times of rare occurrence, showed itself as more true than any learnt knowledge. That inner knowledge emerged as the only thing by which, in the rare moments of crisis, one could be guided.

Aware of her own strength, she had as yet received no revelation of what it would make her do. She had lost all capacity for thought. Insensitive, dumb, and blind, she merely existed, waiting. Sometimes she suspected that some idea lay coiled in the recesses of her mind, growing unseen like a child in the womb, but she could not make the effort necessary to drag it out into the light. At times again she suspected that this conception was of a monstrous nature; of one thing only was she sure, that in the fulfilment of time it would be born. How terrible and agonising that delivery might be to herself or others, she did not contemplate. She knew only that, like other processes of nature, it had to happen. And then the pattern would be complete.

She scarcely thought of people as human beings during that time. The dramatis personae of her life lost their humanity and turned into symbols. Cristina, Venn, and Storn all became symbols, and in the confusion and merging of her mind seemed neither more human nor less human, one than the other. She was no longer sure whether Storn were a person or not, whether Venn or Cristina were people or not, whether she herself were a person or not. She seemed merely to be living in the midst of forces. In spite of her dead and unthinking apathy, it seemed to her sometimes that she perceived things with a new and extraordinary clarity. It seemed to her then that she apprehended a truth transcending the ordinary accepted truths; it seemed to her that she came nearer to the real truth in thus merging Cristina, Venn, and Storn as forces and symbols in her mind.

They were forces that interacted upon one another, and consequently upon her. Storn, she saw now, in this blind unrealised way, had been the influence on her early life. It had meant beauty and escape. Then Venn had killed her love for Storn, and all that that love had carried with it. Then after years of thinking herself dead and broken, she had found Cristina. After many struggles and much caution,—the caution of a person who has been very badly hurt,—she had allowed Cristina finally to replace Storn in her heart and soul. Then Venn had killed Cristina too. So Venn had killed her, Shirin, a second time. He had killed, successively, the two things she cared for: Storn, and Cristina. The first she had accepted, since it concerned her and her only; the second she could not accept, since it concerned not only herself but another person. Herself she could allow to be hurt without retaliation; Cristina she could not allow to go unavenged.

Very few days remained before the date fixed for their departure. Shirin continued her preparations mechanically, with the inner (though, again, almost unexpressed) conviction that they would never go. Venn, on the other hand, appeared to have no such hopes or misgivings. He grew more and more dejected, and Shirin could see that he had now resigned himself hopelessly to a future consisting entirely of fear and illness,—months of humiliation and invalidism, bounded only by the supreme horror of the end. But for this resignation, she would have expected him to rebel suddenly; to say, as he had said at first, that a short life running itself out on Storn was preferable to the protracted purgatory of the sanatorium. Of late, he had ceased to say anything of the sort. She was unaware, of course, that he knew he would fear her less, away from Storn.

He had begun to hate the island; he felt it to be in league against him, in league with Shirin and the ghost of Cristina.

No, thought Shirin, if so unrealised and inarticulate a process could be called thought; it was not from Venn that cancellation would come. That cancellation would come from somewhere, she was sure, but the practical side of her nature held good, and she continued to make lists and to supervise the future ordering of the house which she had never regarded as her own. Even up to the last, she would neither fail nor procrastinate in the performance of her duty.

Abruptly she realised that she was very tired. She had spent a long morning with Jolly, and Jolly was not easy to manage during these days when Shirin must prevent her at every turn from bursting out with the things she wanted to say and must at all costs be stopped from saying. The necessity of keeping Jolly corked down, when Jolly wanted to explode, added to the strain imposed upon Shirin. Jolly had never considered herself quite as a servant, never as a person whose employer might occasionally desire to keep her in her place. She had, indeed, never regarded Shirin as her employer; Shirin whom she had petted as a child, comforted as a girl, counselled as a young woman; Shirin whose children she had nursed; whose intimacy she had thereby necessarily shared; Shirin whose fortunes she had followed, loyally, angrily. Poor Jolly, had she been less wise a woman, would have been hurt to the soul by Shirin's sudden withdrawal of her old easy friendliness. True, Shirin had always kept her at a certain distance over essential matters; Jolly, for instance, had always been promptly snubbed when, her tongue running away with her, she had started to say something furiously critical of the Ranger or Madame. She was accustomed to that, and had accepted it, respecting Shirin for a loyalty she could understand. She had argued it all out with herself, arriving at the conclusion that just as she would have allowed nobody to criticise Shirin, so would Shirin allow nobody to criticise the Ranger or even his grandmother. It irked her, for it always irked her to have to control her tongue, but she respected it. It increased Shirin's dignity in her eyes; dignity; a word she only half appreciated, but which had held a strange fascination for her ever since she first met with it in a novel; she liked to think that to Shirin, her child, her darling, could be attributed that mysteriously alluring quality. But it went almost beyond her powers of self-suppression when Shirin would not let her say that the Ranger had killed Miss Rich. It was hard to have to suppress oneself when one's child, one's darling, was in greater trouble than she had ever been in before. Trouble enough she had had, but nothing like this. And so dumb about it, too. It made one feel so helpless, when one's heart was so full, one's tongue so ready to move in one's mouth, one's arms so ready to go round the slender shoulders. Only her wisdom stopped her from breaking out irretrievably; only her wisdom, and the skill which Shirin displayed in turning her away from the dangerous subject. Especially the skill which Shirin displayed.

This skill, Shirin discovered, had tired her very much. It seemed to have tired her beyond all reason. Jolly had not really been very difficult to manage. She had stopped herself several times of her own accord, and had gone dutifully back to lists of sheets and blankets as befitted an alpaca-gowned housekeeper of a castle on a dark island whose owner was about to absent himself for several months, perhaps for ever. Jolly, thought Shirin, knowing Jolly as she did, had really proved herself quite reasonable and amenable. She had frequently passed through far more difficult hours with Jolly. Jolly had behaved well and with discretion. Still, she was very tired.

She was so tired that she realised she must be ill.

She then discovered that she felt ill. She ached in every joint. Her throat burnt like fire. This was something not attributable to the difficulty of poor Jolly. Wearily, and without much interest, she took her temperature; it showed a hundred and two.

I mustn't go near Venn, she thought instantly and instinctively; *any illness, the doctor said, might be attended by the most serious consequences; he must take no risks. I mustn't go near him*, she thought; and then her practical, protective mind ran at once forward to the necessity of changing their tickets, unless Venn, which was very unlikely, could be persuaded to travel by himself, letting her follow him later. *I wonder what's wrong with me?* she thought; but she was so well used to being ill that she scarcely took any personal interest in the nature of this attack. At most, she wondered for a moment whether this were the thing which should prevent them from leaving Storn. It was possible, it was indeed probable, that Venn would refuse to travel without her. That discussion, which would be difficult and diplomatic to conduct, especially for someone who was feeling as ill as she was feeling, might be postponed. In the meantime, she must keep herself away from Venn. That was her duty; that was the essential.

She sat down, holding her aching head, to write a note to Venn. When she had written it, she would ring the bell and would send it by the footman. Venn must be prevented from coming near her. Then she would go to bed; she would shut herself away till she had recovered. She would deal competently with her own illness, whatever it might be,—she tried to believe it was probably only influenza; Venn should not be worried, Venn should be kept away. Her only anxieties were lest Venn should refuse to leave England without her, or lest he should refuse to believe in the veracity of her illness. She could hear him saying, *You have made yourself ill in order to prevent me from going to Davos. You like thinking that you are ill, when it is I who am mortally ill. Your own illness is mere hysteria.* That was the sort of thing he had said to her in the past, when she had been far iller than he then was, and yet had forced herself to nurse him and give him strength. She was afraid he might say it again; might be angry with her for upsetting their arrangements. But she must risk his anger; she must keep herself away from him.

"Dear Venn," she wrote; "I've got a temperature,—very slight, but still a temperature,—and I don't think you ought to see me. You know the doctor said you ought to take no risks. I hope I shall be all right to travel on Tuesday. If not you must go without me and I will follow. I would risk anything so far as I myself was concerned, but I can't risk any infection for you. Don't think me selfish. It is really you I am thinking about. I will let you know if I am better tomorrow.—Shirin."

Before she could ring the bell, Venn came into the room.

She sprang up and away from him, retreating against the opposite wall. "Don't come near me," she cried; "stay where you are."

She saw at once that he had taken her cry as a movement of repulsion. The expression which she knew so well came over his face. She had not seen it there since Cristina's death. But it was there now, unmistakable: cruel, vindictive, sly. Seeing it, with all its associations that had made her suffer so bitterly, something seemed to fall into place in her brain. Her brain, after all its deadness and unconsciousness, suddenly became extraordinarily aware and lucid. She now knew perfectly clearly what she had been meditating all this time; she accepted the thought which she had been pressing down out of sight. She saw also, as by supernatural revelation, exactly how she should accomplish her intention. Everything had come together at the right moment, both her own realisation and the means for its satisfaction put into her hand.

She was astonished to hear Venn saying, "So you've come out into the open at last." It sounded almost as though he were reading her thoughts.

He came across the room towards her; stood over her as she shrank against the wall.

"I took you by surprise, didn't I?" he said. "I trapped you into showing your real feelings for me? You fled away from me before you knew what you were doing. All these years, you've at least kept too good a guard upon yourself to allow yourself to do that. But then of course you had Cristina; you could go to Cristina afterwards and pour out your grievances to your heart's content. Now that you've lost Cristina it's easier for me to make you give yourself away. Is that it?"

"No," she said, "that's not quite it."

"You hate me, don't you?" he continued, "but what good is your hatred going to do you? You're tied to me, and you can't desert a dying man. You may thank your stars that I *am* dying. But it may take a few years to kill me, and during those years I swear I'll make your life hell as I've never made it before. I'll break you yet, before I've done with you.—Why are you looking at me like that?"

"How was I looking at you, Venn?"

"Not at all as though you hated me," he said. He put his hand on her shoulder, turning her, but not roughly, towards the light. "You had the strangest look," he said; "almost as though you loved me, almost as though you were saying good-bye to me. What is it? what has happened?"

"Kiss me, Venn," she said. She put her arms round his neck and drew him down. She let him kiss her mouth, long and closely, as she had never willingly let him kiss it in all those years. Making herself small and soft and confiding in his arms, she stayed there, inviting his repeated kisses.

"Now go," she said, pushing him away from her.

Venn le Breton died after a very short illness. People in Port Breton began to say that the castle of Storn was a house of tragedy: first Miss Rich, and then the Ranger, and now it looked as though the young Madame were going to die too. It was terribly sad, they said; all comparatively young people, carried off one after the other, one by drowning, the other two by illness. True, the Ranger couldn't have lived very long. Perhaps it was merciful that he should have been taken quickly as he was: it might have spared him years of suffering. But it would be bitter for the young Madame, if she recovered, to feel that her husband had probably taken the fever from her, the fever which had killed him. For of course stories of the whole circumstance leaked across to Port Breton through the channel of the servants, the fishermen, and the villagers of Storn. It became known that after the young Madame had been found lying unconscious on the floor of her room, a note in her handwriting addressed to Sir Venn had also been found lying on her writing-table, warning him that she was ill and that he must not seek to see her. Of course it was clear that the poor lady had been too late with her warning: the contagion must already have taken effect, and to a man in the Ranger's state of health had proved fatal. It now remained to be seen whether it would prove fatal also to a woman in the prime of life.

The morning after the Ranger's funeral the flag on Storn, which had been flying at half-mast, was hoisted again to its normal position. The people at Port Breton watched it daily with anxiety. They had loved the young Madame. She had been good to them and theirs, not with usual dutiful interfering goodness of charitable ladies, but with a warmth and a simplicity they had never met elsewhere. She had been good to them in their troubles as though she really minded. She had never censured them or lectured them, but although she neither censured nor lectured they valued her good opinion even above that of the parson. When prayers were offered for her in church, a real hush came over the congregation, which was no conventional tribute; a hush that deepened when the parson, an unorthodox man of some imagination and culture, followed up the prayer by reading:

There is a lady sweet and kind . . .

The flag, however, did not flutter down to half-mast. Shirin did not die. It was a matter of some surprise to her when she found herself returning to life; not a matter of very great surprise, for she was far too weak to wonder much at anything. She merely lay in her great bed, knowing that Venn and Cristina were dead and that she was still alive. They had broken it to her very gently, that Venn was dead, in answer only to her insistent questions. He had been dead a week and buried four days, before they told her.

She was too weak to think back over what had happened. She lay in bed gazing out towards the hurrying clouds and the gulls that cried outside her window. It seemed to her that for the first time in her life she had peace and leisure to watch them.

III

ONLY when she was strong enough to talk for half an hour a day did they allow her to see Tracey, who had been sent down as the representative of Messrs. Block and Arrowhead. He came into her room on tiptoe, in the frightened way of someone unaccustomed to illness. Her bed seemed a long way off, across the spacious room, and she looked very white and small, in the shadow of the vast four-poster, but apart from her physical weakness she struck him as mentally quite in her normal mind. She even greeted him with a characteristic joke: "Hullo, Tracey; this isn't the first time you've seen me in bed, is it?"

Her smile took away any possible hurt.

He did not stay very long, that first day. Talking tired her, and very soon a nurse came to send him away, rather to his relief, for he found it difficult either to avoid the subjects which were in both their minds, or to decide how to touch upon them in such a manner as not to distress Shirin. He had no idea what she felt about her husband's death. The nurses, from whom he had made tentative enquiries, could tell him only that Lady le Breton never mentioned it. He thought that the Scotch night-nurse especially looked at him rather oddly as she gave this reply, but being as unaccustomed to nurses as he was to illness he was unable to interpret the look.

Two or three days later, however, he was allowed to stay for longer and then his visit became a daily habit. Shirin liked seeing him. "You mustn't mind, Tracey dear," she said, "if I don't talk much. Bring your ledgers and papers or whatever it is you have to do, and work here." Still, she was anxious lest he should find it irksome. "Are you quite sure you don't mind?" she asked repeatedly. She seemed far more concerned with his welfare than with her own. The nurses told him they had never known so considerate or plucky a patient. "She never seems to think of herself at all," they said.

So Tracey would go and sit in her room, and often when she shut her eyes, thinking that he was working at her writing-table, he would sit watching her asleep as once he had watched her asleep before. He recognised then the same attitude, in which she would lie with one arm flung out and her head turned aside, so that her curls framed the childish curve of her cheek and temple. It gave him a secret life with her, thus to watch her asleep. She inspired him then as the very incarnation of purity and innocence. He was glad that he had remained faithful to her all his life, and that, unlike other men, he had never fallen to the temptation of other women.

He told her this, timidly, one day, so convinced of the sacredness of his devotion that it could not offend her even in her bereavement.

"Yes,—you're a monk really, by vocation; not a hearth-rug at all," she said, stretching out her hand to him.

He took the hand; it was small, soft, and boneless, and without any strength. He felt a passionate desire to look after her, and told her so. She smiled.

"Dear Tracey,—no one will ever look after me again."

He thought she was referring to Venn. He scarcely knew of Cristina, save by a stray reference.

The habit of his daily visits had been established for a week when he first heard her talking in her sleep. At first he thought she was calling him, and went quickly across to her bed; "Tracey!" she was saying; "Tracey! oh Tracey, please be good to me."

"Shirin!" he said, astonished and moved.

Then he saw that she was asleep. He wondered what he should do. It seemed dishonourable to listen to something she might not wish him to overhear. Perhaps he had better leave the room quietly and call the nurse? But she was groping to find something; he could not resist the pathos of that wandering hand; he laid his own hand over it.

"Hush, darling," he said, pressing it; "hush; of course I'll be good to you."

Her fingers returned a light, weak pressure.

"Cristina," she murmured, content, and for a few moments she slept peacefully, retaining his hand, without speaking.

Tracey looked cautiously round; he wished the nurse would come in; he was afraid lest Shirin should begin to talk again. The nurse was not likely to come in, however; they had fallen into the habit of leaving him alone with Shirin every evening now for two hours or more, having noticed that he had a soothing, not a tiring effect upon her. He was alone with her, without hope of interruption, and he dared not disengage his hand, for fear of waking her.

He sat there, loving her.

Presently she stirred a little in her sleep, moving her

head uneasily on her pillow, but never letting go of his hand.

"Cristina!" she said suddenly, and in so loud a voice that he thought she would wake herself, "the child was run over,—really it was,—the lorry did it,—I didn't do it."

"Of course you didn't do it, darling," he said soothingly, thinking that she was dreaming. He had been able to soothe her before, when she asked him to be good to her; he hoped he would be able to soothe her again.

"There was blood on my shirt," she said, clutching his hand tightly as though in fear.

That startled him, for this time he knew what she was talking about, and his mind flew back to the first time he had ever seen her, thirty years ago, coming into the lamplight of the little commonplace dining-room at Dulwich. Little had he thought then that he would ever sit by her bedside in a gaunt and beautiful room, hearing her refer to that incident over which he had kept so discreetly silent.

She murmured now too low and too incoherently for him to catch what she said; he heard the name Luke uttered in a whisper of anguish, and then: "No, Venn, I can't; for God's sake, Venn, have mercy."

Poor Tracey could scarcely bear to hear these pitiful ramblings. He began to realise how much she must have suffered. Nor did he think he ought to listen any longer, but whenever he tried to take his hand away she grasped it more tightly. Should he wake her? He had heard somewhere that sleep-walkers should never be awakened; perhaps the same applied also to those who were talking in their sleep? Anyhow, her secrets were safe with him; she should never even know that he had learnt them. Perhaps the very fact of knowing them would enable him to serve her more usefully and with greater enlightenment.

She was talking again.

"He killed her," she said, "he killed her. Venn, you killed her.—Venn, I can't; Venn, spare me, spare me!—I never hurt the child.—I'll hurt Venn, I'll kill him.—Cristina, be good to me, I'm so unhappy, Cristina,—I must go and look for Cristina."

She flung back the bedclothes and sat up, her eyes wide open.

Tracey made her lie down again; he covered her up very gently.

"That's you, Cristina, isn't it?" she said, content again for a moment, but then she cried out "Cristina's dead!" with a terrible cry, and woke.

She was trembling all over.

"Tracey! Tracey!" she said trembling and clinging to him. "What's happened? where am I? what have I been doing?" She seemed utterly lost and bewildered, so he held her in his arms, rocking her and comforting her.

"Tracey," she said, looking at him very seriously, when she had recovered herself, "tell me the truth: have I been talking in my sleep?"

"A little," he replied. "I didn't know whether I ought to wake you or not."

"What was I talking about?"

"Oh, all sorts of things," he said lightly; "nothing very coherent."

"Did I talk about Venn?"

"You mentioned him."

"I've never mentioned him to you consciously, have I? Not since he died?"

"I don't remember, Shirin; no, I don't think you have."

"You remember perfectly well; you know I haven't. Did that strike you as odd?"

"Of course not," said the wretched Tracey, who had no idea of how he ought to deal with this situation; "there's no reason why you should mention anything you don't want to mention."

"When I spoke about him in my sleep just now, did I say that I had killed him?"

"Shirin! no, of course you didn't."

"Tracey, is that true? On your honour?"

"Yes, it is true," he said after a slight hesitation.

"Why did you hesitate? You're concealing something. Tell me exactly what's in your mind."

"Shirin darling, I think you ought to rest now; you're flushed and your eyes are too bright. We'll go on with this conversation tomorrow, if you like."

"You can't treat me like a child, Tracey. Listen: you love me, don't you?"

"More than anything on earth; you know that."

"Well, then, tell me what was in your mind and why you hesitated. Did I or did I not say I had killed Venn?"

"You said you would," said Tracey finally, seeing that he could not appease her otherwise.

"Well, I did," she said. "You'd better go away now, and tomorrow I'll tell you anything you want to know.—Don't argue now; just go. I'm so frightfully tired."

Outside the door he met the Scotch night-nurse coming on duty.

"I was just coming to see if Lady le Breton wanted anything, Mr. Tracey," she said, giving him another of her enigmatic glances. "I thought I heard her call out just now, but Mrs. Jolly told me you were with her. Did she call out in her sleep, perhaps? She does, sometimes."

"Yes, that was it," said Tracey, relieved; "she called out in her sleep."

"Did she by any chance talk in her sleep?" asked the nurse. "The doctor particularly wants me to keep a record."

"Why, does she usually?" he said, to gain time.

"She has rambled a bit."

"Yes, she rambled a bit, as you call it, this evening. Just nonsense. Pure nonsense."

"Yes, poor bairn," said the nurse, suddenly becoming sympathetic and human; "she has got strange imaginings sometimes on her mind. Better not repeat them to her if she asks you, Mr. Tracey. It does no good, upsetting her. I forget them myself as soon as I've heard them."

Tracey, for all his legal training and experience, felt that he could place a little wary confidence in this woman who stood looking at him with such kindly eyes.

"You said something about the doctor wanting you to keep a record," he said cautiously. "Did you mean a record of what she said, or a record of how frequently she talked?"

"Now where would be the sense of passing on what she said, Mr. Tracey? Do you fancy we are not accustomed to hearing laughable things from our patients? No, you need have no fear of that. I simply have to let the doctor know how frequently she talks. If he asks me what she said,—well, I haven't been able to hear. And my advice to you is, take no more heed than I do of anything she may say. Remember she's been very ill, and people when they are very ill churn many things round in their poor brains.—

But you must let me go now, Mr. Tracey; I must go to my patient."

She nodded cheerfully to him and disappeared into Shirin's room. He went away, understanding now what the night-nurse had meant by her enquiring looks. He felt, however, that he possessed in her a tacit and reliable ally.

Tracey did not sleep much that night, although the nurse's words had almost persuaded his simple mind that no facts lay behind Shirin's wanderings. He was bothered only by the idea that on the morrow Shirin had promised to tell him anything he wanted to know. He did not in the least want to know anything, but was haunted by the unpleasant foreboding that Shirin would insist upon telling him a great many things of which he would have preferred to remain in ignorance. Although he did not really believe that Shirin had killed Venn, or that Venn had killed Cristina, his lawyer's training had taught him that unlikely people did improbable things in the most unexpected manner, nor did his knowledge of Shirin do anything to convince him of her inability to act secretly and disconcertingly when circumstances challenged her to such action. He knew that she could be apparently tame, accommodating, and reasonable for months at a stretch; then suddenly turn arbitrary, wilful, and high-handed. So it was in no easy frame of mind that he knocked at her door next day.

She looked more alert than he had yet seen her; she was propped higher on her pillows, and round her shoulders she had thrown a short cloak of sable which almost exactly matched her hair. He noticed that her hair and the sable shared the same lights and darknesses. He had seldom seen anyone who looked less like a murderess. Her very appearance dispelled his dark night-thoughts; *what mad things one thinks in the night*, he thought; *just as mad as people may think when they lie ill and half asleep.*

"Hullo, Shirin," he said, as he said every day.

He had brought a large ledger under his arm. *Sir Dominic le Breton*, it said on the cover; *Storn Estate.* He felt that his work would ease matters, had she thought better of that ominous promise to tell him anything he wanted to know.

She had not thought better of it.

"Sit down beside me, Tracey; there's your chair. I promised to talk to you. You can't work this evening."

"I thought you might have regretted your promise."

"Don't you know me yet well enough to know that I never regret and never repent?"

"Shirin, you forget: I don't know you very well. I've known you for thirty years, it's true, but you are not a person of whom one ever knows more than they are willing for one to know."

What has happened to her? he thought; *she is as firm as ever: she seems her old self.*

"You shall know much more of me now. I shan't trouble to conceal anything from you. I won't go into details, but I will tell you the facts.—Are facts ever facts, though, Tracey? Are they ever communicable to anybody who hasn't known their whole background? Aren't they always the outcome of something which has gone before? something whose effect one was quite unable to foresee?"

"I certainly never foresaw what would be the outcome of Paul's asking me to supper at Dulwich that night," he said, smiling; "I never foresaw that thirty years later I should sit with you here at Storn. . . ."

". . . listening to my account of how I killed Venn?" she finished for him. "Don't wince, Tracey; if I don't wince, why should you? I did kill Venn, as surely and as deliberately as if I had knifed him. Listen, and I will tell you why."

She told him.

"Then," she went on, "I passed through a strange, short period of refusing to know what I was going to do. I suppose I knew all the time, really, but refused to admit it to myself. From the moment that I knew Venn had killed Cristina, I suppose I knew that I should have to kill Venn. He couldn't be allowed to go on killing people, as he had killed Cristina once and me twice over. Besides, you must remember that I knew him to be a very ill man, with no future before him except misery and death. That gave me a sort of additional justification,—not that I want to justify myself in your eyes, Tracey, or in my own; I am simply telling you how it happened, and how it had to happen. I see it all now much more clearly than I saw it at the time. But although I now realise that I knew it all along, I refused for a time to accept the truth. I stuffed it away into the very darkness of my mind. I was aware only that some strong purpose was forming in me, but I suppose that my strength failed me, in some way, in examining that purpose. Perhaps my strength was saving itself up for that very purpose, not allowing me to waste it over a vain and weakening analysis. Then, when the moment came, it all went very rapidly. Surprisingly rapidly. I saw the whole thing in a flash. (Venn used to play chess, you know,—he used to play chess with Cristina; not with me, for I never could understand it,—and he used to tell me how a whole situation would suddenly shape itself before him, so that he saw exactly what was going to happen and how he would quite quickly get the better of the other person. I never quite understood what he meant until it happened to me, —only, of course, it happened to me in rather different terms. Poor Venn; I liked him when he talked intelligently about things like chess, or when he sailed his boat or played with his dogs or the children. He was always charming then; he was happy and natural. It was really I who sent him wrong; it was I who developed the other side of his nature. I don't blame him; he couldn't help it.) That's in parenthesis, Tracey. I was saying, wasn't I, that when the moment came, everything went very rapidly. I know that I acted quite suddenly on the idea which had been at the back of my mind, unrealised, for weeks. I knew then that I had been wondering how I could avenge Cristina. Even up to the last moment I had been trying, consciously, to do my best by Venn. You know, Tracey, the last conscious thing I did was to write him a note saying that I was ill and that he mustn't come near me. I knew he oughtn't to come near me if I had diphtheria, as I believed I had; I knew I must prevent him from running any risk. The specialist in London had told me that any additional illness for Venn might be fatal. When I say, *the last conscious thing*, I mean the last thing I consciously remember. But subconsciously I suppose I had been thinking all the time of the other thing. So when I kissed him I knew I was killing him. I gave him the kiss he had always wanted, only, when he got it, it was the kiss of Judas."

Tracey did not know what to say in answer to this stark account. He could only say feebly, "Thank God, you killed him in a way that can never be discovered."

Shirin laughed; it was long since he had heard her laughter.

"My dear old hearthrug, how like a lawyer! Does your mind work in terms of detectives and detectives only? A clue-proof murder? Motiveless? The ideal crime? You'd better recommend the method to all your clients."

"Shirin," said Tracey, really shocked, "don't talk like that."

"Oh God, Tracey, you fool," she said, "don't you see that I talk like that because I can't talk otherwise?"

"What shall you do now?" he asked her one day. "What shall you do with your life?"

"I really don't very much care," she replied. "You mean, I suppose, that I am free, rich, young enough to make a fresh start. But I am not. It's too late; the spring is broken. I suppose I shall stay here till Dominic marries, if he wants me."

"You used to say that you wanted to travel,—that you wanted to go back to Persia."

"Yes, I used to say so," she replied. She did not add that all her dreams of going back to Persia had been associated with Cristina.

Tracey looked at her with an aching heart. He longed to say that he was there if she would accept his comfort and protection, but he knew well enough that she would never be meant for him. The most he could do for her, indirectly, was to devote all his zeal and all his experience to Dominic's interests. Even that task would come to an end before very long. He would have to go back to London, leaving her ill, fragile, and unutterably lonely.

"You have always had so much courage, Shirin," he said; "when you get better you'll lift up your head again."

She smiled, as one who is grateful for a well-meant encouragement, knowing that the words are vain.

"The moment comes, you know, Tracey, when one gets tired of living on one's own courage and nothing else."

Dominic came in to see his mother and Tracey left them. Like Cristina, he could not wholly like the boy. He could only hope that he would not hurt his mother in his turn as Venn had hurt her.

"How are you, Mummy?"

He sat down beside her, dutiful but not really affectionate. For all her training, she had never been able to warm him. She supposed it was her own fault, though she had tried hard enough to show him the love she had never really felt. He had been Venn's son, too definitely, from the first. Looking at him now, in the half-light, she saw again how like Venn he was, even to the slightly pointed ears, the pointed teeth.

"I'm all right, thank you, darling."

"You still look awfully ill, though," he said, considering her.

He felt suddenly sorry for her. *She must have suffered a lot,* he thought, *in these last weeks, being so ill herself and then Daddy dying like that.* For he had never doubted that their marriage had been an exceptionally happy one. His mother had been so gay, always; nobody who wasn't happy could possibly be so gay. But he was growing up, and he realised how little he knew of her. She had been there always, watching over him, though she had seemed to interfere with him very little, knowing how independent he was and how resentful of interference; but how much had he ever thought of her? Even in these last weeks, when the bewildering rapture of having Storn for his own had thrown him temporarily and secretly quite off his balance, he had scarcely given her a thought save on the dreadful day when they told him she was not expected to live through the night. He had somehow taken it for granted that the doctors and nurses would look after her, and then that Mr. Tracey would give her all the comfort she needed. It had not occurred to him that he himself might have any responsibility.

"I say, you've had a rotten time," he said awkwardly.

"Dominic," she began, seeing that he was in a soft mood, and remembering Tracey's question, "we've had no chance for a talk, you and I. But sooner or later, you know, we shall have to think of the future. The next two or three years are quite easy, because you will have to go back to Oxford, and I imagine that you would like me to look after things here for you until you are able to look after them for yourself. Have you thought at all what you want to do after that?"

"I want to live here, of course," he said, surprised.

"You've given up the idea of having any profession?"

"Of course, Mummy, *now*."

By "now," she knew he meant, *Now Storn is mine.*

"But, Dominic, you can't be altogether idle."

"There's plenty to do down here."

"Plenty of work, you mean? Not just sailing and fishing and enjoying yourself?"

"Plenty of work, I mean. Look at Daddy. He had the County Council and the Roads and Bridges Committee, and the hospital, and the Bench, and the Grammar School, and God knows what else. You know that for five days out of the week Daddy was busy with something, except when it was too rough to get across. You can't say that Daddy hadn't got a sense of duty.—He rather liked the days when it was too rough, though, didn't he? He liked Storn best."

"Yes, I think he liked Storn better than anything."

"Better than anything except you, Mummy."

"Perhaps he liked it even better than me."

"Oh no, Mummy; never."

"Anyway, you'd like to lead the same kind of life?"

"You wouldn't despise me for it?"

"Not if you led it conscientiously. I should mind very much if you adopted it only through self-indulgence. How much should you mind if you thought I despised you?"

"Oh, Mummy, how can you ask? Of course I should mind terribly. But as a matter of fact I've never heard you say you despised anybody. I can't think why, because I know you have terribly high standards. I've noticed only that you kept silent when somebody or other was discussed. And I've heard you say they were made like that and couldn't help it. I've never heard you condemn. Cristina said once that you judged by generalities rather than by personalities. I didn't understand then, but I think I'm beginning to understand now."

"Well, I promise not to despise you if you do your duty like Daddy."

"Public duty?"

"Yes, public duty."

"Daddy was rather fine, wasn't he, Mummy?"

"He had a great sense of public duty, yes.—So that's decided, is it, Dominic? You finish your time at Oxford, and then you come home?"

"Mr. Tracey would help me, wouldn't he? I like Mr. Tracey. I mean, there are lots of things I don't know about estate management. I asked Daddy once to teach me, but he snubbed me so much that I got frightened. I think perhaps it was tactless of me,—was it? I mean, it was rather assuming that I should have to look after the estate some day? I felt he didn't like the idea that anybody might have anything to do with Storn except himself."

"I expect that was it,—quite naturally, too."

"You and Daddy always divided it so perfectly, didn't you? He looked after the estate and you looked after the house."

"You and your wife must divide it equally perfectly," said Shirin, smiling.

"My wife! I don't suppose I shall ever marry."

"Darling, of course you will. Why not?"

"I don't think I should ever like to share Storn, even with my wife," said Dominic judiciously. "Except, of course," he added, "I should want a son. Would it be possible, Mummy, to find a woman who wouldn't want to interfere with Storn and who yet would marry me and give me a son?"

"Would that be much fun for her, Dominic?"

"Well, she could live here. That would make up for a lot, wouldn't it? I would give her a bit of the garden for her own."

"That would be kind of you. And she could have this room, couldn't she? Such a lovely room,—it ought to satisfy her and keep her quite happy."

"It *is* rather a lovely room," he said, looking round, quite unconscious of his mother's sarcasm; "but," he added, "it's your room."

She thought that he said it tentatively, to see what answer he would draw from her. He had that sly look, which she had known so well in Venn.

"I shouldn't be here then, Dominic."

He affected surprise.

"Not here, Mummy? but you belong here."

"Oh no, Dominic, I don't. I don't belong anywhere. I've never belonged anywhere. You wouldn't want me to stay here, would you, once you were grown up, whether you were married or not?"

He was embarrassed. He was very young. He was not old enough to be coldly cruel; not yet.

"Mummy, of course I would never want you to leave Storn until you wanted to leave it."

"Now think. Be honest with yourself. Would you want me to stay here as Granny has stayed? Would you want me to stay watching you and your wife?"

"I've told you, Mummy, I don't think I shall ever marry."

"You're evading the point. Would you want me to stay here, watching you, even if you didn't marry? Would you? Would you?"

She saw a cautious expression come into his eyes. She read him rightly. He was not yet sufficiently developed to be deliberately harsh; he wanted to avoid hurting her; yet at the same time he was determined to protect himself against the future.

"Mummy, ought you to talk so much?"

"Don't worry about that; now that we've begun this conversation we must finish it. What do you really want me to do?"

"Well, Mummy, if it isn't asking too much of you, and if

you don't want to do anything else, I would be awfully grateful if you would stay and help me at any rate until I can manage by myself."

"Stay until you leave Oxford, you mean?"

"Of course,—and longer if you wanted to."

"Well, we'll leave it at that, shall we, Dominic?"

"Mummy, you are a dear."

"Darling, it's you who are a dear, wanting me to stay here until you are twenty-one."

"You look tired, Mummy; would you like me to say goodnight to you now? I don't think you ought to talk any more. I'm sure Mr. Tracey would say you oughtn't to talk any more. Cristina would certainly have said so. Cristina looked after you, didn't she, Mummy? In some ways, I always thought Cristina looked after you better than Daddy did. She seemed to notice things about you that even Daddy didn't notice. When you got tired, for instance. . . . She looked after you even better than Mr. Tracey does. Shall I say goodnight, now, if you're tired?"

She knew that he wanted to escape. He had said all he wanted to say. And indeed, she was desperately tired.

"Yes, perhaps you'd better go, darling. Goodnight. Kiss me,—no, don't."

The doctors were surprised to find that Lady le Breton did not pick up her strength. *Heart*, they said, *affected by her illness*. They noticed that she drooped more and more after Mr. Tracey had gone; and, consulting together, in veiled professional language, wondered each separately how much Mr. Tracey had meant to her, that she should fail so rapidly after his departure. They said nothing in words, but the glances that passed between them said a great deal. There was, quite obviously, a difference in Lady le

Breton now; it seemed as though she had no wish to live.

Crudely, they attributed it to some estrangement between her and Mr. Tracey. That was the way their minds worked. Mr. Tracey had sat in Lady le Breton's room every evening from five to seven. Lady le Breton, therefore, after a decent interval, intended to marry Mr. Tracey, who, clearly, was in love with her. Something had gone wrong between them. What other conclusion could be drawn?

Shirin was to be misjudged to the end. They knew nothing, of course, of the conversation which had taken place between her and her son. They knew nothing of Venn or of Cristina. They knew nothing of the pattern which had drawn itself out to its full design.

They were naïvely surprised when she died quietly in her sleep on a spring morning. *Heart*, they said; *her heart never recovered from that illness*. They did not know that she had let herself die, knowing that it was better to have apprehended perfection than to have achieved it. They did now know that she had let herself die, because life had nothing more to offer.